*April,
thanks so much -
Hope you enjoy it.*

DEATH IN SIGHT

BONNIE BURNATOWSKI

Bonnie Burnatowski

ACKNOWLEDGEMENTS

There are so many people who helped make this book possible. My sister Dawn helped me with every facet of the book other than the writing, tech wizard that she is. Heather Ehresman Johnson thanks for being my toughest critic. You really know your stuff. For their expert advice I must credit Kathy Denman, Chris 'Rainman', and Josh Rogalski. Without them my characters wouldn't have had a clue. Bethany Beard and her partner at Last Draft Editing were fantastic and really helped tighten up the book. They edited tirelessly and with incredible skill. To all my friends and family who served as my readers and discussed plot, characters, dialogue, etc, you are truly the best.

Chapter 1

Everyone kept trying to bring her back, but she liked it where she was. Drifting somewhere between life and death, she could hear both the living and the dead. She'd made it through the accident. Her husband John hadn't.

Yet he was here with her now. If she gave in to the increasingly insistent pull of consciousness, then John would have to go. He'd been with her since the accident, as soon as she was aware of anything. But he wouldn't be here forever. She knew that.

Soon he would no longer come and lie beside her. He would never touch her or talk to her the way he did now. Things would never be the same. So she stayed where she was, tucked away in her cocoon, taking in everything around her as though it were happening to someone else.

Disembodied voices rose in the background: her mother's and someone else's, voices heard at a distance, but coming closer... dangerously close. A shiver of both longing and dread ran through Alexandra. Things were changing. The pull felt inevitable, still she turned away.

"My mother's talking to the doctor again," Alexandra murmured.

"Mm-hmm," John replied. "He says that you're ready to wake up."

"I'm not!" Alexandra said, refusing to open her eyes. If she really opened them, what would she see? Who would she see?

"Soon then," he whispered.

She tensed.

He kissed her forehead, shifting slightly in the bed to hold her more closely. "Don't worry about it right now. Just rest." Alexandra relaxed into him, sinking deeply into her sanctuary of oblivion.

When she resurfaced, it was dark against her closed lids. It felt so right to be where she was, nestled in John's protective arms. Why would she ever choose to leave this place? I won't think about it, she told herself.

"It'll happen soon though," John said, his voice calm, turning his head her way. "We both know it. We both have somewhere else we need to be."

This limbo they existed in was so much more real to her than her parents' voices, the intrusive rustle of sheets, the beep of machines, the smell of disinfectants, the pain that tugged at her whenever she drifted in that direction. Alexandra felt the pull from that place again, and again she denied it. She belonged here with John.

"There is no here. We're both somewhere between your world and mine." John sighed.

"Stop saying that!"

"Think about it, Alex. We can't stay here forever. You have to go back... and I have to go forward."

She pressed her lips together stubbornly. "I'm not ready!"

John smiled sadly. "Will you ever be?" He kissed her forehead tenderly.

"I don't know. I don't think that I'm strong enough to leave you behind." Reaching down, she took hold of his hand. As

3

she did, she heard the opening of a door, the whisper of rubber soles against well-worn floor tiles. It was so much closer than ever before! It was the nurse her mother called Kimberly. Alexandra knew why she was there. She came every night at this time. Most of the time she did her job in silence, but tonight Kimberly spoke to her.

"How you doin' tonight, Alexandra?" Alexandra heard the roll of wheels and the snap of the plastic IV cord against the metal of the pole as the nurse dragged it closer to the bed. Kimberly wrapped the blood pressure cuff around Alex's upper arm. "You know, you really need to wake up soon. You're missing all the action around here. We've had three new admissions in the last hour and then Mr. Phillips in 5405 coded. It took us forty minutes to bring him back and get him stabilized. At least you never give me any trouble. You let me do my job without a fuss." She hit the button on the monitor and the bag inflated. Alexandra felt the now familiar pressure. When the cuff was off, Kimberly lifted Alexandra's hand, placing thumb and finger on her wrist.

A searing streak of white-hot pain arced through Alexandra's head, and she found herself torn from John's arms and the hospital bed to a room she'd never been in before. Except that she somehow knew it intimately. She remembered shopping for the chocolate brown couch and chair. She'd paid a fortune for the plush earth-toned carpet because it matched the furniture so perfectly. The paint color she'd loved so much; iced coffee... was the color on the walls. The black and white framed photos adorning the walls were the one's she'd taken in Colorado the previous summer. Except that this wasn't her house, and she'd never been to Colorado.

It had to be a dream!

A slight evening breeze drifted through an open window to her left. A small table lamp cast a soft circle of light into the living room. She'd spent the day outside catching up on yard work and enjoying the gorgeous hot summer day.

Her hair was still damp from the shower, and she realized she was standing outside of the bathroom door gazing into the living room. The skin on her shoulders felt tight and hot. Were they sunburned? She turned and went back into the bathroom to check. She glanced into the mirror. She gasped inwardly!

4

The woman in the mirror had brown, shoulder-length hair, green eyes, and a pert little upturned nose. Her cheeks and nose were pink from the sun as were her shoulders. She was slim, petite, probably in her early forties. She wore a gray tank top with no bra and cut-off jean shorts. Alexandra stared at the woman in the mirror. She'd never seen her before in her life. Who was she? What the hell was going on?

Wait! She'd noticed a purse on the coffee table in the living room. There had to be ID inside. Alexandra tried to move in the direction of the purse, but found she was unable to go anywhere under her own authority. Frustrated by her inability to move, she waited impatiently in front of the mirror as the woman applied lotion to her shoulders. Finally, she turned and left the bathroom, padding barefoot toward the living room and the purse. Maybe Alex had some control after all.

As she walked through the archway that separated the two rooms, someone grabbed her wet hair from behind and yanked hard. Her eyes watered. Something slammed into her back and she went down, scraping her chin on the carpet as she went. Someone flipped her onto her back.

The carpet, so plush and soft on her bare feet just moments earlier, now dug painfully into her tender shoulders. She found herself trapped under the weight of a man wearing a black ski mask. Every muscle in her body went taut with terror. All she could see in the muted light of the table lamp were a set of starkly white teeth, a pair of dark eyes, and the deadly glint of the knife he held in his left hand. In spite of the heat, his body was covered from head to toe with a long-sleeved shirt, worn faded jeans, and the ski mask covering his face and neck. Even more chilling were the latex gloves that covered his hands.

She wasn't sure what frightened her more, the wicked-looking blade at her breast or those empty, glittering eyes. She had to get away! She remembered that the window was open. If she screamed, maybe someone would hear her. She opened her mouth, but no matter how hard she tried, no sound made it through her tightly closed throat. She met his inky cold gaze thinking to plead for mercy. He stared back at her, his lips twisted into the most grotesquely sick smile she'd ever seen.

5

Slowly he brought his hand up, and then the knife descended with excruciating leisure, slicing through her tank top as though it were warm butter, leaving a thin line of blood from her breastbone to the point where the waistband of her shorts lay against her stomach. Panic seized her. She bucked wildly trying to free herself, but it was as though the man was formed from solid rock. He laughed. She prayed she wasn't going to die horribly.

Then the blade was back. He separated her tank top with the tip of the knife, running the side of the blade over her exposed breast.

Leaning forward, he whispered, "Does that feel good? I can make you feel good, but I won't. I'll make you beg... beg for mercy, beg me to kill you. And after I'm done playing... I will." He laughed again.

In the next moment, everything faded and with that, Alexandra was back in the hospital bed... all of her, every aching molecule. She gasped, struggling to get enough air into her lungs, clawing her way up from the nightmare she'd been caught in. After opening her eyes, she stared up at the brown-haired, green-eyed woman in front of her. It couldn't be. She closed her eyes and then opened them again.

Oh sweet Jesus, it was the woman she'd seen in the bathroom mirror.

Chapter 2

Alex pushed a button on the remote again, staring blindly up at the television screen suspended from the wall in front of her bed. Apparently she'd been in a coma for almost two months. After ten frightening, pain-filled days of being 'awake,' she wished to hell that she could find a way to get back there. She picked up the plastic cup on the tray by her bed and took a sip of ice water in an effort to ease her endlessly dry throat. Idly, she worked the end of the straw with her teeth.

As she caught a glimpse of the large black and white clock on the wall next to the TV, she experienced a familiar chill of foreboding. Any time now someone would be in to check her vital signs, or worse yet, the physical therapist would be in for what Alex had deemed her daily 'torture' session.

Something had gone horribly wrong when that nurse had touched her, wrenching Alex back into the here and now. Alexandra shook her head. Or maybe it had to do with the accident. She must have suffered some kind of brain injury that had left her damaged in some way, something that none of the scans or tests could detect.

After setting the cup with the flattened straw down on the bedside tray, Alex carefully shifted to take some of the pressure off of her aching hips and pelvis. She grimaced, taking in a breath and then blew it out slowly. The pain subsided somewhat, and she relaxed back onto the pillows supporting her.

Was she just imagining that every time anyone touched her, her brain lit up like the grand finale at a Fourth of July fireworks display? Or that the moment it happened she would be literally drowning in that person's emotions and even sometimes their physical pain or pleasure?

If it weren't for the pain of her broken bones and her reawakening muscles, she'd have suspected that she was still in the grip of the coma. Had the blow to the head warped her brain, or maybe it was the swelling in her brain that caused this bizarre reaction?

Whatever the explanation, the whole thing scared the hell out of her. As desperately as she wanted to tell someone, she feared the outcome of that almost more than the delusions. Would she then find herself a permanent resident of the hospital Psych Ward, pumped full of medicine until she lost every shred of herself? No way would she risk that happening. She'd just made it back. She didn't want to go away again.

Added to that, she missed John with an ache that lay like a boulder on her chest. Even though she'd had that stolen time with him, they hadn't really said good-bye. According to her mother, per John's wishes, he'd been cremated. Jace Moseley, his best friend, had given an extremely moving eulogy. She'd missed her husband's funeral. The only things she had left of the man she'd loved were a metal urn full of his ashes and a closet full of clothes he would never wear again.

Tears spilled over and ran down her cheeks. Alex lifted the neck of her hospital gown and wiped them away. She wished fervently she were still drifting in Lalaland, where nothing could reach her. Somehow that was more real to her than the life she was living now. Alex pushed the off button on the remote and the screen went black.

There was so much to deal with on this side of consciousness. She thought she'd at least be returning to something familiar, but was this any more recognizable than the void where she'd been talking to her dead husband? Of all the things that were true or illusion though, she knew with absolute certainty that where she'd been with John had been real. At least she had that to hold on to.

The things she felt now when she 'went away' were as tangible as the remote she held in her hand. They were so believable she was tempted to tell the second-shift nurse to see her gynecologist and request a sonogram of her ovaries. She wanted to urge the night nurse Kimberly to lock all her doors and windows and be vigilant at all times. She'd had to bite her lip to keep from telling her neurologist that his chief resident was having an affair with his wife.

What if it never went away? What if, for the rest of her life, whenever someone touched her, her mind would just go to that place? What if it happened while she was driving or crossing the street? She wondered if she'd ever be able to casually shake someone's hand again or stand in close contact with someone on a crowded bus.

What if more than one person touched her at once? Surely she'd go insane, if she hadn't already! There had to be some kind of medicine that could stop her brain from short-circuiting that way. Surely there must be others who'd experienced this same type of thing after a brain injury. She needed to figure this out.

The door to her room opened. Her pulse leapt.

"Hey there, Alexandra, you ready to work?"

Alexandra forced a smile. "Ken, weren't you just telling me yesterday that I'd done a week's worth of work? Can't we skip a day?"

"No can do, Alexandra. You want to get out of this place as soon as you can, right? So let's get to work." He adjusted the bed so that she lay flat. She steeled herself against what was to come, even as she prayed that nothing would happen this time.

He reached out, grasping her stockinged foot with one hand and positioned his other hand on the bare skin just above her knee. She closed her eyes tightly against the sudden onslaught of familiar pain in her head as she once again made the unwelcome journey into her own private hell.

Chapter 3

The lounge was the only place Alexandra could be alone for any length of time since she'd transferred to the North Shore Rehab Center. The excessive fluorescent lighting, along with the fact that everything in the room was beige, discouraged most patients from actually using the lounge. Therefore, Alex found it the perfect place to be. She sat in a chair facing the TV, which wasn't on, listlessly resting her head on the back of the chair.

"Good God! What are they doing to you? They're supposed to be rehabilitating you, not starving you."

Alexandra sat up straighter in the padded chair, staring at the tiny gray-haired woman bearing down on her. The woman continued talking as she approached. "And when was the last time you slept? You could check those bags at the airport, young lady!"

The woman sat down in the chair across from Alex. "I'm Grace, by the way. I volunteer here a couple days a week." She smiled over at Alex. She was touched by the woman's concern and mustered a smile in return.

The woman leaned forward, placing a hand on Alexandra's knee. Alexandra flinched and then relaxed. Her eyes locked with Grace's.

"Why can't I feel you?" Alexandra asked.

"Because I blocked you," the woman said calmly, patting Alexandra's knee a couple times. "You're not crazy you know. If you don't want to let anyone in then you just have to learn to close the door."

"Close the door?" Alexandra gazed at the woman, thoroughly confused.

"That's what I said. If you want to be alone then you must learn to keep the door closed." Grace patted her knee again and then turned and left the room.

Every time someone came into contact with Alexandra after that, she imagined a door in her head and then she made herself close it. At first, she was too tense to focus, but she was determined to make it work. And then one day it did. She sobbed with relief. She wasn't crazy, or if she was, at least she had some control. For the first time, Alex felt hopeful that she could have a life of her own, without the invasive presence of everyone she made contact with. She began to relax and heal.

****

The breakfast crowd had thinned considerably by the time Alexandra arrived at the diner. She pushed through the door, happy to see that her favorite booth was unoccupied. After grabbing one of the leftover newspapers off the breakfast counter, she crossed the room and slid into the seat facing the windows, so that she could enjoy the sunshine and people watch if she got tired of reading. The waitress came, and she ordered her usual.

She was feeling exceptionally pleased with the world right at the moment. Things were finally beginning to turn around for her. Two days ago she'd signed the papers to finalize the sale of the house she'd owned with John, which had been on the market for several months. This morning she'd been offered the job she'd interviewed for weeks ago.

It was perfect timing actually, considering that she'd found a house she loved very close to the radio station where she'd be working. It was vacant and since she could now pay in cash, the sellers had agreed to let her take possession immediately. She wouldn't be starting at the radio station for another five weeks, which was when the current deejay was due to retire, so she'd have time to paint and settle in.

The waitress set her breakfast down in front of her. Alex smiled and thanked her. She picked up her fork and unfolded the paper, setting it on the side of her plate. She skipped the lead story. She wasn't in the mood to read about politics this morning. A picture caught her attention further down on the page. The fork fell from her fingers, and she grabbed the newspaper with both hands, bringing it closer to read the article.

Kimberly Haas, 41 years old, was found dead in her home late last night. When she failed to show up for work, a co-worker went to check on her and discovered the body. No details have been released, but the police confirmed today that her death was not from natural causes.

Alex set the paper down. Oh God, it was her, the nurse from the hospital… it was summer and she was dead. A frisson of panic shivered through Alex. Had it happened the way she'd seen it?

She threw some money on the table and ran out of the restaurant, walking in the direction of her car with absolutely no idea where to go or what she should do.

She had to find out how the woman had died. But how could she find out? She couldn't go to the police and say, "Hey, was she murdered with a big knife? Did she have a cut down her breastbone?" She unlocked the car and sat down. What should she do? Who could she talk to? She tried to think.

You need to calm down, she told herself. She took a deep breath, letting it out slowly, the way she did at yoga class. Even if it had happened in the way that she'd seen, what could she do about it? She'd never seen the man's face.

If she went to the police and told them what she'd seen, how would that help? And how would she ever convince them that she wasn't certifiable? She groaned. What if she had told the woman what she'd seen just before she'd woken up?

She wouldn't have believed me, that's what would have happened, she told herself. Hell, she hadn't even believed it herself. She'd just woken up from a coma, for God's sake. She shook herself mentally. She told herself that it could be a coincidence, but she didn't really believe that.

If Kimberly Haas had died at the hands of the man Alex had seen in her dream, did that make Alexandra responsible for her death? And if she couldn't change anything, she needed to find a way to let the guilt go and go on with her life.

She remembered Kimberly taking care of her for all those weeks while Alex lay in the hospital. Then she remembered being Kimberly, or at least being with her. And now Kimberly was dead. How could Alexandra let that go? She didn't know if she ever could.

Chapter 4

She was stalling. Toying with the letter in her hand, she took a moment to calm herself. John had written this letter to Jace, and she was sure that he'd want him to have it. She just needed a few more minutes to collect herself. She didn't know why her heart was beating so fast.

She hadn't seen Jace in a long time. Sure, she'd talked to him on the phone. He'd made it a point to call her at least once a month to see how she was doing. But seeing him was going to be so much harder. And when he heard the other reason for her visit, he'd probably assume that she'd lost not only her husband, but also her mind in the accident.

She wouldn't have been sitting in his driveway if she'd been able to think of any other alternative. Even though he and John had been best friends since grade school, things had always been awkward between her and Jace. Alexandra was momentarily assailed by the old familiar guilt. She hadn't meant to come between John and Jace. They were both such amazing men, and their friendship was one that most people only wished for. She hadn't wanted that to change because of her, but it had. She'd always felt the weight of that. So this was the least she could do for both of them. If things didn't go well then she wouldn't even bring up the other reason for her visit.

She pressed the doorbell and waited. The door opened and there he was, taller than she remembered, a little older, looking tired and maybe a little thinner, but he still looked gorgeous and dangerous, just the way he had the first time they'd met. His brown hair was shorter than the last time she'd seen him. Her roommate in college had referred to his eyes as 'take me' eyes. He wore jeans and a white tee shirt, both of which had seen better days. The tee shirt only served to accentuate his dark tan.

He gazed down at her with those piercing steel gray eyes and bam! That same quiver of something she could never quite name went through her, the way it did every time she was near him. It wasn't sexual, but something deeply sensory, like she could suddenly feel every cell in her body and maybe some of his too. Whatever it was, it was damned uncomfortable. She hated it and she'd really hoped that she'd moved past that.

"Alex! My God." He seemed to take in every inch of her, as if he were making sure that everything had ended up in the right place. She wondered what he was thinking as he gazed down at her. She'd never been heavy, but she'd lost some weight after the accident and kept it off. Since they'd shaved her head out of necessity, her hair was shorter than he'd ever seen it. Now that she'd finally gotten back to running several times a week, the sun had given her dark blonde hair some interesting highlights. She had some scars, but luckily none of them were visible to him.

"Hi, Jace. Sorry to surprise you like this. Your secretary told me a few days ago that you were back in the States."

"Yeah, the case took longer than I expected. I just got back three days ago. Please, come in." He stepped back and she moved into the entryway.

"Lexi... about John..." His voice cracked.

Her eyes filled and the tears rolled down her cheeks. He moved quickly. Suddenly, she was in his arms. His intense sorrow and a swell of some other emotion caught her unaware and nearly floored her. Grief? Sympathy? She couldn't quite pin it down.

And then… nothing! It had to have been him. Had he felt her reading him? How was that possible?

They stood like that for a few minutes. She'd missed this so much, being held close to a warm masculine body, being able to touch another person without being dragged through a psychic wringer. It felt good to lean on someone, even for a short time. It was so hard to be strong all the time.

He stepped away from her, clearing his throat. For a second, she felt just as she had while she'd been trapped in the front seat of the mangled car, snow falling through the shattered windshield onto her face. She felt bone cold and so terribly alone.

"Come in and sit down," he said. She followed him, taking a seat on the black leather couch.

Jace took a seat across from her in a matching leather chair. "So, how are you doing? For that matter what are you doing these days? Sorry I haven't called in a while. There's no cell phone service where I've been." He smiled, a sad smile that never quite reached his eyes. "Actually, there wasn't much of anything where I was, except for trees and dirt and insects. Oh, and rain."

"Did you find what you were looking for?" Alexandra asked.

"Yes, we did," he said, his expression grim.

"And that wasn't a good thing, apparently?"

Jace got up and paced the room. "Well, yes and no." He adjusted a small statue on the mantle an inch or two to the left, and then he moved on, running a hand along the shiny surface of an end table as he spoke. "An old friend of my father called me. He hadn't heard from his daughter for almost a month, and he was afraid that something might have happened to her. He asked me to look into it." He sat down on the edge of the chair he'd so recently vacated. "She was an environmental biologist doing research in the Brazilian Rainforest."

"Was?"

"Yeah…" His jaw clenched. "Was." Exhaling, he focused on her again. "While she was out doing fieldwork, she was bitten by a poisonous snake. It took us quite a while to find her and even longer to get her back home. Her father was devastated, but at least he has some closure." He leaned forward, picking up what looked to Alex like a yellow Nerf ball and began tossing it back and forth between his hands. "Some of the people I work for never get that."

He looked so desolate in that moment it made her want to wrap him in her arms and comfort him. "So anyway," he said, "change of subject! What are you doing now? I was going to call you tomorrow."

Alexandra jumped into the conversation. "I've been keeping busy the past two months. You know I've had the house on the market for a long time. Well, it finally sold. I bought a small house not too far from here, and I start my new job with WJAM radio in a week."

"You have been busy." His eyebrows rose in surprise. He held the ball in one hand for a bit. "That's great. I'm glad that you're finally done with the physical therapy. You seem to be getting around really well. No more limp and no more cane, huh?"

"Amen! Just a little pain sometimes, not to mention I'm a walking weather vane." She laughed. "When it comes to changes in the weather, my body is a better bet than the local forecast."

"Good to know." He chuckled. "Maybe when you start your new job, you can do the weather too." He squeezed the ball in his hand and then threw it up and caught it. "So what brings you here? Mattie, my secretary, told me that you showed up at the office a few weeks ago. As much as I'd love to think you just dropped by for a friendly visit, somehow I doubt that's why you're here." He smiled sardonically.

She sat up, moving to the edge of the cushion. "I have something for you." She placed John's letter on the coffee table in front of her and slid it toward Jace. It lay there between them. Jace looked at the letter and then back at her. "I found it when I was packing up the office. It had fallen down behind a drawer. That's probably why John never mailed it. I'm sure he'd want you to have it."

After taking the letter in his hand, he stared at it for a long moment. "Would you mind if I wait until later to read this?"

Although she was aching to know what was in the letter, she knew that it was a private thing between John and Jace, the last precious bit of communication between two lifelong friends.

"No, of course not. It's for you."

They sat quietly for a minute, both lost in thoughts of John.

Alexandra took a deep breath. "There's another reason why I wanted to see you in person." Her eyelid began to twitch, something that only happened when she was around Jace, and she resisted the urge to reach up and try to capture the tic.

"I need to hire you to find someone," she said.

The ball dropped to the table between them. Leather creaked as Jace turned slightly in his chair.

"That was probably the last thing I expected you to say," he said. "Who's missing?"

"First, I need to tell you my story, and I need you to hear me out before you say anything." She told him everything that had happened from the time of the accident to the time she'd moved to town.

"I had everything under control... until I moved here and bought a dining room set—"

"A dining room set?" Jace asked.

This time her laugh was genuine. "After everything I've just told you, that surprises you? That's your only comment?"

"For now," Jace said. "You asked me to hear you out. Believe me. We'll talk after you're done explaining. So you were saying you bought a dining room set?"

"You're telling me you're not freaking out and wondering how soon you can get me out the door?"

Jace smiled calmly over at her. "Do I look like I'm freaking out?"

She cocked her head to the side. "Why aren't you? I have been and I'm living it."

"Why don't you just tell me the rest of your story and then we'll finish this conversation."

"Well, I was looking for some furniture. I'd been to about a hundred antique shows and shops looking for a dining room set, but nothing seemed right for me. It had become kind of an obsession with me. I had no idea why, but I had to have the perfect table and chairs for my dining room. So, anyway, Olivia... you remember Olivia?"

He smiled. "How could I forget Olivia?"

She chuckled. "Well Olivia recommended this antique shop down on Broad Street that one of her clients told her about. John wasn't that fond of antiques, but I've always loved them, so I went down there and I found this incredible dining room table and chairs. The minute I saw it I felt this tremendous pull towards it, felt compelled to buy it. I just had to have it! So I bought it, and they agreed to deliver it." She was too restless to sit any longer. She stood and walked over to examine a large painting on a wall near the hallway. "Where was I?" Oh yeah! After they got it into the dining room, the sun was shining on the table, and honestly, it took my breath away. The grain in the wood was so beautiful and rich that I couldn't help running my hand over the surface.

"But as soon as I touched it, I saw a woman." She turned to face Jace again. "She was lying halfway under the table on a hardwood floor in front of a huge window in a pool of her own blood. Her shirt was cut down the middle, just like the nurse's, and there was a man standing over her with a knife in his hand, his left hand. Just like the man I'd seen in the vision or whatever. I couldn't see his face. It was blocked from view by the table. It felt like I was looking up at him from the floor. The things he'd done to her…" She shuddered in revulsion. "I don't know how, but somehow I just know that it's the same man who killed that nurse. And I need to find the woman who owned this table before he kills her too, if he hasn't already. I have to try to stop him.

That must be the reason I'm seeing these murders. The problem is I don't know who she is or how to go about finding her." She realized that her hands were clenched so tightly in front of her that her nails were digging into her palms. She dropped them to her sides, relaxing her posture with an effort.

Jace stood and walked over to where she was standing.

"Let's go into the kitchen. I'm sure you could use a drink and so could I." He led the way and she followed behind him. "So have you done anything else to try to find her?" he asked, opening the fridge. "How about a water? Or I think I have some tea bags somewhere."

"Water's fine, thanks." He handed her a bottled water and pointed to the bar stools beside the island. She pulled herself up onto one. Jace leaned back against the counter by the sink, taking a long drink from his bottle and then he screwed the cap back on, giving her his full attention once again.

"Well," she said, "I went back and talked to the woman at the antique shop, but it turns out that she just works there part time. The owner buys all the furniture for the store. She had no idea who'd owned the table before or where it had come from. I asked to talk to the owner, but she was out of town on a buying trip. The clerk gave me the owner's business card."

She took a sip of water and then continued. "I called her and left a message on her voice mail, but she hasn't returned my call." She pushed a stray lock of hair back from her forehead. "I know it sounds like I'm crazy. I'm not even sure why this is happening to me."

He went over to her and reached out, intending to take her hand, but she pulled her hands close to her body. He drew back and waited.

"Anyway," she said, "I've run out of ideas, and I know that you do this kind of thing for a living. John told me that if I ever needed to I should come to you, that you would help me. So here I am. Even if you think I'm nuts, you will help me find this woman, won't you? I know that you're really in demand. I can pay you whatever the going rate is."

"Of course I'm going to help you and you damned well are not going to pay me!" Jace said. "John was my best friend and you're his wife. My God, you really don't think much of me do you?"

"That's not true!" She raised her hands. "It's just that when I talked to your secretary, she told me that you were so busy she wasn't sure that you even took the time to sleep anymore."

Jace rolled his eyes in annoyance. "I can't believe she talks to my clients that way. If she weren't the only person who's ever been able to put up with me, I'd force her into an early retirement." Running a hand over the back of his neck, he said, "She's right though. I have been busy. Way too busy! But that's about to change. I've been looking for someone to help me for a long time. Someone I could stand to work with, or rather someone who could stand to work with me." A rueful smiled appeared. "When it comes to work, I've never really played well with others."

Alexandra snorted. "When have you ever played well with others?" They both laughed.

"Anyway, I've been asking my brother Eli to join me for years. He's perfect for the job and he and I have always gotten along great. He's sold his business and he's finally agreed to come out here. If it works out, I'll have myself a partner." He blew out a weary breath. "He's due in later today, as a matter of fact. He's helped me on a few cases before, so it should be a snap showing him the ropes. Then I'll get started on finding the owner of the antique shop and tracking down the table."

Alexandra took the shop owner's business card out of her wallet and handed it to Jace. "Here. This should help."

"Thanks." He stuck it in the pocket of his jeans. "I'd like to come take a look at the table, maybe tomorrow if that'll work for you."

Surprised, she said, "What do you think you can learn from the table? I checked the bottom of the table, but I didn't see any markings on it or anything."

Although she'd come to his house at the urging of his secretary, for some reason it felt strange to think of him coming to her house. This was business, but having him in her home felt personal. She was just being silly, but her body was still humming with heightened awareness. The image of him walking around in her house, filling up all the light and space with his magnetism felt really strange. Way too personal.

Although, she thought, looking him over covertly as he opened a door and tossed his empty water bottle into a bin just inside the door, he didn't seem affected in the least by her presence. So she was probably making a big deal out of nothing. The truth was that she needed his help.

He turned back to her. "You really don't know do you?" He shook his head in disbelief. "John told me that he had never once mentioned it to you, but I always assumed that that was the reason you always felt so uncomfortable around me."

"What are you talking about?"

"I'm talking about my seeing."

The hair rose on the back of her neck. "Seeing what?"

"Missing people, dead people, places where they've been, places where they are now, all kinds of symbols and clues that I don't understand and have to piece together." He waved a hand in frustration. "Half the time it's already too late to help them, and I just have to be content with helping the family to find some peace of mind. Most of the time I'm afraid to go to sleep while I'm on a case for fear that someone will be dying while I'm sleeping. What if I could have saved them if only I'd stayed awake?"

"Oh my God, you're psychic?" Alexandra gasped. "How could I not have known? I can't believe John wouldn't have told me. I didn't think we had any secrets between us. Why would he keep that from me?"

"Are you kidding?" Jace said. "You believe in psychic abilities? Yeah, right. You wouldn't even admit to having your own, let alone acknowledge anyone else's."

Alexandra jumped down from the stool. "Because I didn't have any abilities back then. How could I admit to something I didn't have?"

Jace shook his head at her with a look of disgust. "Oh you had them, and you'd go to any lengths to deny them. Anything the least bit spiritual was anathema to you. Christ, you wouldn't even consider taking that yoga class with Olivia because the instructor was 'so out there!' All of a sudden he just looked sad. "You know, for some reason I always thought that deep down you knew about me and that's why you didn't want to be around me."

He turned and walked back though the kitchen toward the living room, effectively ending the conversation. Alex had no choice but to follow behind him.

He led her to the door and opened it. His voice was polite, the voice of a stranger. "I'll call you later and we'll set up a time for me to see the table. Thanks for bringing John's letter. I really appreciate it." She stepped over the threshold and he stepped back, closing the door. She walked to her car and sat in the driver's seat, trying to assimilate everything that had just happened.

She'd met John in college and had fallen instantly and madly in love with him. She'd been so sure then that nothing on Earth could burst her bubble of happiness. That was until John had introduced her to his best friend Jace, a man she'd encountered numerous times on campus and given a wide berth. That was when she'd experienced a bubble burst of cosmic proportions.

She'd seen Jace many times but had never been close enough to feel the power of his persona. The power he exuded seemed to actually pull at her. She could feel it vibrating around her when they were too close to each other.

She both resented and was terrified by the fact he could have that kind of sway over her. John was the one she loved. So why should Jace affect her this way? She hated it…hated it so much that she began to find excuses to avoid his company. John noticed it. He'd called her on her lame excuses, and they'd ended up having a huge fight. The worst part of it was that she knew she was being unreasonable.

Since she couldn't even understand why she was so uncomfortable with Jace, there was no way she could hope to explain it to John. He finally told her that as much as he loved her, anyone who couldn't accept his best friend wasn't the right woman for him, and he'd walked away. She loved John so much. There was no denying it had all been her fault. The truth of it was that Jace was a great guy and he was John's best friend. If she wanted a life with John, then she'd have to learn to deal with her issues with Jace.

Finally, she'd called John and asked him to come over and talk. When he appeared at her door, it was clear that he hadn't slept in days. He'd just stood there looking at her and she had flown into his arms, crying and apologizing all at the same time. After that she'd decided that she would do whatever was necessary in order to make it work.

She did her best to hide her feelings whenever they got together with Jace, and everyone had accepted the status quo. Nevertheless, it was always there between the three of them. After a while Jace started making excuses of his own. A few months later, John was offered a great job in downstate New York and had asked Alexandra to marry him. They'd had a small wedding, with Jace and Olivia standing up for them and then they'd moved. It wasn't far away, but it could have been the other side of the world.

John had found them a house and Alexandra had taken a job doing the news at a small radio station in the town next to theirs. The move had placed them a couple of hours from Jace. With John free and Alexandra working weekends, it had seemed perfectly natural for John to go by himself on the weekends and visit Jace while Alex was working. Even after Alexandra had been promoted and had weekends free, John had always gone to Jace, never the other way around.

Chapter 5

For about the tenth time, Alex adjusted the pillows on the couch. Jace had called over an hour ago. Why wasn't he here yet? This was ridiculous. She had butterflies in her stomach, and for some reason she was feeling a little breathless. This was Jace, her husband's best friend for God's sake, the guy she'd never even wanted to be around in the past. He was only coming over to look at her dining room table. The table she hadn't been able to make herself go near after that first telling touch.

As she walked through the first floor of her new home, she wondered what he'd think of it. The only other place she'd ever decorated had been the home John had found for them. Not that she hadn't loved that house, but this house was hers and hers alone.

Every color on every wall, every stick of furniture, every rug or pillow she'd picked out was a direct reflection of her personality. She loved everything about the house, which made introducing it to anyone else seem deeply personal, like an artist's painting or a writer's prose. His approval shouldn't feel so vital to her, but somehow it did.

The doorbell rang. With one last sweeping glance around the rooms, she went to answer the door. Steeling herself, she opened it. With every nerve in her body jumping to attention, she greeted him, stepping aside to let him pass. He handed her a huge bouquet of flowers wrapped in tissue paper.

"Happy new home," he said.

"Thank you," she said around a sudden lump in her throat. "They're beautiful. Come on in. I'll just get something to put these in. Can I get you something to drink?"

"No thanks, I'm fine," he said, his tone polite, impersonal.

Alexandra sighed inwardly. It seemed that things were never going to be easy between them. She grabbed a vase and filled it with water before arranging the flowers in it. When she turned, she found Jace standing next to the antique table.

"Wow, this place is great, Alex."

She felt a swell of pride. "Thanks. I can't really take credit for a lot of it. The house was in good shape when I bought it, but I've had a great time making it my own."

"And it is totally you." He turned, indicating the dining room table with a tilt of his head. "So this is the table you were talking about." It was a statement, not a question.

"Yes, this is it."

"Have you gotten anything else from it?"

"To tell you the truth, I haven't been able to get up the nerve to touch it again." She shivered. "I'm still having nightmares from the first time."

"I know what you mean. It's not the stuff of warm fuzzy dreams. On another note, I did manage to get in touch with the shop owner last night. She remembers buying the table, but unfortunately she bought it at an out of town auction house, and she had no idea who the previous owner was."

Disappointment showed on Alex's face.

"I called the auction house today," Jace said. "They are going to check into it and call me back. Hopefully we'll know something soon."

"I hope so. Thank you for working so fast. I'm so afraid that it might already be too late." She rubbed her hands up and down her arms as if she were cold.

"Alex, I'm going to see what I can get from the table now. Don't worry if it seems like I'm gone for a few minutes. That's the way it works with me."

Standing close to the table, he leaned down placing both palms on the tabletop. His eyes remained open, which surprised Alexandra. The silence was intense. She stood there quietly, hardly daring to breathe. Suddenly his eyes opened even wider into a glassy unfocused stare. He stayed like that for what seemed like hours but was probably no more than a few minutes.

Just as Alexandra was ready to shake him and make sure he was okay, he straightened up, swaying slightly. Moving quickly, she pushed a chair at him and he dropped into it. His breath came in shallow puffs. His face had lost all color.

"Are you all right?" Alex asked, worry making her voice quiver.

"Yeah, just give me a minute. This really wipes me out for a while."

"Whew." Alex whistled through her teeth. "Now I know why everyone looks scared to death whenever I do my thing. That was quite a show."

He grimaced. "Thanks a lot."

"Be right back."

She was back in a minute with a bottle of water. She handed it to him. After twisting the cap off, he gulped the water down until the bottle was empty.

"How did you know?" he asked.

She shrugged. "That's the first thing I want when I come up for air. Did you see anything?"

"Yeah… a few things. I'm not sure if mine works the same way yours does. Mine is kind of like a slide show sometimes."

"So what did you see?"

"I saw water dripping from the table onto a hardwood floor. Then I saw a woman's hand hanging off the edge the table.

There were lines of blood running down her hand. She was still alive. If her heart weren't still beating, the blood wouldn't have been running that steadily down her arm. She must have been standing and then been pushed back onto the tabletop. The blood was dripping into the water already on the floor." He pressed his lips together, breathing out through his nose. "Then I saw another room. There were charcoal drawings of women plastered everywhere on the walls, and there were a few more on a long table. Whoever drew them is a very talented artist and very, very twisted. The women in the drawings were all dead. And their deaths were not peaceful. This guy has killed before, and he really enjoyed it. The only other things that I saw were the numbers three and five. I don't know what that means yet."

"The woman I saw was lying on the floor. And I didn't see any water. It has to be the same woman though, right?"

Jace shrugged. "The woman I saw was still alive. I don't know what happened after that. I did notice that on the woman's wrist there was a sliver bracelet or watch with some kind of black etching on it. I could see the indent on her finger. It was her left hand, so I'm assuming she had been wearing a wedding ring at some time in the recent past."

Alexandra shook her head in disbelief. "You only saw her hand, and you noticed all that? I saw all of her, and I don't remember any of that."

"Don't forget, I've been doing this for years. I've made it my business to notice every detail. I also had some forewarning of what to expect. It's hard to be objective when you see something like that and you're not expecting it. I think that if you can stand to look again, you'll notice a lot more."

"I know that I have to look again, but I've been a coward. I didn't notice much of anything the first time. I was really freaked out about seeing a dead body. She was just staring up at me. I let go of the table, so I wouldn't have to see her anymore." Unhappiness colored the tone of her voice. "I was thinking that if I tried while you were here it might be easier. That maybe I wouldn't feel so alone and terrified." She bit down on her bottom lip, avoiding his eyes.

"If you're sure you want to do this, then I'm glad I'm here with you. I know firsthand just how scary it is to see things like this."

"All right then. Let's do this right now before I lose my nerve." Alexandra moved closer to the table and Jace stood beside her.

"Remember, all you have to do to stop seeing at any time is to just let go of the table," Jace told her.

She took a calming breath and a moment to prepare herself. She placed her hand on the shiny surface of the table. There was the arc, the white-hot pain, and then she was back in the room with the dead woman. She tried to look around, but when she did, everything went out of focus, so she focused on the woman lying on the floor.

Dark red blood pooled beneath her body. There was a thin line of blood down the middle of her body and her nipples had been removed. The killer had traced around her navel and her pubic areas with the knife, and there was a deep cut across her throat. Random cuts had been made, as though the killer were drawing with a crayon or playing with chalk. Except that everywhere he'd cut, there were congealing trails of blood. So she had been alive when he cut her. Oh my God, what kind of a monster would do this? What the woman must have suffered. Look at her, Alex! She thought. Look for anything that will tell you who she is.

Alex forced herself to look more closely at the woman. Her hair looked like it had been highlighted and was cut stylishly short. The woman was in her mid to late thirties. She was trim and fairly tall, Alex guessed, and had the body of someone who exercised on a regular basis.

Alex looked at her hands. Her palms were up, her fingers curled up towards her body. Her nails were well manicured and polished in a light beige color. She had rings on her left hand, one silver band and a thicker one, silver but edged in gold. There were no rings on her right hand. On her left wrist, the woman wore a gold watch or bracelet with a band in a woven pattern. Alex looked down. The woman's feet were bare, and her toenails were also manicured and painted with the same beige as her fingernails.

Every beat of Alexandra's heart pounded through the blood in her brain. As much as she dreaded it, Alex ran her eyes back up the woman's body, looking for anything else that might hold a clue.

On the woman's right hip, she noticed that there was a patch of darkly pigmented skin, a birthmark roughly in the shape of the state of Florida. It was the only thing she could find aside from the series of cuts and twisted artwork and the clouded sightless stare of the dead woman's eyes.

Alex let go of the table. She could see that she was back in her own dining room. The intense pounding pain in her head remained. Her body felt suddenly weak, boneless, as if every drop of her blood was flowing out of her brain at hyper-speed. Her knees gave out. Jace caught her, supporting her. His strong emotions coupled with her own exhaustion proved too much for her. Her brain did the only thing it could to protect her. It shut down.

✱✱✱✱✱✱✱✱✱✱✱✱✱

She woke up on the couch with a dull, throbbing headache. Jace was leaning close to her.

"Are you all right?" he said. "I was really starting to worry."

"I'm fine," Alex said. "But I could really use a drink of water."

Jace went to the kitchen and came back with a bottle of water. Handing it to her, he said, "Does this always happen to you?"

"No, no. I think I stayed there too long. My head was splitting and then you touched me and I wasn't blocked and it hit me like a freight train. Sorry if I made you nervous."

"I was trying to decide whether to call 9-1-1. Are you sure you're okay?" Jace took the half-empty bottle from her, setting on the coffee table.

"I'm fine. I hope I never have to see anything like that again." She sat forward on the cushion. He sat next to her, taking her hand in his. This time she felt nothing, and she realized he must be blocking. She heaved a sigh of relief.

"What did you see?" he asked her quietly.

"It's not the same woman. It's not the one you saw."

"How do you know?" Jace asked.

"I saw her hands. The rings on her left hand are silver with gold. She's wearing a gold watch or bracelet."

"Shit. I was afraid of that," he said. "When you feel like you can, tell me everything you remember."

She gently pulled her hand from his. After picking up the bottle of water, she downed the rest of it.

Then she told him everything she could remember.

"How about the things around her: furniture, knick knacks, pictures?" Jace asked.

"That was really weird," Alex said. "I could see her so clearly, but whenever I tried to look around everything was indistinct, like it was in shadow, or really blurry."

"Hmm…probably because all the violent energy was centered around her."

"Except that when the nurse touched me I could look around and see everything in the room," Alex said.

"But she wasn't dead at the time. I think that you were using her energy and experiencing all those things through her."

"Oddly enough, that makes some kind of sense. So now we have two women to search for, one of whom we have to identify by just her hand and the back of a watch. How the hell do we find them?"

"We keep digging," Jace said. "While you were out of it, Eli called me. The auction house called back. They gave us the name and address of the woman who sold them the table. It's about an hour and a half from here. I'm going to talk to her tomorrow."

"I want to go with you."

"You sure you don't want to wait until I check it out? I'll take a picture of her on my phone and send it to you."

"No, I want to see her. If it's her I'll know and I can talk to her. You can help me make her believe."

"If she had a New York state driver's license, I could just show you her picture. Unfortunately, she didn't come up in the database. So if you really want to go with me, I'll pick you up around nine-thirty tomorrow morning."

"This is taking up a lot of your time. You must have other cases you're working on. You could give me the address and I could go myself."

"No way are you going to investigate this by yourself. You might just find yourself in the path of a killer. No, I'll pick you up. You doing all right now?"

"I'm fine now. Thanks for catching me before I fell flat on my face." She smiled up at him.

"No problem." He leaned down, planting a warm kiss on her cheek.

"Jace, about yesterday…"

"Yeah?"

"I hated to leave things that way. It was never about me not liking you. I've always thought you were a great guy."

"Then what was it about, Alex? Because it was very apparent that you avoided me like the plague, that you made every lame excuse not to spend time with John when I was around."

She struggled with a way to tell him about the instant wake-up call her body experienced whenever she was near him. Apparently he didn't get the same shot of molecular zing when he saw her. So what could she tell him?

Was it a psychic connection? Was it just plain old chemistry? She'd denied that for years. If it was that, how could she have been so physically attracted to the best friend of the love of her life? She had loved John, deeply, and sex with John had always been amazing. So, how could she explain something to him that she couldn't even understand herself?

"Never mind. It doesn't matter." Jace was already turning away.

"Yes, it does, damn it!" Alex said. "You're my husband's best friend for God's sake. I don't want to have these bad feelings between us."

"John and I being best friends has nothing to do with what goes on between you and I." He growled in frustration. "Look, let's just leave it for now. You have a headache and I have to get back to the office. Take it easy today and I'll see you tomorrow morning. And don't go around touching things you shouldn't."

"Don't worry. I'm a hands-off kinda girl."

He laughed. "Okay, I'll see you tomorrow." He let himself out.

Chapter 6

Alex said. "I thought that men never needed directions, that they just genetically knew how to get places. At least, that's what John always told me."

Jace shot her a look and then returned his eyes to the road. "Yeah well, guess what? Real men use GPS these days. When I'm on my own dollar, I'm not going to waste my time being lost for the sake of my manhood. Besides, everyone knows that men love gadgets, and I'm no exception there."

"My, aren't we both being stereotypical today?" Alexandra grinned. There was a benefit to spending time with Jace. Whenever she was near him she felt alive again in ways that she hadn't in a very long time. Her body's instinctive reaction to him still left her feeling off kilter, but in some sense she felt more comfortable with him than she had with anyone else since the accident. She decided to just enjoy the moment.

"How is Eli making out, considering you dropped him into the middle of the job and then left him to fend for himself?" she asked.

"Are you kidding? He's like a kid in a candy shop. His laptop is practically a part of him. He's already done more research then I could have accomplished in a week's time, and he was still going strong when I left the office. I think this is gonna work out just fine."

Just as he finished speaking, the GPS announced, "Take the exit on the right in point five miles and then turn right onto Route 163." Jace turned right off of the exit and onto Route 163. "Drive one point two miles and then turn left onto Sixth Street."

"Almost there," Jace said. "You ready for this?" He glanced over.

"Stop worrying about me. I just recently woke up from a coma and I managed to come out of it relatively intact. I shouldn't have any problem getting through this."

"Turn left onto Sixth Street in one tenth of a mile."

Jace turned left. They drove for a minute. "That's it, 309."

What had once been a very handsome example of Victorian splendor had obviously seen better days. It certainly didn't come across as the home of a wealthy socialite, which was what Alex imagined the dead woman to be. Jace pulled over and parked. They walked up the stairs without a word. Jace rang the bell.

They heard footsteps and then a woman's voice. "Hello?"

"Hello, Mrs. Branson. I'm Jace Moseley and this is Alexandra Pope. My secretary talked to you on the phone yesterday."

The woman inside pulled at the curtain on the sidelight, fixing them with a piercing gaze. "Please show me some identification, Mr. Moseley."

He pulled out his license and held it up to the window. She slid a pair of reading glasses out of her pocket and put them on. She thoroughly examined his license. The curtain snapped back into place and they heard the click of the deadbolt. The door swung open. An older woman opened the door—not the woman Alex had seen in the vision. Alex could have cried she was so disappointed. Maybe there was someone else in the house.

"I'm sorry," Mrs. Branson said. "But a woman can't be too careful these days."

"No, don't apologize. You did everything just right. I wish everyone were as careful."

Her cheeks grew pink. She led them into a room with very high ceilings and a beautiful white fireplace against one wall. They sat down, and Mrs. Branson offered them refreshments. They declined.

She got right to the point. "So I understand that you're interested in the history of the dining room set I used to own."

"Yes," Alexandra spoke up for the first time since their arrival. "I recently bought it and we're trying to track the history of the table. Anything you can tell us would be appreciated. Were you the original owner?"

"Oh no," the older woman said, "my second husband bought it for me as an anniversary gift."

"Oh how nice!" Alex said.

"Yes, I thought so too, until three weeks later when the rat bastard took off with my accountant and the bulk of my estate."

Alexandra and Jace exchanged glances. While Alex wrestled with an appropriate reply to that, Jace stepped in.

"I'm sorry to hear that. That must have been really hard for you."

"Damn right it was! I had to close out all my credit cards and learn to cook. I was bitter for quite a while, until I realized that I liked to cook and hated to shop. It was during my bitter period that I sold the table. I didn't want to be reminded of what a foolish old woman I'd been."

"Do you have any idea where your husband bought the table? Whom he might have bought it from?" Jace asked.

"I found a receipt when I was throwing out all of the things he left behind. I saved it, so I could figure out how much to ask for the table when I sold it and then I forgot all about it." She slid a manila folder across the low table between them. Jace opened it and they both bent to look at the receipt. It was from an antique shop in town and it was dated almost seven years to the day. Seven years! What on earth had made the woman hold on to a receipt for seven years? Thank God she had, though.

Picking up the receipt, Jace asked, "Do you know if this shop is still in operation?"

"I'm not sure," the woman said. "I haven't been over that way in years. I usually shop in Sheffield, the next town over. The shops are better there. You're welcome to take the receipt with you. I certainly don't need it anymore. I didn't even realize that I had kept it until I decided to clean out my file cabinet the other day. Must have been fate."

"Do you know where this shop is located?" Jace asked.

"Oh sure. Let me write down the directions." She turned the receipt over and wrote on the back. "It's pretty straightforward. You won't have any trouble finding it." She handed the paper back to Jace. "I'm afraid I wasn't much help."

"No, this is great." Jace smiled warmly.

"Thanks so much for seeing us," Alex said. "This will be a big help."

They thanked her again and left.

"Well, she wasn't the woman I saw," Alex said.

"She wasn't the woman I saw either," Jace said.

"How could you tell? You only saw a hand."

"The hand I saw was the hand of a much younger woman. I don't know why I say that, but I got the impression that the woman I saw was younger."

Alexandra looked up from the directions. "Turn right here."

Jace turned the corner.

"Hopefully we'll have more luck at the antique shop," Alex said.

Jace glanced over. "It'd certainly be great if it turned out to be this easy."

Alex consulted the map. "Take a left at the blinking light. That's route 153. Then it's about six or seven miles."

"Okay, thanks."

"This is crazy. Even supposing we find the woman who owned the table, what the hell do I say to her? 'Excuse me, I bought your dining room set and I saw you lying dead under it?'" Eyeing Jace, she asked, "How do you make people believe you?"

The corners of his mouth turned up slightly. "What makes you think that anyone believes me?"

"You've built quite a reputation as an investigator. Someone must believe you," Alex said.

"I don't tell many people about my talents. When I first started to 'find' people, I tried to talk to the police a few times. I always ended up being considered either a suspect in the case or a whack job. You said take a left here?" he asked as they approached the blinking light.

"Right. I mean yes, turn left here."

He smiled.

"So you do everything on your own and never confide in anyone?" Alex asked.

"No, I do as much as I can without mentioning how I got the information or by fudging just a little bit, and I've finally managed to make a few believers within the departments. After while a few of the more open-minded detectives realized that I was consistently on target and that I couldn't possibly run a successful business and still have time to lead such a varied life of crime. Once they realized that I could be useful to them, they started to call me when they needed help and helping me when they could."

"And just how long did it take to make someone believe you?" Alex asked.

Smiling over at her, Jace said, "Oh, give or take a few, I'd say about twenty years."

"Great! By the time I can convince anyone I'm not a lunatic, I'll have Alzheimer's and even I won't believe it."

He chuckled.

"It's down there on the corner according to the map." She pointed as she spoke.

He slowed and slid neatly into an empty parking spot.

"This is really a cute little town, you know," Alexandra mused looking around at the shops. "Quaint... kind of a throwback to the sixties."

Jace hit the lock on the key ring, and they crossed at the corner to stand in front of the shop. It had obviously been vacant for quite some time.

"Damn, it's not here anymore," Alex said. "What do we do now?"

"Now we do it the hard way," Jace answered. "As soon as I get back to the office, I'll start digging. I should be able to find a record of the business certificate and then we'll go from there."

"Okay, thanks. Listen, I know you're a busy man. If you just give me some direction, I can probably do some investigating on my own."

"Listen, Lex, I've been doing this for a while. What I can find in a few minutes would take you hours."

She started to protest.

He held up his hand. "Hey, that's not just my ego talking here. I do this for a living. Trust me."

"Okay, sorry. I'm just frustrated. The clock is ticking on this. I feel so powerless. Just like I did in the hospital."

"Well, you're not in the hospital now, and you're definitely being proactive here. I hate to tell you, but you're about to find out that frustration is a big part of your 'gift.' Give me one minute and then we'll go."

He ducked into the shop next the empty antique store. As good as his word he was back in less than a minute. "Okay, let's go."

Jace hit the button, unlocking the car doors and they climbed in. "The guy next door told me that he's been there for almost two years and the antique shop was gone by the time he moved in."

"Crap."

"Don't worry. We'll find her." He pulled out into traffic. "We won't stop until we do. And we'll find the other woman too."

Chapter 7

Alex toed off her sneakers and headed into the kitchen. After grabbing a drink from the fridge, she plopped down onto the couch to check her email. There was one from her best friend, Olivia. Smiling, she opened it and read:

Hi,

How's the new job? You started yesterday right? Any luck finding the table woman? How are you doing with your new improved life? When we talked the other night you sounded lonely. It's been a long time, you know! You should definitely do something about that.

I loved the pics of your house. Can't wait to come visit. Should be really soon. Oh, by the way, about that guy from the dating service I was texting. Well, he's a great texter (is that a word?) He's funny, quick, and intelligent. So we were going to meet for drinks, but it turns out that he's only available from 3:30-

5pm Monday thru Friday. (Can you say married?) Then yesterday he sent me a picture...of his penis!

Alex laughed out loud.

What a perv! And the sad thing was, it wasn't all that impressive. And that's only the first guy. This is about as much fun as the divorce so far. (Grimace) Wait till I tell my mother what she's gotten me into. You know she'll be riddled with guilt. Good deal. Maybe you should try the online dating thing :) Okay, gotta go for now. Meeting with my boss in five. Call me with the full scoop on the new job.

Love ya,

Olivia

She read the other three emails and then logged on to check her work email. Two meetings tomorrow and an email about a promo she would be doing on Saturday at the Kingston Auto Mall. There was one more. She didn't recognize the sender. She clicked on it. It was from a listener.

Alexandra, I've really missed you. I'm so glad you're back on the air. Your voice sounds even sexier since the accident. I can't wait to hear your voice again tomorrow. I imagine how it'll be when you're talking only to me. I wish I could be right there in the room with you. I know that's not possible right now, but I'll be seeing you soon. I try to be patient, but it's so hard.

There was no signature. It had to be a joke. Her second day of work and she already had a quasi-stalker. How had he known who she was and how had he known about the accident...unless he was from back home. Digging her cell phone out of her purse, she dialed the station.

"Hi, Jean, it's Alex. Is Paulie around?"

"Yeah, hold on a sec."

"Paulie Boyd."

"Hey, Paulie, This is Alex."

"Ah, Alex, missin' me already?"

"Big-time," she answered. "Listen, I have a question for you."

"Shoot."

"Is there a regular listener at the station who emails all the DJs?"

"There are a few prolific e-mailers, but no one who stands out. Why do you ask? You making friends or enemies already?"

"Come on, I'm good, but I'm not that good. It's probably nothing. Sorry to bother you. Get back to work and I'll talk to you tomorrow."

She closed her phone and read the email again. He was probably just some lonely guy who had nothing better to do than send emails. She told herself not to make a big deal of what was bound to be nothing, but it still gave her the creeps. Why had he said he'd see her soon? Did he work at the station maybe? Or somewhere nearby?

Her stomach growled loudly and she realized that all she'd had to eat was some yogurt for breakfast. She got up to go find something. Her cell phone rang.

Her pulse raced as she checked the number.

It was Jace. She snapped the phone open.

"Hello?"

"Hi, Lex, it's Jace. I wanted to let you know that I finally tracked down the owner of the antique shop."

"You did? That's great."

"Yeah, I have a picture of her for you to look at. I can send it to your email if you want me to, but I found out a few other things. I wondered if you have a few minutes. I just left a client's house. I'm about ten minutes from you. I could stop by."

Maybe Olivia was right. Maybe she really was lonely. That was the only reason she could think of to explain the fact that she was so damned glad to hear from a guy she'd avoided like the plague for years.

"Have you eaten yet?" she asked impulsively.

"Actually I haven't."

"There's this great little Mexican place a few blocks away. I could meet you there. We could get something to eat while you fill me in. I'm anxious to see the picture and to hear what you found out."

"Mexican sounds great. Why don't I swing by and pick you up?"

If he picked her up, it would be too weird.

"No, that's okay. I need to pick up a few things on my way. I'll meet you there."

She gave him directions and they agreed to meet there in ten minutes. She ran into the bathroom to run a brush through her hair and brush her teeth. She checked the windows and doors and left for the restaurant.

As she drove to the restaurant, she realized that she was chewing on her thumbnail. She only did that when she was really nervous. You're being ridiculous! she thought. It wasn't like this was a date or anything. God, she hadn't dated in what, 11 years? She'd only had sex with two men in her whole life. That in itself was pathetic.

For that matter, Alex couldn't begin to imagine getting carried away enough to even consider dating and then getting to the point of undressing in front of any man other than John. It seemed foreign and embarrassing to her. And why was she thinking of this now when she had no interest in Jace other than the fact that he might well have a picture of the dead woman she'd seen in his pocket? She hoped to God it was the right woman so that they could get to her in time.

Alex pulled into the parking lot just as Jace was approaching the door. He stopped and waited for her. When they were seated in a booth, their waitress took their drink orders and left them menus.

Alex looked at Jace. "Actually, I already know what I want. I try to get here at least once a week. I love Mexican food."

Jace smiled at her over his menu. "Yeah, I remember. You were always trying to convince John that if he kept trying it he would learn to like it. I also remember that it never happened."

Alex laughed. "That's true, but he got even. He knew I hated shrimp, so he always made me try it 'just one more time.'"

As soon as they placed their orders Alex asked, "Okay, where's the picture?" He pulled some papers out of his pocket and handed them to her.

She opened the picture up and felt like screaming in frustration. It wasn't her.

Jace could see her disappointment. "I didn't really think it was her, but we had to try. She told me that she and her husband bought the table and chairs at an estate sale somewhere in Ohio."

"She didn't tell you the name of the town?"

He dipped a chip into the bowl of salsa and bit into it. She waited for him to answer.

"Sorry, I'm really hungry. I think she mentioned 'Outer Mongolia.'"

"She doesn't even remember where she bought it? Doesn't she keep records?"

"Lexi, it was eight years ago. I guess she ran the business and her husband was the buyer. We're lucky that she remembers the table. She did say that after her husband picked it up, he went on and on about what a huge estate it was."

Alex picked up a chip and scooped up some salsa. "So did you ask the husband where he got it?"

"Well, that's kind of a problem. As of four years ago, he's her ex-husband. They had no children and she owned the business. Apparently they really hate each other, so they've had no reason to keep in touch."

"In other words, she doesn't have a clue where he is now."

"Bingo. Eli's tracking him down for me, since I've been busy with a new client. And believe me, it's giving him fits."

"The ex is that hard to find, huh?"

"The guy's name is John Smith."

"You've got to be kidding me! He'll never be able to find him."

Jace put his hand over hers on the table. Her body went on alert.

"We will find him," Jace said, "and we'll find the owner of the table. We won't quit until we do."

"Thanks, Jace. I don't know why you're being so nice to me. I was never very nice to you."

"Lex, this is what I do. I find people who are in trouble. Believe me, I know how it feels to know just a little about someone, where they've been, what's happened to them. It's frustrating and sometimes futile, but I can't stop because sometimes… not often, but sometimes, I can save someone. And then maybe I can get a few good nights of sleep and possibly even have a decent dream for a change. Besides," he winked, grinning across the table at her, "John liked you. You must have some redeeming qualities." He spied the waitress walking toward them, a large tray on her arm. "Ah, here comes the food."

The waitress set the food in front of them. Jace moaned in pleasure. "Oh yeah, this smells great."

"It is, believe me!" Alex said. They both ate in silence for a few minutes, enjoying the spicy flavors.

Jace sat back, taking a short break. "So how's your new job going? You've only been there a couple of days, right?"

"Yup, I've been there for exactly two days. It's great so far. I spent the first day learning how the station works and familiarizing myself with everything. Then today I went on the air. I used to do a talk show, but I didn't want all the pressure and stress of that this time. And, to tell you the truth, I love deejaying. I love the music and the mix of things. I'm even looking forward to going live to different locations."

She took another bite of her burrito and a sip of her frozen margarita. "Everyone I've met so far has been really friendly and helpful. And the producer is great. Actually, I think he's the Wizard of Oz. He has this huge high-tech board that he runs the show from. I really think I'm going to be happy there."

She remembered the email on her computer.

"What?" Jace asked.

She looked at him, a question on her face.

"You just frowned over something."

"Oh, it's nothing. I was just thinking about this email I got from a listener today at the radio station. I'm sure it's harmless, but it was a little creepy."

"Creepy how?" He set down his bottle of Dos Equis.

"Well, he knew about my accident, and he said he'd be seeing me soon. It was just weird."

"Let me take a look at it. Eli and I can trace it back to the sender, just to make sure he is a harmless creep."

"You don't have to do that. I'm sure it's nothing."

"I hope it is nothing. Let's find out. Indulge me in this."

"Okay, thanks. It seems like I'm always saying that to you."

"Then please stop. I'd do it for any of my friends." He smiled at her. Alex was filled with surprising warmth at the knowledge that he considered her a friend.

"Tell me what else you found out. You said you have some other things to tell me."

Jace signaled the waitress for another beer. "Well, I talked to one of the guys I've worked with quite a bit. He found out who's handling the Kimberley Haas homicide."

"The nurse," Alex said, pushing her plate away.

"Yeah. The MO is almost exactly the same as the woman in your vision. Her nipples were cut off and there were the same type of cuts. He cut her shirt and bra off with the cut down her sternum, and then there were the same kind of cuts on her body, kind of like he was trying to make art out of it. He came in through the side window that you said was opened. There were no prints, no DNA. The victim did receive some calls in the days before the murder. They traced them to several public phones in some very public places."

He stopped as the waitress set down his beer. Alex asked for a glass of water with lemon and the waitress left.

"So they have nothing really."

"Right, and it gets worse." He brought the bottle to his mouth and took a swallow. Alex absently watched his Adam's apple move up and down. How could it get any worse? No evidence meant that there was no chance of catching the killer. That meant that there were bound to be more victims. She couldn't bear the thought of any other women dying like that. There must be something more she could do! Maybe if she touched the table again she'd see more, maybe even the face of the killer.

Jace set his beer down. "When he checked the database for similar crimes, there were eight hits in New York and Pennsylvania."

"Oh God." Her food sat like a rock in her stomach. Eight women! And there could be more that they didn't know about.

"There weren't any in Ohio?" she asked.

"Not that he could see, but he's still checking. I'm sorry, Lex. But you have to see that this was happening before you started 'seeing' the victims. He was already out there."

"But I could have saved one of them, and I have to do whatever I can to save the ones who are still alive. The other woman I saw could still be alive. We have to catch this monster somehow."

The waitress set her water on the table and asked if they would like any dessert. Jace looked over at Alex and she shook her head no. He asked for the check.

"Sure, I'll be right back with it."

"Alex, this is a guy who's been killing for at least ten years and hasn't left a single clue to work with. Some very good men have been working these cases. In fact, the FBI is involved now that they know the guy has killed in several different states. And let me tell you, their forensics lab is state of the art."

They paused as the waitress set the bill on the table.

As she walked away, Alex said, "I don't care. We have other ways of finding information. Maybe we could get something more off the evidence they already have."

"Alex, it's evidence in a murder case. Having people handle the evidence would contaminate it."

"Well, how good is the evidence if they weren't able to get anything useful from it in the first place!"

"Hey, I agree with you, but I doubt seriously that anyone else will." Jace shrugged. "We'll just have to work backwards from the table and hope that it leads to the killer or at least to the victim."

"I don't know how you do this for a living, Jace. It's so damned frustrating. Are we getting any closer?"

"Patience was never one of your virtues, was it?" He smiled. "Don't worry. I'm like a bulldog. Once I get my teeth into something I never let go until it's finished."

He handed the waitress a credit card as she approached the table. She left to run it.

"Hey, I should get that. I'm the one who invited you," Alex said.

"You can pick up the tab the next time. Besides, we discussed business. I can claim in on my taxes as a business dinner."

"Fine, but I won't forget. Next time's on me."

"Sure."

The waitress set the check down. He signed it and they got up to leave.

"I'll meet you at your house. We'll take a look at that email."

He read the email twice and then sat back on the couch. "Okay, I agree that the guy is a little strange. I'm going to forward the email to my office. We'll find out where it originated. Let me know if you get any more from this guy. I wouldn't worry. He's probably just a harmless admirer." He turned to her. "I'm sure that your accident was reported in the newspapers at the time and you were fairly well known there, so that's most likely how he knew so much about you."

"Yeah, I'm not really too worried about it. I'm just a little freaked out about everything right now I guess, lots of changes in such a short time. Jace, do you think that Eli will ever be able to find John Smith?"

"Positive. The ex-wife was able to tell us his middle name and his birth date. So we'll find him. As soon as we find anything I'll let you know."

Restless and unable to sit still, Alexandra walked to the window. She stood with her back to the room, looking out into the darkness. "It's so hard to wait! I feel like I need to find out everything right now and that every day that I don't find that poor woman is just wasted time. Sometimes I imagine I can actually hear the minutes ticking away."

Jace came up behind her and put his hands on her shoulders in what was meant as a gesture of comfort. She stiffened, her body jerking slightly. He held on.

"Are we ever going to get past this, whatever it is? You asked me to go to dinner. I know you wanted to find out what was going on, but you seemed to enjoy yourself."

"I know. I did. It's not you. It's me."

"That's a bunch of bullshit. I hate when people say that. It's not an answer." His smile was bitter. "It's really kind of funny, you know. That's exactly what Natalie said right before she left me. As far as I can tell it's never completely true. It may be about you, but it's also about me. It's gotta be."

"I'm sorry about Natalie. I never told you that."

"Don't be. I'm not. Turns out she was right to leave. She hated my 'seeing' and that made me feel like I was a schitzo or something. She said she loved the 'normal' side of me, but that she was actually repelled by my 'darker side,' as she put it."

Suddenly restless, he turned and moved around the room. He poked his finger into a bowl filled with polished rocks. Moving on, he picked up a picture of Alex and Olivia from the fireplace mantle. "I tell myself that there are women out there who will understand the seeing, that it's really just the result of genetics, like my ability to play the guitar, or the way I can add numbers really quickly in my head." After placing the picture carefully back onto the mantle, he sat on the arm of the couch. "But so far, I've seen no evidence to support that theory. Even you, similarly blessed with the same genetic quirk, practically shudder whenever I touch you." He shook his head.

Alex crossed the room to stand in front of him. "The way I reacted has nothing to do with the seeing."

His head came up. He looked her in the eye. "Oh that's right. You couldn't stand my touch long before you knew I had psychic abilities."

"What are you talking about?" Alex said.

"I'm talking about your wedding day. Remember how John insisted that I kiss the bride. When I did you pulled away like you'd been burned. Then you turned away and wouldn't even look at me. You did everything but wipe your lips with the back of your hand."

How could she explain that every time he touched her she felt like she'd been burned? How could she tell him that every time he came near her, each and every cell screamed in awareness? How could she possibly justify the fact that from the moment she'd met him, she'd felt more alive somehow when she was with him then she had with any other person on earth aside from John.

How could she feel that way about him when she'd always been so in love with John? If she said it out loud, then it became a betrayal. She couldn't do that to John, to the memory of John and their life together. What could she possibly say to Jace? So she went on the defensive.

"Oh poor, poor Jace. Nobody loves you. Please… you've had a constant stream of women throwing themselves at you since the first day I set eyes on you at college." He opened his mouth to say something. "And don't try to deny it! I remember you were a tour guide at my freshman orientation, and they had to split up your group because you had twice as many people in your group as anyone else – all of them women."

She poked him in the chest with her finger.

"And you know how I said that I was sorry that Natalie moved out? Well, I lied! She was a stone cold bitch from day one. If anyone was schitzo, she was. The only time she was ever nice was when you were around."

"What do you mean?" Jace said.

"Remember when the four of us went to Tim's wedding, and we all sat together? When you left the table the first time, she acted like John and I weren't even there. I mean, she never said one word to us the whole time you were gone. It almost drove us crazy. We actually said a few things to her and she acted like we hadn't even spoken! Then you and John went to get us drinks and left me alone with her and the little witch threatened me."

Jace grinned. "She did? What possible reason would she have to threaten you?"

"I'm sorry I mentioned it. Forget it."

"Oh no you don't. Now that you brought it up I want to hear it all," Jace said.

"It's ridiculous and embarrassing."

"Tough. Spill it."

"Okay, well, she told me that she could see the way you were looking at me and that whatever you and I had going had better end right then and there or else she was going to 'make my life a living hell.' She wouldn't believe me when I told her that we didn't even get along. She claimed that she could feel the 'sexual tension' flowing between the two of us and that she couldn't believe we could treat John like that."

Jace laughed. "I always wondered why you were so pissed when we got back to the table. You usually got along great with everyone, except me that is. That theory she had about the two of us... interesting!" He shook his head. "I must say, though, you guys were good. You and John never let on that you didn't like Natalie." The amusement left his face. "But all that still doesn't explain the way you act around me."

Alex sighed. "Jace, can we just table this discussion for tonight? It's late and I haven't been sleeping well since the accident."

"Bad dreams? Still? It's been a long time."

"I know. There are long periods when I sleep just fine. I only get them now when I have big changes going on in my life. Once I feel more settled at work and we get this other thing settled, I'm sure they'll go away."

He stood up to leave and suddenly they were close, very close. Alex knew it was a test. Her first instinct was to take a step back, but she kept her feet firmly rooted to the floor. Jace reached out, gently cupping her chin in his fingers. She felt the hum, but she didn't move away.

"You've had a really bad time of it this past year, haven't you? I think you've had enough bad dreams. You deserve some of the good kind. Go to bed and dream something mindless for a change. That's an order." He leaned forward and placed a chaste kiss on her forehead. She closed her eyes, deeply touched by the gesture. He stepped around her and crossed to the door. "Night Alex. Get some sleep."

Chapter 8

Jace stared at the computer screen in frustration. He tried something else. Another dead end!

"Damn it!" He sat back in his chair, rubbing the back of his neck with one hand.

"Up with the chickens, bro?" Eli set a large cup of coffee in front of Jace.

Jace reached for it. "I definitely made the right decision when I took you on as a partner." He lifted the plastic tab. After blowing on the steaming coffee, he took a careful swallow. "Ahhhh. Better than a blood transfusion. I needed that. Thanks, man."

"No problem. So what are you doing here at the crack of dawn, and what were you swearing at when I came in?"

He took one more gulp of hot coffee. "I'm trying to find out where this email originated, but this guy is better than I am."

"Well, move aside and let's see if he's better than I am. Somehow I doubt it."

"Whoa, so much humility from one guy." Jace rolled his chair to the side to make room for Eli.

"Hey, there may be a few things I'm not good at." Eli grinned over at Jace. "Although nothing comes to mind at the moment, but this stuff–" he pointed to the computer–"is as natural to me as mother's milk." Eli pulled a chair up to the computer and tapped a few keys. He took a minute to read the email. Turning to Jace, he said, "Is this email to your Alex... Lexi?"

"She's not 'my' Alex, but yeah it is. She started her new job a few days ago, and this was in her email yesterday."

"Man, she must really be something. She comes to see you a week ago, and she's already got you wrapped around her little finger. Now two days into a new job she's got a psycho stalker? I gotta meet this woman."

Jace smacked Eli on the back of the head. "Hey, show a little respect. She's John's wife and she needs help."

"No, actually she's John widow. Big difference there! Believe me, I'm all admiration. Any woman who can hop you up like this has got to be really something. She's gotta be a major babe to have you so tied up in knots. I've never seen you act like this with any other woman, period. You couldn't have cared less when Natalie left." He continued to tap on the keyboard. "Of course she was a total bitch, so no great loss."

Jace laughed. "How come I never knew that everyone hated Natalie? I've always placed myself somewhere above the average guy in the intelligence department, so how could I have had such bad judgment where she was concerned?"

"Dude, the woman was 5'9", all legs and talk about flexible! Must have been all that yoga. I'm sure whatever she lacked in the personality department, she more than made up for in the sack."

Jace grinned. "Yeah, but it's nice to have someone to talk to once in a while." They both laughed. Jace said, "It's a good thing Mattie wasn't here to hear us talking about women like that. She'd knock us both on our asses."

"Gotcha!" Eli shouted. "There's the little geek. Just another minute, and we'll know where he sent this sucker from."

The only sound in the room was Eli furiously tapping on the keyboard. Jace drank his coffee and waited. Eli hit the return button and sat back in his seat. "There it is! This guy knows his stuff. That was better than the game of chess I played last night." He shook his head, grinning.

"The guy really had me going. He had me bouncing around all over the world, but he made one mistake. He doesn't know his stuff as well as I do. After all that subterfuge, it turns out that the guy sent the email from the public library. He must have been using someone else's time because I think the IP address he used is a woman's."

"How the hell would you know that?"

"Well, the screen name is 'Barbiedoll22' so unless he's a serious Barbie doll collector, I'm thinkin' that he used someone else's screen name."

"But why would he go to all the trouble of disguising the IP address if he's using someone else's email in the first place?"

"He's peacocking. He wants to show us how smart he is. Or maybe he's just paranoid and does this kind of shit all the time. The guy's a little bit of a nut case if you ask me. That email was just strange, man."

"Yeah, I gotta agree with that. Okay, smartass, where does that leave us?"

"Well, we could go to the library and talk to the people who work there. Maybe they know who the girl is and maybe, she let someone use the computer while she was online, but I doubt it. But my guess is that either she didn't use up her whole hour, or she got up to go to the can and the guy either offered to hold her place or used it while she was away. Or maybe the guy watched her sign in. It might be worth talking to her if we can find her, but I doubt it. If he's going to all this trouble to hide, he's smart enough not to be seen."

"Okay," Jace said, "Let's wait and see if the guy sends another email to Alex. If he does, then we'll go talk to the people at the library."

"Sounds like a plan," Eli said.

"So, any luck finding John Smith?" Jace asked.

"Not yet. I've been through the DMV records for just about all the eastern states, but no one with that birth date comes up. She's absolutely sure of the date right?"

"Yeah, she was very definite. And you remember how Mom was about birthdays, always making a big deal about celebrating everyone's birthday. I think most women are better at that kind of stuff than we are."

"You got a point there, bro. Okay then, I'm gonna work my way through the rest of the states. Let's hope I get a hit soon and it doesn't end up being on the west coast. After your trip to Brazil, we could stand to build up some money in our coffers, ya know?"

"Coffers? Where do you come up with this shit?" Jace said. "And our 'coffers' are pretty well filled. But you're right. It never hurts to tuck some more away. Plus, we've got three other cases on the front burner. By the way, Eli thanks for dropping everything and coming here to work with me. You've already taken the pressure off considerably. I've managed to get in about seven hours of sleep three nights this week! That's a personal best for me in I can't tell you how long."

Eli smiled. "As you know, there was very little left to drop and I've been itching for a change for a while now, so this was perfect for both of us. I'll keep working on John Smith. We have to find this dickhead before he kills anyone else."

They touched base on a few other cases, and then Eli left to go to his own office. Jace got up, stretching muscles stiff from sitting for so long at the computer. What he needed was a nice long run to clear his head. He did some of his best problem solving while running.

In the bathroom, he changed into shorts and put on his running shoes. He poked his head in to let Eli know where he was going. Eli nodded absently, not bothering to look up from the computer.

He stretched and then set out at a good pace, heading toward the park about ten blocks away. So many things were going on right now, he could hardly keep up. Taking on a partner, the letter from John, seeing the drawings of all those women murdered so brutally captured in death all for the pleasure of a maniac.

Who was he kidding? The thing that was having the largest impact on him was the arrival of Alexandra on his doorstep! He never saw that coming. She'd been avoiding him for so long that he had given up hope of finding a way to somehow make a connection with her.

Jace had been so sure that he'd never let on to John how Alex affected him, but of course John had known anyway. He would rather have cut off his own arm than do anything to hurt John. But John even apologized for stealing Alex out from under Jace's nose, which was ridiculous when it had been plain to see from the start that Alex and John belonged together.

There'd always been something about Alex that pulled at Jace, and from the moment he had held her in his foyer, he knew that whatever it was, it was still there. Well, he'd just have to deal with it.

He picked up the pace. He could feel the sweat running down the curve of his spine. It felt good to use his muscles instead of his brain for a change. He was tired of seeing everyone's worst nightmares come true. He was due for something good to happen, but he couldn't shake the feeling he'd had in the pit of his stomach ever since Alex had involved him in this case.

He knew from experience that whenever he felt like this it was bad news. Every time he'd felt this way in the past, something had gone horribly wrong. He couldn't let that happen this time. Not with Alex involved. Feeling the burning in his calves, he looked around him. He'd run much farther than usual. He headed back to the office.

Chapter 9

Alex drained the pasta and poured it into a bowl, tossing it with the roasted tomatoes, garlic and olive oil fresh out of the oven. Steam rose in a fragrant rush. Leaning forward, she inhaled, closing her eyes to better savor the heavenly scent.

She was starving. It was eight pm, and all she'd had to eat all day was a package of instant oatmeal and a small bag of stale oyster crackers she'd found in her purse. If they kept her this busy all the time at work, she'd have to buy some new jeans.

She finished the pasta off with salt, pepper, and some fresh Parmesan cheese she'd grated. She put some pasta on a plate and then poured herself a glass of white wine. She wiped down the counter, stacking the pots and colander in the sink. She stacked the dirty dishes in the dishwasher racks.

Stop stalling! she told herself. She'd decided that it was time to eat at her new table. She'd almost died in the accident, but the fact was that she hadn't. So she'd take John's advice and really live the life she'd been given. If that meant learning to embrace her 'gift' and all that it entailed, then she had to stop avoiding anything that might trigger it. She needed to learn to use it and control it instead of letting it control her.

So tonight she was eating in the dining room. After piling the silverware on the side of her plate, she picked up her glass of wine and her plate. She straightened her shoulders and strode through to the dining room. She set everything on the table, unconsciously avoiding touching the shiny surface. After taking a deep breath, she quickly pulled out a chair and sat down.

She pulled the chair closer to the table. A hot, searing pain moved into her hands. She winced, squinting her eyes closed. She let go of the chair like she'd been burned, but as soon as the pain passed and her eyes opened, she knew she wasn't alone in the seat.

A white damask tablecloth covered the table. There were flowers and two heavy candlesticks in the middle of the table. The table was set formally for five people, as if for a special occasion, but there were only four people seated at the table. Dinner had already been eaten and in front of her she saw a half-eaten piece of cake. Lemon. She could taste it. It was his favorite.

He wasn't hungry for cake. She looked to her right at the woman delicately dabbing her mouth with a snowy damask napkin, and she felt the sick desire well up inside of him. It had been almost three years since David had married her and brought her home. He'd watched her with his hot dark eyes for three long years. Alexandra's stomach turned as he imagined all the things he would do to her. Soon. Very soon.

Alex felt his giddy excitement and deviant lust. As he gazed at the blonde woman seated at one end of the table, Alex could see that this was the woman she'd seen lying bathed in her own blood on the floor. As the woman looked over at the occupant of the chair Alex was sitting in, Alex could see the fear and disgust in her eyes. The woman knew what he was thinking.

The woman's gaze went to the opposite end of the table. The man's eyes followed hers. The man at the other end of the table was obviously the woman's husband. He looked to be at least fifteen years older than the woman. Alex felt the hate and contempt welling up inside of the younger man. He hated David as much as he lusted after Ann.

"Do you have to go away right now, David? Couldn't they manage there without you this once?" the woman asked her husband.

The look he bent upon her was both loving and a tad patronizing. "You know I wouldn't leave if it wasn't necessary, Ann. The manager there is new and hasn't got a clue how to handle the production problems there. Hopefully I'll only be gone for a few days, a week at most."

Alex felt her mouth — no not her mouth – the man's mouth tilt upward into a sly smirk. The young man across from Alex resumed eating his cake. But she felt her own face turn towards Ann. The stepmother's face drained of all color.

Alex felt his excitement and lust rising as he looked at the woman named Ann. His feelings were so intense that blood was pounding through his/her veins at a truly alarming rate. If her head were a melon, it would have burst with the pressure. He lifted his fork and took another bite of cake.

Alex stomach turned. The thoughts going through his head were so scattered now that she couldn't keep up. She had to get away. Scenes of his depravity flashed through his head like a slide show.

Turning back to her husband, Ann said, desperation in her voice, "Why don't I come with you this time? It's been a while since we've been away together."

"Any other time I'd say yes, but I won't have any time to spend with you. Why don't we plan a trip when I get back? I thought you said you were really backed up at the office. You never take time off during tax season."

"Yes, of course. You're right. It was just a thought." The woman sat back in her seat, looking both trapped and terrified.

The pressure in Alexandra's head was building. Black appeared around the corners of the dining room. She had to break away now. Using every ounce of concentration she could muster, she lifted her hand and pushed the chair back from the table. She shot up out of the chair, her upward momentum causing the chair to topple over backwards onto the hardwood floor. She registered the crack of wood on wood. She let go of the table, taking a deep breath. The room came back into focus. Her room… in her house.

Thank God.

She stumbled to the couch. She lay down, closing her eyes against the blinding glare of the floor lamp spilling light over the end of the couch. The pain in her head was tremendous. She lay there, her breathing shallow, her skin cold and clammy with sweat, waiting for the pain to recede. The pain would go away, she told herself. It always had before. But it had never been this bad before.

She breathed evenly, forcing her mind to be a blank page, as she had learned to do while at the rehab center. After a while the pain eased, until it was just a dull throbbing behind her eyes. She sat up, checking the digital clock on the cable box across the room. Only 8:42! It seemed more like hours since she'd sat down at the table.

She needed a drink badly. A wave of dizziness washed over her as she stood. Her body was telling her that it needed fuel. She grimaced at the thought of eating now. She thought she could still detect the slight tang of lemon on the back of her tongue. She poured herself a tall glass of tap water and guzzled it down at the sink. She didn't even want to think about what she had felt inside the mind and body of that sick bastard.

She returned to the dining room, giving the fallen chair a wide berth. She picked up her wine glass and her pasta now cold and somewhat congealed, careful not to touch the table in any way. She set her meal on the coffee table and picked up the remote turning on the TV. It didn't matter what was on. She felt the need for the comforting white noise of a sitcom.

Taking a forkful of the pasta, she forced herself to take a bite. She stared at the soothing wash of color on the TV screen. She took another bite, carefully focusing on the mindless action taking place on the screen. A few minutes later she glanced down at her plate, surprised to find that it was empty. She picked up her wine glass and took a drink, enjoying its fruity flavor and the ensuing warmth as it made its way down her throat.

The woman she'd seen crudely slaughtered and lying in her own blood on that floor was already dead and had been for a long time; she was sure of it. In fact, she was certain Ann had been the first one to die at the hands of that monster. And Alex would bet he hadn't been so careful when he'd killed her. She'd felt everything he was feeling, and she was certain his feelings were way too violent and uncontrolled when he'd been thinking of what he had planned for Ann.

Tears spilled from her eyes and ran down her face unheeded, tears for the woman she's sat at the table with. Tears of helplessness and futility, tears full of knowing with certainty that there was nothing she could do that would save this woman from an excruciatingly painful death. Ann was already dead. Alex felt tired to her bones. She sat limply on the couch, her head resting on the back cushion.

Her head snapped up. Maybe they couldn't save her, but if they could find her body, she felt certain that they would find evidence they needed to nail the sick bastard. But where was the body? Why hadn't she come up in the crimes database? Alexandra needed to talk to Jace about this, but not tonight. First she needed sleep, and some distance.

Chapter 10

Friday turned out to be just as crazy a day at the radio station as the rest of the week had been. They were down a DJ and behind on recording some commercial spots, so Alexandra worked a double and then recorded some commercials. She'd tried to reach Jace in the few minutes she'd had free, but apparently he was out of town for the day. She'd grabbed a yogurt and some Cheez-Its from the vending machine and went back into the booth.

She was afraid that she was beginning to depend too heavily on Jace. She'd been alone and handled things just fine for quite a while. Even when she'd been married to John, she had basically taken care of everything but the yard work and repairs on the house. It bothered her that it seemed so important to have this lifeline with Jace. Come on Alex, she told herself, you've never handled anything like this. You're severely out of your depth.

She felt this burning impatience to talk to him about what had happened last night. They just had to find the woman, Ann. It seemed more urgent than ever now that she had been inside the killer's mind. She was certain he would never stop killing.

There was something inside his brain that wasn't wired right. The thought of killing seemed to be a deep-seeded craving. The experience of killing and carving those women was a thrill he would never be able to pass up. Even worse, when she'd been inside the twisted miasma of his brain, she had sensed that there were no boundaries in place, no natural instinct for self-control. No, he was never going to stop until they found a way to stop him.

Pulling on her headphones, she resolved to call Jace as soon as she was done at work. She'd take all the help she could get. "Don't forget we'll be live from the Kingston Auto Mall tomorrow from ten to two. So stop by for some great deals on a new or used car, truck, or SUV. They've got it all there in one place. And there's easy financing available on site. We'll be giving away some free Jam T-shirts and lots of other free stuff. So come out and take a look at all the great bargains and stop by and see us." She went into a rock song.

She dug her cell phone out of her purse and texted a message to Jace. I have some new info. Call me when you get a chance, leaving work in about an hour. The song ended and another started. Her phone beeped and she flipped it open. U going right home? I'll be back in town then. I'll stop by your house?

She typed, "Okay. See you then."

****

Alex closed the car door with her hip, shifting the plastic grocery bags from where they were cutting into her fingers. She was glad she'd made it home before Jace arrived. After sliding her key into the lock, she pushed the door open, slipping out of her shoes as she entered.

She went through into the kitchen, setting everything on the counter. She turned and then stopped dead. The hair on the back of her neck stood up and a chill passed through her.

Something wasn't right. She turned and looked around the room. What was it? What was it that was bothering her? And then it hit her. She turned again, going back through the kitchen to the dining room.

The flowers she had bought two days ago were no longer in the vase on the small table by the window. In fact the flowers in the vase were not the ones she had bought at all. The vase now sat in the middle of the dining room table, and it was filled with a huge bouquet of brightly colored flowers. She felt lightheaded and her hands were suddenly tingling.

Without thinking twice, she turned and ran for the front door. She flung it open and barreled through. She slammed into an immovable object. She opened her mouth to scream.

"Whoa!" Jace said. "Where's the fire?"

The moment she heard his voice, the tension left her and she flung her arms around him in relief. His arms came around her, enveloping her trembling body and pulling her closer.

"Hey, what's wrong? Are you all right?"

She held on tight. Was she all right? No, definitely not. His energy flowed through her body as always, but this time it was calming instead of scary.

"Someone's been in my house. And they left me a present on the table."

"In your house? Didn't you lock the doors?" Jace asked.

"Of course I locked the doors," Alex said, her voice tight. "I had new deadbolts put on the minute I moved in. I don't know how they got in."

"Okay, stay here." He set her aside and went into the house. She heard him moving through the house, opening and closing doors. God, her closet was a mess. Had she left her underwear on the floor after her shower this morning?

Why was she even thinking about that now! Someone had been in her house. All of a sudden, she was furious. Everybody should have one safe haven, that one place of their own where they felt cozy and secure. Alex loved her new home so much, and now she wasn't sure that she'd ever feel totally safe there again.

Jace appeared in the open doorway. "All clear. You can go in now. I just want to look around outside, see if I can tell where he got in."

"I'll go with you," Alexandra said. No way was she going back into that house by herself.

Jace walked slowly around the house, stopping to check each window. When they reached the back of the house, he squatted in front of one of the cellar windows. "This is where he got in. See how the dirt is all scuffed up and the grass is flattened."

She bent down. One pane of glass had been cut out of one of the basement windows. The window folded in and down, but whoever had opened it had closed it again, minus the pane of glass.

"We need to call the police," Jace said.

"That's fine with me. I've got a permanent case of the creeps. Right now I'm seriously considering buying bars for all the windows."

Jace put his hand on the small of her back, guiding her to the front door. She went back to the kitchen and he followed. Her bags were still where she'd left them on the kitchen table. She hoped the ice cream wasn't melted. She moved to put the groceries away while Jace opened his phone and called 9-1-1.

"Okay, they'll be here in a few minutes. Why don't you sit down while we wait?"

She opened the freezer door and stuck the ice cream on the top shelf. "No, I need to keep moving. I'm so mad, I swear that if blood really could boil, mine would." She closed the freezer door with unnecessary force.

Turning around, she said, "Who breaks into someone's house to leave flowers, for God's sake!"

"A stalker maybe," Jace said.

Her laugh held just a hint of hysteria.

"So this is my new life! John wouldn't let me go with him. He insisted that I stay here because I have this 'gift,' this mission, and I have to 'help' people. So far all I've done is help a woman die. So now I'm seeing another woman and it turns out she's been dead for years! Who the hell am I supposed to be helping here? Every time I get near my new dining room set all I see are scenes from hell and when I sit in the chairs I'm looking at life through the eyes of a monster. As if that's not enough, now I've added a stalker along the way... really? Welcome to my new improved life."

"Hey, hey." Jace gathered her close again. She felt his energy and comfort filling her. "Calm down, Lex. It may take a little while, but we'll get this all straightened out."

She took a shuddering breath. Her hands stopped shaking and she felt her strength returning. In his arms she felt safe again, calm. She'd been through a lot, but self-pity wasn't going to help. She'd led a very lucky life for a long time. Until John's death, nothing bad had ever touched her. So now she would learn to deal with adversity. After all, adversity built character, right?

They heard the crunch of tires in the driveway, then the police were at the door. Alex answered all their questions. By the time they left, it was after eight. Alex looked over at Jace as he closed the door on the last of the officers. He looked as beat as she felt.

"Go pack a few things, Alex. We both need a good night's sleep, and neither of us will get one if you stay here."

She looked around the room and then further into the dining room where the flowers still rested in the vase on the table.

"I know I should be brave and say I'm fine here, but there's still a hole in the basement window, so give me ten minutes.

She followed him to his house and parked behind him. After they were inside and he'd dropped her bag in the spare room across from his, they went downstairs to the kitchen.

"How about grilled cheese and soup?" he asked.

At the thought of food, her stomach growled. "Sounds great."

He got out a small pot and a frying pan and set to work making the sandwiches.

"What can I do?" Alex asked.

"Just sit and relax. I think I can manage to whip up soup and sandwiches."

She sat on a stool, leaning her elbows on the breakfast bar and watched him in action.

"So," he said, "you said that the woman we've been looking for is already dead. What happened that I don't know about?"

"The funny thing is," Alex said, "that I tried all day to get hold of you to tell you about it and then with everything that happened, it flew right out of my head."

"Understandable. I'm sorry you couldn't get hold of me."

"Yeah," she joked, "you really should quit your job, so you can be available to me at all times of the day and night."

"Wow, you want the nights too?" He grinned over at her. "That'll definitely cost you extra." Then the grin was gone. "So tell me."

She told him about her decision to start eating at the table and what had happened after she had sat in the chair.

"So you couldn't see his face?"

"No, I told you, I was in his seat and he was sitting in it."

"But you saw the rest of the people at the table. Did you get a feel for when it might have taken place?"

"I've thought a lot about that," Alex said. "The killer was much younger then. I could feel that his body was lean and muscular, but he handled himself like a younger man. The killer who attacked Kimberly Haas was older, more solid. He carried himself like an adult. I can't really tell you how I know that, but trust me. He was a younger man when he killed the woman I saw. And she was his first victim. I would guess maybe about ten or more years ago."

Jace poured the hot soup into two bowls with handles on the sides and set them down on the bar, then went back for the sandwiches. "You want something to drink? Beer or water, those are your choices."

"I'll have a beer."

He grabbed two out of the fridge and took a seat next to her.

Alex took a bite of the sandwich. "Mmm, so good. I'm beginning to think that I'm doomed to be eating just one good meal a day at nine o'clock at night."

Jace smiled over at her. "If you think this is a good meal, guys must love you. You're a very cheap date."

She chuckled. "Hey, I'll have you know that when I was little, grilled cheese and cream of tomato soup was one of my favorite meals. In fact, it's still really high up there." She took a spoonful of the soup and let the warm liquid slide down her throat. Comfort on a spoon, she thought. She felt much better already.

"To say that the house was very upscale would be a gross understatement," she continued. "You know what the dining room set looked like. But the table was set very formally, lots of silverware, water glass, wine glass, etc. And they were using linen napkins. I saw the woman, Ann, raise the napkin and daintily dab at her mouth, with a linen napkin." She tilted her head, spoon poised in mid-air. "I thought people only did that in the movies."

Jace smiled at that.

"Anyway, they were all dressed very well, expensively I mean. The young kid across the table was wearing stuff that today would probably come from Gap or J. Crew. Ann had on a cashmere tank and sweater. The husband was in a white dress shirt, like maybe he'd just come from work. They were all very beautiful. The boy I could see was blond with blue eyes and a finely sculpted face. He looked pure-bred through and through."

"So, we know a lot more about them now," Jace said.

"Yeah," Alex said. "We know that the victim's name is Ann and that she's already dead."

"We already knew that it was a strong possibility, Alex. I'm sorry it turned out that way, but you just told me a few minutes ago that you don't think he'll ever stop killing. So we still have some women to save."

"I know. I'm just wallowing a little. You know, the other reason I think he was pretty young is because he's a hell of a lot more organized now than his thoughts led me to believe he would be. I think that practice makes perfect, that he's really honed his methodology. I can't believe he's never made a mistake that would give anyone a clue. You should have seen the inside of his mind, Jace." She set down her spoon and reached for her beer.

"He's extremely intelligent, but his thoughts were all over the place. The only time he was focused was when he was zeroed in on Ann."

Jace wiped his mouth, crumpling the paper napkin and tossing it onto his plate. "Eli was going to work on John Smith today, but I haven't had a chance to touch base with him. Hopefully he'll find him soon and then we'll see. Any more emails today?"

"Not as of three o'clock this afternoon. I haven't checked since then. Did you find out who sent it?"

"We traced it and found out that it was sent from the Dayton Library, but we weren't able to find out who sent it. We were going to wait, but Eli decided to stop over there when he went out for lunch and see if the people who work there remembered anything, but we're probably not going to find out a lot. It's a large branch and they have a ton of people in and out of there every day. We'll see."

Alex finally brought up the subject she'd been avoiding. "So who do you think put the flowers on my table? And what do I do now?"

"While you were talking to the police, I called a friend of mine. He's a retired cop and he works for a security company. If you give me the okay, he knows a contractor who will replace the basement window, and if you agree, the company can install a home security system sometime very soon."

"Damn, I hate to have to do that. It's a nice neighborhood. I don't want to have to be on lockdown all the time. I just want to go back in time and feel safe in my home again." She sighed. "But since that's not going to happen, I guess you'd better call the guy and set it up."

"What's on your agenda for tomorrow?" Jace asked her.

"I've got a remote tomorrow at the Kingston Auto Mall. After that I have some laundry to do."

Jace pushed his plate back, leaning his arms on the countertop. "Why don't I meet you at your house when you get out of work?"

"You don't have to do that, Jace. I'm a big girl."

"Believe me," he said, "I'm well aware of that. Just humor me. I'll feel better if I go in there with you the first time." He picked up the dishes, rinsing them and stacking them in the sink. "Now let's go watch TV for a little bit before we hit the sack."

They watched TV until Alex could no longer keep her eyes open. "Come on, light weight," Jace said. He stood and then offered his hand to pull her up. "Bed time."

They walked up the stairs and down the hallway. At the door to her room, she turned to Jace. "Thank you for everything you've done for me, not just tonight, but from the beginning. I can see why John thought the world of you."

She reached up to kiss his cheek, but he turned his head at the last minute and their lips met. His lips were warm and firm. It was just a quick kiss and then he stepped back, but it was enough to set every cell hopping. Her stomach dipped, the same feeling that she'd experienced when she was a child and her father had taken a hill too fast in the car. Why the hell did this stuff always happen with him? Why him and not anyone else?

"You're welcome," Jace said tightly, his hands clenched at his sides. "The bathroom's the next door down. Night, Alex."

With that he went into his room, closing the door behind him.

She went into the guest room, shutting the door. She leaned back against it. What the hell had just happened? She'd kissed Jace, and she'd been disappointed when it ended. She must be missing sex more than she thought, that's all. Don't make a big deal about it, Alex. It was just a mistake. He turned his head. That's all it was.

Chapter 11

Alex was afraid there would be some awkwardness in the morning, but when she followed the smell of freshly brewed coffee to the kitchen, she found Jace by the door tying the laces to his running shoes. He was in t-shirt and shorts and was obviously on his way out for a morning run. He looked up and smiled.

"Morning. Did you sleep well?"

"Like a rock. Thanks."

"There's coffee and some fresh bagels on the counter. Help yourself. What time do you have to be there?"

"I'll have to leave in about forty-five minutes to get there on time."

"Well then I'll see you after at your house. Call me when you're leaving the mall, okay?"

"Okay."

"Sell lots of cars. I'll see you later." And he left.

She poured some coffee into a thick mug he'd left on the counter for her and toasted a bagel. As she sat down to eat, her phone rang. It was Olivia.

"Hey, Liv, what's up?"

"I'm bored and I'm sick of dating weirdoes, and I miss my best friend. That's what's up. How about some company this weekend? I could leave now and be there in a couple of hours."

"Well, I have to work until two, but why don't you meet me at my house at about two-thirty. I can't wait to see you. I have so much to tell you."

"Juicy stuff I hope. Okay, it's a date." She groaned. "Did I mention the word date? Hey, listen. Could you email me the directions? You know how directionally challenged I am."

Alex laughed. "You and me both. No problem. I'll send 'em in just a few minutes. And Olivia... I'm really glad you're coming."

"Me too. See you later."

****

Alex was surprised at how many people had shown up at the Auto Mall. She found it hard to believe that there were that many people at any given time that actually needed a new car. Either that or they were just hungry for free hot dogs, burgers and soda. It turned out to be a lot of fun though and the time went quickly. She was looking forward to seeing Olivia and catching up on things.

She checked her phone for messages. She hoped Olivia had found the house okay. There was a voice mail from Jace. "Alex, I'm really glad Olivia's coming into town. I'm sure that will be fun. I just wanted to tell you that I have to go out of town this morning. There's an elderly gentleman missing, and they called me to help in the search. I called my friend and he's sending someone out to fix the window. They should be there around four-thirty. Make sure you check their IDs. Even though they're contractors, they're under contract with the security company, so they should have badges from TK Security. I'll try to call later. Bye."

What a job Jace had chosen for himself. Or had it chosen him? Please God, let the man be okay. Alex put the car in gear and drove off.

Olivia was waiting on the doorstep when she got there.

"Aren't you proud of me?" she said. "I even left a few minutes early, so I could get lost a couple of times, but your directions were so good I didn't even get lost once."

A dimple appeared in her left cheek.

They hugged and went into the house. "Yes, I'm very proud of you," Alexandra said, "and impressed. Even I got lost finding this place the first time."

"Why are we both carrying overnight bags? Where have you been, you naughty girl?"

For some reason Alex blushed.

"It's not what you think, Liv. Just give me a minute to send a quick email to work about the remote we just did and then I'll tell you everything."

"Okay, but make it quick," Olivia said.

"Go put your stuff in your bedroom. It's the second one down the hall on the right."

"So bossy." Olivia picked up her bags and headed out.

Alex opened her laptop and waited for the Internet to kick in and her mail to download. She looked around. Everything looked the same as last night, but she had the urge to go and search through every nook and cranny to make sure no one else had been there. She knew it was just nerves, but she almost felt like someone was watching her.

Her email dinged and she shrugged off the uncomfortable feeling. She logged onto her work email. There were several emails. She composed hers first and sent it off then started to sort through her incoming messages. The first two were reminders of things she already knew about. The third was from a woman's organization wondering if she were available to speak at a dinner. She opened the fourth one.

Dear Alex,

You looked so beautiful today. Blue is definitely your color. I wanted to speak to you so badly, but I don't want it to happen like that, with all those strangers around. Did you like the flowers?

The color drained from her face.

I spent a long time picking out just the right ones for you. Each one of them reminded me of you in some way. Every time I hear your voice I can feel that you're reaching out to me. I hope you are as anxious as I am.

"This house is fantastic! And you did this all by yourself?" Olivia came back into the room. "Alex, what's wrong? Your face is as white as a sheet." She rushed over and sat down next to Alex on the couch.

"I just got another email from my own personal stalker."

"You're kidding!" Olivia turned the laptop so that she could read the email.

"Geez, this guy is a nut! How long has this been going on, Alex? You just started the job a week ago or so. You must sound really sexy on the radio."

"Not funny. And this is my second email from him. But he broke into my house yesterday and left those flowers." Alex pointed to the vase filled with flowers still sitting on the dining room table.

"Okay, Alex, I think you better tell me what's been going on, and don't leave anything out."

She let Alex speak without interrupting and then she flopped back against the couch cushions, amazed and at the same time deeply disturbed.

"I don't even know what to say, except pack everything you can carry and come home with me."

"Sounds good, Liv. I'm tempted, but it would really cramp your style. How would you explain to your date that he'd have to share the one bed you have with both of us?"

"Are you kidding? With the men I've been dating, I'm sure that would only be seen as a plus." Olivia frowned. "I'm seriously worried about you here all alone, Alex. I happen to know that John left you in good shape. You don't need this crummy little job. With your rep in the business you could have snagged a job just about anywhere making a lot more than you are here. Stick a for sale sign on the lawn and come on home."

"It is not a 'crummy little job,' and thanks for being so supportive and reassuring. What are best friends for?"

Olivia jumped up from the sofa, throwing her arms up the air. "The hell with being reassuring, Alex. We almost lost you once, and I don't intend to sit by and let something happen to you again."

Alex closed her laptop, and stood facing Olivia. "Olivia, the first time was an accident! You couldn't have done anything to prevent that. And nothing is going to happen to me now. If I need help I've got Jace close by."

"I still don't like it," Olivia said. "I could take some time off and stay here for a while."

"No you can't! You used a lot of time while I was in rehab and when you were going through your divorce. You know you can't afford to take more time off now." Alex pushed Olivia toward the door with a hand on her arm. "Stop nagging me and let's have some fun. I know this place that has the absolute best frozen margaritas."

"Unfair!" Olivia groused. "You know my weaknesses too well." She shook a pointed index finger at Alex. "You haven't heard the last of this. And I fully intend to speak to Jace about this."

"You mean grill him don't you?" Alex grinned. "You're not in court now, counselor. Come on, we have to hurry. We've only got till four thirty. There's someone coming to fix the basement window."

"All right, let me get my purse."

****

They got back just after four. A white van with TK Security emblazoned on the side pulled up just as they were walking up to the door. They were both feeling a little buzzed from the drinks, which had seemed quite a bit stronger today than the last time Alex had them. Two men stepped out of the van and they walked up the driveway.

"Yum," Olivia said, openly leering. "If this is how they make them here, I need to consider relocating."

"Shhh. They'll hear you."

"I have a feeling they already have."

One of the men was trying valiantly to hide a smile, but the other one sauntered up, a blatant grin on his face.

"Hi, ladies. We're here from the security company. We're going to replace a window."

"Honey, you can replace anything you want," Olivia drawled.

The other guy grinned.

"Olivia, shut up. I'm sorry. She had a drink on an empty stomach and now... anyway, can I see some ID please gentlemen?" Alex tried to sound like she was totally sober. She realized belatedly what a bad idea it had been to have drinks before the repairmen came.

They both got out their badges and she examined them thoroughly, pretending that she would know a real badge from a fake one. At least they could go in through the cellar doors in back, and she wouldn't even have to let them into the house.

Handing the key to Olivia, she said, "You go on in and I'll show these gentlemen where to go."

"Why do you get to show them?"

"Because it's my house and you don't have a clue where the broken window is," Alex ground out, giving Olivia a gentle push toward the front door. Alex felt guilty. She hadn't realized how bombed Olivia was getting until this moment.

She led them around to the back of the house. After locating the window they went back to the van for the new window and the tools they'd need for the job. Alex went into the house and down through the basement to open the cellar doors.

Both men came down the steps and she turned on the lights. "I'll check back with you in a while to see if you need anything. Thanks for fixing the window. I know security companies don't normally do windows. I appreciate the favor."

"No problem," the taller of the two said, "Tom said to tell you that if it's convenient we could look around before we leave and see what they'll need to do for the new system and then we can work up an estimate."

"Tom?"

"Yeah, Tom Knight, the owner of TK Security."

Duh! "Oh right. Can I let you know in a few minutes?"

"Sure, it'll take a while to fix the window."

Alex went upstairs, locking the door after her. Ignoring Olivia for the moment, she went to her computer and looked up the number for TK Security. She made a quick call to confirm what the two men had told her. She was relieved when everything checked out. At least one thing seemed to be under control.

While Olivia was in the bathroom, she dialed Jace expecting to leave a voice mail, but he answered on the second ring.

"Hello?"

"Hi, Jace, didn't mean to bother you. I was just going to leave you a voice mail. How's it going there?"

"Better than usual. I was able to zero right in on him and we found him about twenty minutes ago. He just went for a walk and got lost, thank God. His family is ecstatic. I really love it when there's a happy ending. How are things going there? Did the guys get there yet to fix the window?"

"Yes they did. They're down there now. Liv and I went out to eat and we had a few drinks. You know she gets a little bold when she's had a few. Well, I almost feel sorry for those guys, if she gets her hooks into them."

He chuckled. "So what's up? I know you didn't call to tell me that."

"No, I just wanted to let you know that I got another email from the stalker today... turns out he's the one who brought me the flowers."

Jace swore. "I'll be leaving here in a few minutes, but it'll take me a few hours to get there. Get some paper and write this down." He gave her his email address. "Send the email to me so I can have Eli look at it. I'll see you in a few hours. And call the police."

"I'll call them later. I don't want to spoil my time with Olivia. And you don't need to come over. There's nothing you can do."

"I'm coming over. Deal with it."

Olivia walked back into the room. "Fine. Gotta go. See you later."

"Who will we be seeing later?"

"Jace. He insists on stopping by."

"Oh goodie!" Olivia waggled her eyebrows. "Haven't seen him in ages. Is he still as gorgeous as ever?"

Alex grinned, rolling her eyes. "You have a one-track mind, do you know that?"

"That's not true. How could I be so brilliant in court if that were the case? The case, get it?" She laughed at her own joke. "Did you tell Jace about the email? Is that why he's coming over?"

Apparently Olivia wasn't as drunk as Alex had thought. "Yeah. I told him it wasn't necessary, but he insisted."

"Such a nice man." Olivia pushed her hair away from her face. "I never understood why you didn't like him."

"I never said I didn't like him," Alex said, not bothering to hide the irritation in her voice.

"Not in so many words," Olivia muttered. She shrugged. "So what are you going to do about this stalker?"

"Well, I know one thing." Alex was suddenly angry all over again. "I'm not going to let him wreak havoc with my peace of mind." She strode over to the table, grabbed the vase, and carried it into the kitchen, Olivia following close behind. She set the vase down on the counter and grabbed the flowers to throw them away.

The pain in her head was just a little zing this time. Maybe she was getting used to it, she mused. The sun was very bright and she had to wait for her eyes to adjust to the light. There were flowers all around her in buckets of water. There were flowers in her hand already, wait, not her hand, his hand.

When she looked down, she could see one hand closed around a growing bunch of flowers. The other was outstretched, reaching for another flower. It was a strong masculine hand dotted with short, dark hair. The fingernails were well maintained and his fingers were long and lean.

He was thinking of her as he selected the flowers. She saw herself lying on a long couch, wearing only a man's shirt. The shirt was open and draped artistically over her otherwise nude body. It wasn't really her body, she realized. It was her body as he imagined it to be. There were flowers strewn all around her. As she watched in horror, he moved closer. She felt his eyes raking over her body. He moved in close to her, close enough to reach out and touch her. She felt his need building. The sexual tension that filled him was almost unbearable.

He would have to do something soon. But he needed more time, more time to woo Alexandra. The urge was getting so strong. It was too much. He would have to find someone else to tide him over. He couldn't wait much longer. It wouldn't be what he really needed. It wouldn't be perfect, like it would be with Alexandra. But it would help him to wait. Yes, there would have to be someone else, just for now.

He looked around him, noticing for the first time the women in the marketplace. Which one would it be? It was so hard to think of someone else when all he wanted was Alexandra. He had to do it though. He stopped and turned his head, searching. Maybe there was someone here… someone who looked even a little bit like her.

The flowers were wrenched from her fingers, then she was back in the kitchen, leaning heavily against the sink.

"Alex, oh my God, you had me scared silly. What the hell just happened?"

"Give me a minute, Liv. I need some water. Get me a glass, would you."

Olivia frantically searched the cupboards until she located the glass cupboard next to the sink. She filled a glass and handed it to Alex. She gulped down the water and then set the glass on the counter.

"Alex, sit down before you fall down," Olivia ordered. She led her to the minuscule kitchen table and forced her to sit down in one of the two chairs. She sat down across from Alex.

"Okay, what was that? Did you have a seizure or something?"

"No, it wasn't a seizure. You know how I told you that I have some psychic abilities since the accident?"

"That was what that was? One of your 'visions'? It seemed like you were in a trance. It scared the shit out of me!" Olivia said.

"Yeah, well you should have been where I was. That would really have sent you running."

"I'm sorry, Alex," Olivia said, squeezing Alex's hand. "Was it bad?"

"Yeah." She blew out a breath. "It's no fun being inside people's heads, especially if they are thinking about you in a very unnatural way."

"Wow! That's how it happens? You're inside people's heads? That's just downright spooky."

"You have no idea."

"Tell me what happened. Do you need some more water first?" Olivia asked.

Alex shook her head no. "I'm okay, really."

"Okay, whose head were you on the inside of?"

"It was the guy who brought me the flowers. He picked them out personally for me, one by one. He was at a flower market somewhere. And all the while he was picking out the flowers, he was thinking about how he was going to 'make love' to me. He had all these scary intense feelings and they were building up inside him. I felt like my... he was going to explode if he didn't do something about it." She reached up, pushing her short hair off of her forehead, running her hand through her hair and down the back of her head. "The good news is that he's not ready to be with me yet. He's thinking it's not time yet. The bad news is he's looking around for someone to help keep his urges at bay. Liv, I'm really scared. I'm not sure what he'll do. His head's not right. I can only describe it as an ugly place. I think I'm even more frightened now than I was before."

Chapter 12

Alex could see that Olivia was as sober as a country pastor at this point, and that she was scared to death. She'd bullied, pleaded, blackmailed, and generally tried everything she could think of to get Alex to pack up and leave right away. She should have known by then that Alex was possibly the only person in the world more stubborn than Olivia herself.

As frightened as Alex was, she didn't want to leave her house. Her stalker obviously wasn't ready to confront her, and Jace had told her that the security company could install the new system in less than a week. She doubted she'd get much sleep, but she didn't want to leave her job so soon. She wasn't going to go home with Olivia. And she didn't want to stay with Jace.

Things were going so much better with him. Too well, in fact. She was afraid of what would happen if she were in close proximity to him for very long. She was feeling things she hadn't felt since before the accident. She hadn't really thought about sex since John's death, until now, and with John's best friend. Somehow that seemed almost like cheating on John.

Had she somewhere deep inside unconsciously harbored feelings for Jace all along? No, until she had that straight in her mind, she couldn't stay with Jace. So she was relieved when Olivia was finally just too exhausted to try anymore. Their margarita buzz was long gone by the time the guys were finished installing the new basement window.

When they were done they took their tools back out to the van and rang the doorbell. Alex went to let them in. At this point, she wanted the new security system in place as soon as possible. They came in and did a walk through, making notes on what was needed and then they left, promising to call as soon as they'd worked up an estimate.

One of the men smiled encouragingly at Olivia, but she barely noticed. As they shut the door, Alex said to Olivia, "If you're going to walk around with that face all weekend, you might as well just turn around and go back home. I thought you came here to keep me company and catch up, not nag me to death."

When she saw the anxiety in Olivia's gaze she relented. "Okay, bad choice of words. Now come on and tell me some more of your dating stories. If they're all as funny as the first one, we'll both get a good laugh in, and lord knows we could use one right now."

They went to the kitchen and made some hot tea. They sat at the tiny table and talked. Alex couldn't help but laugh when Olivia was around. She had a way of turning the most mundane things into something funny. By the time she was done describing her dating woes, they were both wiping tears of laughter from their eyes.

"You know, Alex, when my divorce became final, I felt like I might never laugh again… or date. But look at me now, doing both. It's a good thing, you know?"

Alex smiled over at her. "Yes, it is. Eddie put you through hell enough for a lifetime."

"You know, what was I thinking ever marrying a guy named Eddie in the first place? His biggest talents were watching football and scratching his stomach. Oh yeah, that's right, there was that one other thing he could do well. Too bad he used his talent so indiscriminately."

"He was scum. He never did one thing in his life to deserve a catch like you. Now let's talk about something worthwhile. Like making brownies maybe?"

"Oh yeah, that's why we're best friends. Great minds and all that." They both got up from the table. Alex grabbed a brownie mix from the pantry and they mixed the batter, licking the beaters and the bowl before popping the brownies into the oven.

As they were cleaning up the kitchen the doorbell rang. "That must be Jace, the hunk. Want me to let him in?"

Alex was busy washing the brownie bowl. "Yeah, that would be great. Thanks."

Olivia wasn't taking any chances. "Yes?" she said through the door.

"Hi, I'm Eli, Jace's brother. Our internet is out at the office. Jace sent me to check out Alex's email."

"How do I know you're who you say you are?" she asked.

"Because I just told you. Didn't Alex get Jace's text?" he said.

"No, she didn't get any text that I know of," Olivia said. "So, let's see some ID. Hold it up to that little window near the top of the door."

"How are you going to see it? Climb on a chair?" He sounded amused.

"Just do it." The truth was that although she was pretty tall, she really couldn't see it.

"Just a minute." She looked around for something she could drag over to the door, but the only chair in the room was a huge overstuffed chair and that was all the way across the room.

Alex came in to the living room. "Who was at the door?"

"It's still to be determined," Olivia said. "He says he's Eli. Says the internet's out at the office or something. But I'm not letting anyone through that door until I've checked them out."

Alex walked over to the door.

"Hey," Eli said. "My arm's getting a cramp here. Are you going to let me in or what?"

She opened the door. He brought his arm down. "Thank you." He smiled. "Jace said you were tough, but I had no idea."

"Hi, I'm Alex." She smiled. "And this is my friend Olivia. She's my self-appointed bodyguard this weekend. She's the tough one, just ask anyone who's come up against her in court."

Olivia took a bow. "Thank you, thank you." She liked the look of him. His hair was the same color brown as Jace, but longer, kind of wavy and shaggy all at once. He was built a little more solidly then Jace, but he was still on the slim side. His brown eyes had the impact of soft velvet. He was a tall, cool drink of water in jeans and a geeky t-shirt. She smiled.

Eli chuckled as he came into the room, indicating the space on the coffee table next to Alex's laptop. "All right if I set up here? Jace wanted me to get right on this and there's no power at the office."

"Uh, sure, that'll be fine, but he shouldn't have made you rush right over here on your day off. I'm sorry about that."

"No problem. I don't know anyone in town yet, so I wasn't doing anything anyway."

The oven timer went off. "Brownies are done. I'll be right back." Alex turned and left the room.

"How bad was this email?" he asked Olivia.

"The email was bad enough, but the 'vision' thingie she just had was the absolute topper. I'm tempted to ask for a leave of absence and camp out here for a while," she said with a frown.

"She'll be okay. Jace'll never let anything happen to her," Eli said, setting his computer case aside. "He's a good man, the best I know."

Olivia nodded. "I know he is, but he's got a job to do. This guy is fixated on her now, and there's no way Jace can be with her every second."

"Wait," Eli said, following her lead and keeping his voice low. "Is there something else I should know here? All Jace told me was that she'd gotten another email from the stalker and that he was the one who left her the flowers."

"Stop whispering about me you two." Alex came back into the room.

"Alex, could you open the email for me on your computer so I can get started?" Eli asked.

"Sure." She called up the email. He read it, whistled through his teeth, and set to work right away. Alex said, "If you need anything, let me know."

"Umm-hmm," Eli said, already completely engrossed in his work.

Olivia shook her head. "If it isn't football, it's computers. None of them are worth a damn."

"Oh, some of us definitely are," Eli said, still typing away on the keyboard.

She snorted.

"Olivia," Alex said, "come into the kitchen and we'll have brownies. I forgot I had some ice cream and hot fudge. Eli, would you like one?"

"Not right now, but save me some okay?"

The doorbell rang again.

Alex opened the door.

"Is that any way to answer the door?" Jace said. "You didn't even ask who it was."

"Not you too! There are three people here. Do you think that the guy is going to come knock on the door with all those cars in the driveway? Give me some credit."

"Hi, Jace." Olivia stepped up, giving Jace a hug. "I'm glad you're here. Maybe after you hear what's been going on, you can talk some sense into Alex."

"What's happened now? I just talked to you a couple of hours ago. Eli, thanks for coming over man. I owe you."

"Yeah, you do." He kept typing. "Now everyone get out of here and let me work."

They went to the kitchen. Olivia insisted on making the sundaes so that Alex could fill Jace in. When Alex was done, Jace sat back in the kitchen chair tiredly rubbing his hands over his face. He was quiet for a minute, thinking.

Olivia brought two of the bowls over, setting them in front of them. "Tell her to come home with me, Jace."

He looked over at Alex. "You should consider it."

"I'm not leaving my house, damn it! I've just gotten it exactly the way I want it. I've just started a new life here. I'm not going to turn tail and run. Besides, he said he'd heard me before when I worked at TALK950. So he knows where I used to live. What good will it do to go back there?"

"Fine, then you could move in with me until we find this guy," Jace said.

"I am not leaving my house!" Alex insisted, crossing her arms against her chest.

"You are a very stubborn woman," Jace ground out.

"It's two emails and some flowers!" she shouted, then stopped to take a deep breath. Belligerence turned to reasoning. "Look, he hasn't done anything to hurt me, and the security system will be installed soon. I told you, he's not ready to take any action where I'm concerned. If anything else happens, and I feel like it's coming to a head, then I promise I won't stay here alone, all right?"

"Damn you, Alex, you've always had independence issues," Olivia said.

"Should we talk a little about some of your issues?" Alex shot back.

"All right, all right!" Jace whistled shrilly, touching the fingertips of one hand to the palm of his other. "Everybody just calm down and eat your ice cream. We'll figure it out later," Jace said.

Eli walked into the kitchen. Jace looked over at him. Eli shook his head. "Sorry, bro, but this time he was at some internet café over in Kingston, using the screen name RWallace2. I have serious doubts about whether that's this guy's real email address either. The guy's an opportunist. I think he used someone else's computer again. When I searched the IP for that screen name, it was from a frat house over near the college. I don't think it's him." He pointed to the empty bowl in front of Jace. "Any chance I can get one of those now?"

"Sure." Alex got up and went to make it.

"It didn't take you very long to find him this time," Jace said.

"Yeah, he only did a little showboating this time. I think he might have been pressed for time. Probably working on someone else's dime again." Eli accepted the bowl from Alex. "Thanks, Alex. This looks great." Leaning back against the counter, he took a big spoonful.

"And I thought that online dating services were a nightmare," Olivia said. "So what happens next?"

"Now we get serious... and find us a stalker," Jace said.

"Not to be confused with the killer we're trying to track down," Alex said.

"Don't even go there. You people are giving me the creeps. Now I came here to have some fun. So why don't we all go somewhere and have some," Olivia said.

"I haven't been anywhere but the office since I got into town," Eli said. "I'm definitely in."

Jace looked over at Alex. "Whata ya say?"

Alex squelched the fear that threatened to overtake her whenever she thought about her latest vision and the emotional roller coaster going on inside the guy's head. Fear was not going to rule her life now. She'd fought long and hard to get to where she was today. Standing up straighter and pasting a smile on her face, she said, "I say let's go."

Olivia let out a whoop. "Just give me a few minutes to get gorgeous."

Alex groaned.

"You already are," Eli said. He grabbed her hand he pulled her toward the door.

Alex gathered their purses and they went through the house, turning on a few lights as they left and locking the front door.

Chapter 13

Alexandra sat in a chair, recording some sound bites to slip into the day's programming. She deejayed for two different stations simultaneously, and each one had a different location, so she recorded several different spots for each station, referring to different events in each location. As she edited one of her spots, she thought about Olivia's visit. They'd had a great time together as usual and they'd had a great time with Jace and Eli.

Alex decided that she had been way too serious since the accident. She used to be fun, have fun. Saturday night she'd had a glimpse of the old 'fun' Alex and she liked it. Maybe it was time to start dating again. She quickly squelched the tiny seed of guilt. John was not coming back. She was still young. Looking at the computer screen in front of her, she decided that she would think more seriously about it... later.

Since she had two remote shows during the week, she spent some time familiarizing herself with the venues and the people involved. She'd get there a little early, so she could meet with the advertisers and promoters and get more of a feel for what they needed from her.

She checked her email and sighed with relief. Four days and no more emails. Maybe he'd moved on to someone new. She took a moment to feel guilty for wishing her stalker on someone else. Still, she couldn't help hoping.

Her heart rate picked up as she replayed the moments she'd spent inside his head. The intensity of his feelings had verged on the violent. She'd like to think that maybe he'd moved on or given up, but his focus on her had been so absolute. A chill skittered across her scalp. She reached up, running her hands through her hair, and turned her attention back to her emails. Then she went into the studio and chatted with the deejay until it was time for her to go on the air.

She pulled into the parking lot of Jace's office. He'd lent her his jacket on Saturday night and she was determined to get it back to him. She'd called his cell phone, but hadn't gotten any answer. That had been three days ago.

She told herself that she wasn't bothered at all that he hadn't returned her call. After all, he was a busy man. She'd decided that she'd just drop the jacket off at his office. That way he wouldn't think that she was just making an excuse to see him. She rolled her eyes. She was acting like a silly teenager.

After grabbing his coat out of the car, she slipped through the glass and metal doors. She walked up a few steps and found herself in a small reception area. The woman sitting behind the desk looked up and smiled as she came in. "Hi, welcome to Moseley Investigations."

"Hi, I'm Alex Pope. I just came by to drop off something that belongs to Jace. If he's busy, I could just leave it with you."

The woman's smile widened. "Oh, Alex, I'm so happy to meet you in person. I'm Mattie. We've talked a couple of times already."

"Oh yes." Alex returned the smile warmly. She held out her hand and Mattie shook it. "It's so nice to meet you."

"I'm sorry, Alex, but Jace isn't in the office today."

"Oh well, then I'll just leave this with you."

"Mattie, where's the—" Eli strode into the office. "Oh, hi Alex. I didn't know you were coming by. Is there something I can do for you?"

Before she could speak, Mattie said, "Alex just came by to drop off Jace's coat."

"I left him a message a couple of days ago, but he must be busy so I thought I'd just drop it by here for him," Alex explained.

"Yeah, Jace has had a tough week," Eli said. "He's been on a case and it didn't end well. He's at home right now licking his wounds. He doesn't like to inflict himself on anyone when he's like this. He tends to take it really personally when he can't save someone. I tried to talk to him, but he told me to take a hike." Eli frowned in obvious concern. "I've always hated to see him like that, but nothing I say ever seems to help." Eli tapped his fingers on the coat she held in her hands. "If you just happened to drop by with the coat, maybe he'd talk to you."

Alex couldn't stand to think of Jace all alone and blaming himself for someone's death, just as she had done months before. "Well, if you think it would help him, then of course I'll stop by on my way home."

"It would be great if you would do that," Mattie said. "We worry so much about him after a case like this."

****

Twelve minutes later, Alexandra pulled into Jace's driveway. With his coat in hand, she determinedly made her way to the door. She rang the doorbell. Nothing. She rang it again several times. When she got no answer, she tried the door. Surprisingly, it was unlocked. She stepped into the foyer, shutting the door behind her.

She peeked into the living room. There was a mug on the coffee table. Beside it was a newspaper, which obviously had been read and then untidily folded in three. There was no sign of Jace. After laying his jacket on the back of the leather chair, she passed through into the dining room and then into the kitchen.

The kitchen looked as if it had never been used, not one thing out of place. Unless he was a total neat freak, she doubted that he'd done any cooking.

She walked to the sink and glanced out into the back yard. Her stomach dipped. There he was. He wore only cut-off shorts and he was on his knees, viciously pulling weeds from a garden running along a tall wooden fence on one side of his property. She slipped out through the back door and onto the patio leading to the yard. Her feet made no noise as she padded across the soft grass. She could see that he was wearing leather gardening gloves. High on his back were a set of grimy tracks where he'd scratched an itch or swiped at a bug.

His head was bent in grim concentration on the task at hand. His shoulders and neck were tense and the muscles in his upper arms bulged with the effort he was expending. At this rate, she thought, there was no doubt that he would end up exhausted and with some very sore muscles. She thought that what he was probably aiming for was something closer to numb. She remembered the feeling well.

She stood quietly for a minute, waiting for him to pick up on her presence. When he didn't she laid her hand gently on his shoulder. He jerked around, landing on his jean-clad butt on the grass and sat looking up at her. She waited for him to say something.

"What the hell are you doing here?" He sounded so angry, but his eyes looked dull, dead. He put a hand down on the ground, hoisting himself up until he stood next to her.

"I stopped by the office to return your jacket and they told me you were here," Alex said. He was tall, maybe 6'2" to her 5'6". His skin was golden brown, as if he'd spent some serious time outdoors. She remembered that he ran. His body was angular, tall and lithe like a runners body, yet he had a well-defined six-pack and his chest and arms were hard and muscular, just the right amount of muscle.

"Did they tell you that I was home because I wanted to be alone?" Jace said. He pivoted on one foot and stomped toward the house. She followed, struggling to keep up with his long strides.

"No, actually they encouraged me to come by. They seemed to think you could use some company."

"Well, they were wrong." His words were hard, unyielding. "So why don't you leave and I'll call you later."

"I'm not leaving."

"Fine, suit yourself," Jace said. "Make yourself at home. I'm going to take a shower." He headed up the stairs.

"Fine," Alex said, her voice quiet. "And I'll make you something to eat."

"Don't bother," he yelled down the stairs. "I'm not hungry."

"Tough. You'll eat it anyway." She opened the refrigerator and stood for a minute assessing the choices. She was ashamed to see that he ate much better than she did. Perversely, she decided on fettuccini Alfredo with bacon and asparagus and a salad to go with it.

She set water to boiling. The bacon came already cooked so she crumbled that and grated some Parmesan cheese. She roasted the asparagus just as she had done with the tomatoes at her house with garlic, olive oil and salt and pepper in the oven.

While things were cooking, she made a quick salad, softly singing the last song she'd heard before leaving the station. His kitchen was a dream to work in she decided. She drained the fettuccini, and took the asparagus out of the oven.

Where was Jace? What was taking him so long?

She was really worried. He didn't seem like himself at all. Climbing the stairs, she listened for the shower. She realized that he must have finished his shower because she couldn't hear any water running. She walked to the doorway of his bedroom and she saw him just sitting on the edge of his bed, a towel wrapped around his waist. He looked so defeated that tears sprang to her eyes. He looked up then and saw her standing there.

"Why do I keep doing this? For every one person I save, there are so many others that I can't. The families look at me with such hope in their eyes. I would gladly go to hell and back if that's what I had to do to give them back their daughter or son or maybe their wife. But most of the time it's all for nothing. And then I have to see the hope in their eyes die. Sometimes I don't think that I can stand it anymore. I feel like just walking away."

Alexandra crossed the room and sat down next to him on the bed. "But you can't walk away can you? For most of those people, you are their last hope. Eli was telling me the other night how most of the people who come to you have run out of options." Impatiently she pushed a stray lock of hair off her face.

"Everyone else has given up the search and that's why their families come to you for help. You're their last chance to find closure of some sort. And you do that for them. Whatever happens, whether it's ultimately good or bad news, at least they'll have the comfort of knowing." She placed a hand on his arm. Her voice was thick with tears that threatened. "And that means everything to them."

He'd been staring straight ahead, but now he turned his head and looked her in the eyes. "Thank you for that. Most of the time I know that and I can live with it. It's cases like these, when I know what I'm going to find. I keep seeing in my mind's eye the twisted and viciously brutalized body of that innocent little six year-old girl. That tiny little body with so much living spirit just snuffed out, all for the thrill of some sick, perverted fuck." He released a ragged breath. "So I tell the family as big a lie as I have to in order to try to preserve their sanity. I can't lie to myself about what's happened though, because most of the time I've seen it all. How the hell am I supposed to go home and sleep at night? How do I just pick up my life wherever I left off, like nothing out of the ordinary has happened?"

"I've asked myself that question too," Alexandra said. "I've been where you are now, although not nearly as often. I know the helpless feeling of not being able to do anything. The frantic race to do something, anything to find the person and help them. And then when you find out you're too late, the anguish, the anger and then that empty hopeless feeling. But Jace, you've helped so many families, saved so many lives. You really need to see that right now. Her parents might never have found that little girl if not for you."

"You know," Jace sighed, "When I lived with Natalie, she hated when I got like this. She would just tell me to either snap out of it or go get some therapy. I like your take on it a whole lot better. It's the first time I've felt like someone really understands how I feel. Natalie sure didn't."

"She was such a bitch!" Alex said.

Jace barked out a laugh. "You know, all of a sudden I'm starving. What's for dinner?"

Alex slapped him on the leg and then sprang up. "Get dressed and come find out. All I'm gonna say is that it's totally decadent and I can't wait to eat it, so hurry up."

By the time he appeared in the kitchen in a t-shirt and jeans, dinner was ready and on the table. Leaning over his plate, he inhaled deeply and sighed. "Oh man, that smells great!"

"Wine or beer?" Alex asked.

"Beer's good."

She grabbed two out of the refrigerator and sat across down from him. He picked up his fork, twirled the pasta expertly and took a bite. "Mmmm." He took another bite.

"Usually you eat the salad first." Alex smiled across the table.

"I'll get to it… maybe. I haven't eaten in a couple days, and this smelled too good to wait." He plunged his fork into the pasta again.

"Pasta's my thing," Alex said.

"It certainly is," he said around a mouthful. "If I die of heart disease, at least I'll die a happy man."

They ate in comfortable silence. After he'd cleaned his plate and polished off his salad, Jace sat back in his chair drinking his beer. His eyes were a darker gray than she'd ever seen them and he looked relaxed and at ease sitting there. He was still gorgeous, she thought, even with dark circles under his eyes. "Now that you've had something to eat, you need to get some sleep," Alex said.

He finished off his beer. "You know, you're right. I haven't slept for more than twenty minutes at a time in three, no make that almost four days. You're really taking good care of me here. Are you going to tuck me into bed now?"

"No," she said, stacking the dinner plates, "I'm going to do the dishes and then I'm going home and do some laundry."

"You cooked. I should do the dishes." He got up, bringing the rest of the dishes to the sink.

"I'll make a deal with you," Alex said, "I'll wash these few pots and pans and you stack the dishes in the dishwasher."

"It's a deal. Any more emails?"

"Nope." She wiped her hands on a dishtowel. "Maybe he's moved on. That would make me very happy."

"Doubtful, but we can always hope," he said through a huge yawn. "Hey, I'm sorry about that."

"Don't be. You're exhausted. I'm gonna get going." She walked through the kitchen and he followed.

"Well... good-night." She swung around to face him.

He stepped closer and brought his hand up to rest on her shoulder. His warmth spread through her body. The insidious pull of his sensual being made her want to crawl right inside of him. "Thanks for coming by and forcing me to join the human race again." He smiled.

"Anytime." She smiled back. A sudden onslaught of desire swept through him and then her. She sucked in a breath. His hand came up to cup her chin and then his mouth was on hers. His arm wound around her back, pulling her in against him. She felt every inch of his hard body against her and it fed the fire already raging inside her.

She brought her hands up, pulling him closer and deepening the kiss. Oh God, he was like a drug. She had to have more. She ran her hands up and down his muscular back, reveling in the feel of his hard lean body against her own. His warm hand came up under her t-shirt, sliding slowly up her skin until he reached her breast. Her stomach tightened. A soft moan escaped her lips.

"Yes," she whispered. "Oh yes." She felt the punch of heat low in her stomach. She hadn't felt this way in so long, or maybe she'd never felt this way, this much. She tried to get closer. Right at this moment she couldn't remember ever wanting anything half as much.

She felt him leave her. Why was he blocking her? Why now? She felt like screaming in frustration. He stepped back, keeping his hands on her shoulders. They were both breathing hard. The sound filled the foyer.

Alexandra tried to break free of his hands. She didn't want him to see the puzzled, hurt look she knew was on her face, but he held on.

She took a deep breath, lifting her chin. "Okay then, I should go."

"In a minute," Jace said. He pulled her close once again, resting his forehead on hers. He stood like that, saying nothing for the space of a few very long seconds. Then he said, "It's not gonna happen like this."

"It's not?"

"No, it's not. Not when you've come here to comfort me. If it happens, and you don't have a clue how much I want it to, it'll happen when we're on even ground. That way I'll know that it was totally what you wanted and not just something that happened because you felt sorry for me."

He thought she was feeling sorry for him? That definitely answered her question about whether he got the same vibes from her that she got from him. She'd been ready to rip his clothes off and have sex right here in the hallway, and he thought she felt sorry for him.

"You've got to be kidding!" Alex said.

He lifted his head. "I'm dead serious." He smiled sheepishly. "I'm also dead on my feet. I'd like to be on my game for something this important."

"On your game? Did you really just say that?" She shook her head in disbelief.

"Yes, and that's all I'm going to say on the subject right now. Lexi, why don't you stay in the guest room? I hate to have you go home in the dark. I'd follow you and check out the house, but I'm so beat I don't trust myself to drive right now."

"I'm fine, really. I'm certainly not afraid to drive in the dark and I refuse to let some nut drive me out of my home. I'll be very careful and check all the locks when I get in. Besides the guys are coming to install the security system sometime tomorrow so I have to be there." You can bet your ass I'll be careful, she thought. She'd left almost every light in the house on when she left. There was no way she was going home to a dark house. "So say good-night, Jace and then go get some sleep."

He leaned in, kissing her again and then he turned her toward the front door. "I still don't like it, but good-night Alex. I'll call you tomorrow and we'll talk."

****

She drove home in a daze, her body still humming with need. The house was ablaze with light. She dropped her purse by the couch, took off her shoes and headed to the kitchen. She'd make herself a cup of tea and try to sort out her feelings. She stopped in her bedroom to change into some pajama pants.

She flipped on the bedroom light, the one light she'd left off, and her eyes were immediately drawn to the bed. Right in the middle of the bed sat a brightly wrapped gift. The blood drained from her face. He'd been here again. The nightmare continued. After grabbing a five-pound weight from the floor by her bed, she went through the entire house until she was satisfied that no one was there. Then she threw a few random things in a bag and got the hell out of there.

She thought about sending Jace a text to tell him about the gift, but she knew he'd be asleep by now. Besides, she'd seen his cell phone plugged into the charger on the kitchen counter. She checked in to the hotel, dropped everything on top of the dresser, undressed, and fell into bed. She'd deal with everything in the morning.

Chapter 14

Alex closed the front door and leaned back against it. It was 10:30 in the morning and already she felt like she'd been through the mill. The police had come and gone, taking the gift and the note with them. They hadn't even opened it. The gift was from her stalker of course, along with a note that had left no doubt in her mind he wouldn't be giving up any time soon. They'd even tested her bed for semen. Yuck! Luckily it had come up negative. Otherwise, she could never have slept on that bed again.

They'd told her that they needed to check whatever was inside the package for prints and DNA. She looked around her house. There were dark smudges in every conceivable place that the stalker had likely come in contact with.

The police hadn't found any doors or windows unlocked. So far they had no idea how the guy had gotten in this time. She knew the detectives believed that she had left something unlocked, but she was absolutely sure that she hadn't. She'd been practically manic about locking up since the first break-in.

Glancing into the dining room, she was reminded of another woman who hadn't been safe in her own home. She hadn't heard from Eli all week, so she assumed that they were no closer to finding John Smith. What if they couldn't find him? How would they ever find the owner of the table? How would they ever find the killer?

She looked around her beautiful house, sadness weighing her down. She'd been so in love with it. She doubted that she would ever feel quite that way about it again. She was still waiting for the security company to come and install the system. Ironically, they'd called and they were due to arrive in about thirty minutes.

She got out some all-purpose spray cleaner and began to wipe down the areas where the powder residue remained. There were so many things going on right now. Her head was spinning. A murderer to catch with no clues, a stalker who could apparently enter and exit her house at will, still getting used to her new job, and now this thing with Jace, which she had no idea how to handle.

She only knew that if he hadn't called a halt to things, they would definitely have sealed the deal, probably right there in the foyer. She wasn't sure how she felt about that, except that it had felt good to lose herself like that, even if it had only been just ten minutes of mindless pleasure. She wasn't even going to think about that right now. Sighing, she went into the bedroom to clean in there. As she was dusting the nightstand, the doorbell rang. It must be the security company.

Alex went to the front door and then realizing that she couldn't see who was there, she asked who it was. They identified themselves as being from the security company.

"Hang on a minute."

She knew she was somewhere beyond paranoid, but she slipped out the back door and went around the side of the house. The van was the same one or identical to the one that had come last time. The two men, however, were not.

Retracing her steps, she got her cell phone out of her purse and dialed the number she had memorized from the side of the van, verifying that they had sent two men out and what their names were. She even asked the woman to describe them. The woman thought she was nuts, but described the men anyway. Alex didn't care. She wasn't taking any chances.

They showed her their IDs at her insistence and then she let them in. They set right to work. Alex kept busy paying some bills, doing laundry, and reading a magazine she'd bought on the way home that morning. She was tempted to follow the men everywhere they went and watch them, but since she would have no idea what they were doing anyway and they were both working in different areas in the house, she let them do their jobs undisturbed.

Jace never called. Alex hoped that he was making up for all the sleep he'd lost. She was restless. Maybe some TV would help to numb her overactive brain. She folded a basket of laundry while she watched the local news. Nothing good there. A woman had been raped over in Hamilton. A teenaged boy, a senior at the local high school, had been killed in a car accident. A woman murdered in her home several nights ago. They thought the motive was robbery. Alex sighed in relief. That wasn't their guy then.

She wondered how long it was going to take to get the security system up and running, hopefully not much longer. They'd already been at it for several hours. After folding the last shirt, Alex carried the basket into her bedroom. As she came through the doorway, one of the men, Devon, the blond one, was coming out of her master bathroom.

"What are you doing in here?" she asked.

"I was installing a sensor on your window. We put them on every window."

"The window is over there." Alex pointed to the far wall on the other side of the bed. "There are no windows in the bathroom."

"Yeah, sorry about that. I was rubbing my eye and my contact popped out. I went in there to rinse off my contact and put it back in." His smile seemed sincere.

"Are you done in here?" Was she becoming a paranoid freak, suspecting everyone who came into her house?

"Yes, I was just about to leave." He left the room.

She went into the bathroom and looked down into the sink. Droplets of water clung to the sides of the sink, and there was a small ring of water around the drain. She looked around carefully, but nothing looked out of place. Before leaving the bedroom, she checked out the sensor on the window. She decided that he'd been telling the truth and she was being a suspicious mess.

By the time she put her clothes away and went back out into the living room, the men were packing up to leave. Their tools and equipment stood next to the front door.

One of the men, Devon opened the door and started carting things out to the van. The other guy, whose ID read Hank, handed her a few sheets of paper with instructions on how to set the code and how to arm and disarm the system. They went through the routine until she felt confident and then the men left.

She stood by the door. She should feel so much safer now, but somehow she didn't. No doubt about it. That was going to take some time.

She was working from a new mobile phone store location in two hours, so she showered and dressed. She tried to ignore the creeped-out vibes the house gave her now. She hoped that it would pass with time. She was not going to feel this way about her own house. After arming the security system she left the house.

The remote was outside the store. There was a canopy over the equipment, but the sun was hot and it was shining right into Alex's face. She wore her sunglasses, but the glare was brutal. She spoke to tons of people, but she couldn't really see any of them. By the time it was over, she was sweaty, tired, and, she thought, quite possibly half-blind. Jace hadn't called when she went to bed.

Chapter 15

Jace elbowed the glass door open and then walked into the reception area, setting down the cardboard coffee tray.

"Welcome back. You look rested." Mattie handed him his mail, along with his messages and the morning paper.

"Thanks. It's good to be back and I'm feeling much better. Anything I should know about?" Jace asked.

"Eli's found John Smith. Don't tell him I told you though, he's been like a little kid waiting for you to get in."

Smiling, he said, "My lips are sealed."

He walked into Eli's office and handed him a coffee. Eli said, "Thanks man. Nice of you to finally make an appearance." He lifted the lid of the coffee and took a whiff, sighing in pleasure.

"Seriously though, you look a lot better. So, I guess siccing Alex on you wasn't such a bad idea, huh?"

"I should kick your ass for that, but actually it turned out to be a good thing." Jace smiled. "So what's new here?"

"Other than the fact that you have a partner with a brilliant mind?" Eli handed Jace a folder. The name John Smith was printed in block letters on the front.

Jace opened it. "You're a genius. You found John Smith. Rhode Island, huh? Who would have thought?"

"Yeah, I can't believe that I missed Rhode Island. I owe them a big apology."

"I'm sure they'll forgive you," Jace said.

"Sorry it took me so long to find him, but with so many other searches going on at once, I've had some trouble squeezing it in."

"No, you've done great work. I've gotten so much more done on my end of things since you came on board. Thanks for this." Jace held the folder out in front of him. "Well, I'd better get busy and catch up on some things around here."

Jace went to his office and sat down at his desk to look over his mail. There were a few checks, a couple of bills, and a letter of thanks from a client. Sipping his coffee, he checked his phone messages. There was one from Mike Stone, a homicide detective over in Cherry Hill. For several years now Jace and Stone had worked together on missing persons cases and then later on some homicides. Draining his coffee, Jace dialed Stone's number.

"Detective Stone."

"Hey Mike, it's Jace. Just got your message. What's up?"

"Have you read this morning's paper?"

"No, not yet." Jace picked up the morning paper, unfolding it.

"Well, it looks like your boy struck again."

"My boy?"

"The murders you were asking me about last week. Looks like we've got one of our own."

Jace bolted up in his chair. "You're shitting me!"

"I wish I were," Stone said grimly. "Same MO, the cuts, the missing nipples, no usable prints. The few hair samples collected from the scene were IDed as the victim's and her cat's.

We did get some semen, but just like with the other victims the guy's a non-secretor so we have no DNA. Basically, we got nothing. I was hoping maybe you could visit the crime scene with me and see what you can come up with. We've got to find this bastard."

"I'll do anything I can to help catch this guy. When do you want to do this?" Jace asked.

"I've got a million things on my desk right now. It'll probably have to be later tonight. That work for you?"

Jace looked at the piles of work on his desk. "Yeah, that'll be good. Listen, how would you feel about me bringing someone along with me?"

"Does he see things too?"

"Actually he's a she. And yeah she does. She's the one who saw the nurse's murder."

"Before it happened right?"

"That's right."

"The woman who saw the killer?" Stone sounded excited.

"Yeah, for what that's worth. Remember, she said he was covered from head to toe. But she and I are working on something else that may help us identify the killer. I'll let you know if it pans out."

"Don't tease me like that, Jace. If you know how to find the guy, tell me now. I have tons of resources at my fingertips."

"I'm not sure whether it's a dead end or not. As soon as I know, you'll know."

"All right." Stone sighed. "Bring your friend along. I'll take any help I can get at this point. I'll call you later and let you know when and where."

"Okay, talk to you later." Jace hung up the phone and dug into the piles on his desk.

Chapter 16

Alex slept pretty well in spite of everything. She decided to treat herself to a croissant and a latte. She went through the drive-through and then back home. Sitting cross-legged on the couch, she took a bite of the buttery croissant and then flipped open her laptop, clicking onto her email account from work. And there it was:

Alexandra,

I'm sorry that so many days have gone by since my last email. There was something I had to take care of. Did you enjoy your gift? When I saw it, I knew that it was just perfect for you. I was disappointed to see that you weren't wearing it yesterday, but I could tell by the way you were watching me that you were trying to tell me how much you loved it, that you wished that we were alone, just the two of us, so you could show your appreciation. Soon we will be together my love, my angel, very soon. I'm closer than you know.

Alex sat staring at the screen, hands clenched into fists. It was escalating. He was getting scarier by the minute. He'd been at the remote, standing right in front of her, and she hadn't been able to see him! She wondered if there were security cameras in front of the store. What did he mean by 'closer than you know?' She didn't like the sound of that at all.

At the moment, she felt a strong urge to get into her car, start driving and just keep on going. Not an option! She had to be at work in a few hours.

She closed her laptop and headed for the shower. Ever since they'd found the hole in the window, she had been 'speed showering.' Her house still gave her the heebie jeebies. She'd even started wearing shorts and a t-shirt to bed. And now her stalker was "closer than she knew." Great, just great!

She hated feeling like a wimp. She'd always thought of herself as strong and independent. So why did she suddenly have the urge to call Jace whenever anything came up? Who was she kidding? She had the urge to call Jace even when nothing was going on. She would call him after her shower though, and let him know about the gift and the email.

She showered, dressed, and blew her hair dry. As she came into the living room, she heard the beep of a missed call on her cell phone. She checked the call. It was Jace. A tiny thrill of pleasure stole through her, remembering their last encounter. Would he mention it? She hit send and waited.

"Hi, Alex," came Jace's voice through the phone. Did his voice sound lower and more intimate or was she just imagining it?

"Hi, Jace. Sorry I missed your call. I was drying my hair."

"No problem. Sorry I didn't call yesterday. I slept most of the day and evening, and I've had a crazy day trying to catch up on things at the office. Listen, thanks for coming over and snapping me out of the fog I was in the other night. I felt a lot better after we talked and you fed me. I slept like a baby after you left."

Nope. He wasn't going to mention it.

"I'm glad I could help."

"So what's new on your end?"

"Well, last night when I got home from your house there was a gift in the middle of my bed."

"God damn it! What was it? And how did the guy get in this time?"

"I can't answer either of those questions. When I saw that he had been here again I was so freaked that I just grabbed a few clothes out of my dresser and booked. When the police came this morning they had no idea how the guy had gotten in. You'll be happy to know that after the police left with my little present, the security company came and installed the new system."

"You've had a busy couple of days."

"And I haven't even told you about my newest email. Or about the fact that the stalker was standing right in front of me at my remote yesterday, and I didn't even know it because the glare was so blinding I couldn't see anything at all."

"Shit. For two psychics, we don't have a clue do we? I'll tell you one thing, Alex. You are not staying in that house alone tonight, alarm or no alarm. I don't care what you say. You either come to my place, or I'll stay there with you. It probably won't do much good but send the email on to Eli. We'll see what he comes up with this time. You are giving the police all the e-mails as they come in, aren't you?"

"Yes, the officer gave me an email address to forward them to."

"Good. Maybe they can track the sender down. We'll talk more about this later, I promise you that."

"Fine, I'm not going to argue this time. I'm trying to be strong, but I'm not stupid. To tell you the truth, I was dreading being here alone tonight."

"Just wait until I tell you why I called, 'cause the hits just keep on coming," Jace said. "The good news is that Eli found an address and phone number for John Smith. I'm going to try to call him in a few minutes and see what he can tell us."

"That's great! This could really help us find the bastard. You'll let me know as soon as you talk to him?"

"I will."

She took a breath. "Okay, hit me with the bad news?"

"There's been another murder. This time over in Cherry Hill."

"Sweet Jesus!" Alex said. "The woman in the paper this morning?"

"Yes, and Alex… it's the same guy."

"The same guy… you mean…"

"The guy who killed the nurse, Kimberly, and Ann."

Alexandra dropped down onto the arm of the couch. "What's he doing around here? The last murder was almost two hours away from here."

"Well, Cherry Hill is about fifty minutes from here, so it's about half way between here and there. He's too smart to keep hunting in one area. We know he's been in several states. He stays a while and then seems to move on. Anyway, the homicide detective in Cherry Hill is a guy I work with off and on. He called to see if I could take a look at the crime scene."

"I should go with you. With both of us there, we'd have a better chance of getting something."

"Are you a mind reader now too? That's what I told Detective Stone. He agreed to let you come. Are you sure you want to do this, Alex? It won't be pretty."

"I have to do this, Jace. I need to help find this guy."

"You mean we need to find this guy… and we will." Determination fueled his every word. "So Stone's going to meet us at the crime scene at nine o'clock tonight. Why don't you pack some things and meet me at my house around six? We'll get something to eat and then we'll go together to meet him."

"Make that 6:30. I have to work until six," Alex said.

"Okay, fine. See you then. Be careful today. And Alex…"

"Yeah?"

"I'm really glad that you've decided that you like me better now."

"Who says I do?"

He laughed. "So you were just being polite the other night? Well, if that's so then bring it on! See you later." He disconnected.

Chapter 17

Alex pulled into Jace's driveway at exactly 6:30. She picked up her bag and went towards the house. Jace came out and down the stairs. He took her bag, setting it just inside the front door. He closed the door, locking it behind him. After kissing her lightly on the lips, he led her to his car.

They had a while before they were due to meet Stone and since neither had eaten, they stopped to eat. Alex tried to eat her dinner, but her body refused to cooperate. Her throat was tight and there seemed to be a boulder sitting in her stomach. She finally settled for a glass of wine, hoping it would help her to relax.

Jace filled the tense silence with a steady stream of light conversation. He'd been through this many times before, but for Alex it was the first time. She hardly knew what to expect. Jace thought he knew what she was feeling. He reached over and placed his hand over hers. His warmth and empathy flowed through her, warming her from the inside out. She immediately felt somewhat better.

"You don't have to do this, Alex."

"Yes, I do. I'll be fine once we get there." She forced her tight lips into what she hoped was a reasonable facsimile of a smile.

Jace rubbed his thumb over the back of her hand. She took a healthy swallow of her wine and felt it's warmth trickle smoothly down her throat.

"Jace?"

"Yeah?"

"There's one thing that I've been wondering about."

"What's that?"

She looked him straight in the eye. "What do you think will happen if I'm inside someone's mind at the moment of their death? How do you think I'll be affected by that?"

His hand tightened painfully on hers. She gasped in pain, pulling her hand from under his.

"I'm sorry, but Jesus Alex, I never considered the possible outcome of you being inside people's minds. My visions don't work the same way." He frowned at the coffee cup in front of him. He got out his wallet and throwing some bills on the table he said, "Come on, let's go, I'll drop you at my house before I meet with Detective Stone."

"What? Oh no you won't. I'm going with you. I'll be fine. I was just letting my imagination get the better of me, that's all." She threw the bills on the table back at him, digging her debit card out of her wallet. "And I said I was paying this time."

Jace ignored the last comment. "Your imagination? Yeah, well you forget that I was with you at your house when you saw that dead woman. You were out for quite a while then. Even after you woke up, you said that you felt like your head was going to explode. Alex, neither of us knows what would have happened if you hadn't let go of the table when you did?"

"But I did let go, Jace."

"And what happens if you don't let go the next time? What if you can't?" There was a ferocity in his gaze that gave her pause, but she refused to back down. They had to find this guy.

"I will. I know I'll be able to. Look, I'm sorry I even mentioned it. I was just nervous about going through the crime scene. You've done it before, but I'm fairly new to this stuff."

"Well, you can stop worrying because, you are not going."

"I'm going to the crime scene, one way or another!"

"What's that supposed to mean?"

"I'd rather go with you, but if you won't take me then I'll call Detective Stone on my own. I'm sure he'll be glad to let me in, especially since I may be able to see the killer again."

"Damn it, Lexi, you're driving me crazy! Answer me this. Did John ever win an argument with you?"

"Yes. He won the last one. That's why I'm still alive and that's why I have to do this."

That shut him up. He sat there for a minute, scowling at her.

"Let's go," he growled. "But I'm keeping my eye on you. The minute I have any doubts about what's going on with you, I'm pulling you out of there."

****

They arrived at the house a few minutes before the detective and sat in an uptight silence. Alex spent the time observing the small white house. Yellow crime tape ran over the door and around the lawn. She stiffened. Turning to Jace, she said. "Jace, look at the address."

He turned his head, checking out the numbers next to the door. "Thirty-five. The numbers I saw when I touched the table at your house. But the woman I saw then was still alive." He gazed at the door thoughtfully.

Gravel crunched behind them. Detective Stone pulled in behind them. They got out of the car and waited for him. His salt and pepper hair was sticking up like he'd run his fingers through it and then forgotten it.

"Sorry, I'm late. I hit the ground running two days ago and haven't stopped yet."

"No problem. We just got here. Mike, this is Alexandra Pope. Alex, Mike Stone."

"Hi, Alexandra. Sorry to meet under these circumstances. Not a great way to meet people." He took her hand in a firm handshake.

Alex smiled. "I wouldn't imagine so. Nevertheless it's refreshing to meet a believer, Detective Stone."

"I'm ashamed to say it took me a while, but it's hard to fight the proof when it's right in front of your face."

"So tell us about the crime scene," Jace said.

"The perp went in through a window in the back of the house. Here's how we think it happened. The victim was cooking dinner. We think that she may have heard a sound and left the kitchen to check it out. The perp came down the hallway and met her just as she was coming out of the kitchen.

"We think she tried to run to the front door, but he caught her in the living room. Judging from a cut on her forehead that occurred before her death, we determined that either she lost her balance and fell or he pushed her down, and she hit her head on the corner of the coffee table.

"The perp cut her clothes off. He raped her, carved her up, and then he killed her with a deep cut across her throat that severed her carotid. She bled out right there on the floor. He didn't leave a single clue and the vic's nipples are gone."

Minus the cooking, this was almost a carbon copy of Kimberly's murder. He'd hit her from behind and then cut her and killed her right where she fell. Had he raped her too? She didn't remember reading Kimberly had been raped. She didn't remember much of anything she'd read at the time. She'd been too shell shocked.

Detective Stone pulled something out of the pocket of his sport coat. "You'll have to put these on before we go in." He handed them each a couple of blue paper booties to slip over their shoes. He slipped some over his shoes. "Jace, your prints are already on file, but Alexandra I'm afraid you'll have to agree to come down to the station tomorrow and be fingerprinted, or I can't let you come in. They've already been through the scene, but they may have to come back, so anything you touch—"

"Will have to be verified," Alex finished for him. "I understand Detective Stone and that won't be a problem."

"Please call me Mike." He looked at them both. "You ready to do this?"

They both nodded.

"Okay then, let's go." Stone led them around the house and up the driveway. He unlocked a side-door and swung it wide. They were immediately assailed by the metallic tang of blood coupled with the overwhelming smell of burned food.

Chapter 18

No one seeing the kitchen would ever suspect that a vicious murder had taken place in this house. Except for the smell, the blackened pans in the sink, and a few black smudges, the kitchen looked like any other kitchen on any other day.

Detective Stone led them through the archway of the kitchen and through a formal dining room. They stopped at the entrance to the living room. A large section of both the carpet and the pad had been cut out, but the subfloor held a dark stain where the victim's blood had seeped through both. That's where it happened. That's where he'd killed her.

Jace stepped in front of Alex. He looked her in the eyes. "I go first. Don't do anything until I'm back. I mean it."

She knew she had to do it, she was determined to do it, but making sure he was there to pull her back if she needed it was the only intelligent choice. Besides the fact that she was in no hurry to go there, she wanted to watch him work. "I won't. I promise."

"Good."

The coffee table was gone and there were black smudges on every conceivable surface. There were some framed pictures on tables and on the mantle of the fireplace. Jace moved forward into the room, automatically stepping around the hole in the carpeting. He stopped in front of first one picture and then moved on to another.

"This is the victim?"

Mike Stone crossed the room to stand beside Jace. "Yes, that's her."

"What was her name?"

"Marie. Marie Flores. She was thirty-six years old, a school teacher," Stone said.

"Was she married?"

"No. But she lived with the guy in the picture for about eight years. He's an engineer. His job took him overseas a couple of years ago. According to him, he asked her to go with him, but she refused. The guy was pretty broken up when he found out about the murder."

Jace picked up the picture and closed his eyes. He saw the couple standing on a huge boulder by the ocean. They were facing each other and laughing, their clothes and faces wet. Then it was gone.

He walked around the room searching for something that might tell him more, something she might have touched recently. He left the living room and walked down the hall to her bedroom. He looked in a clothes hamper near the door. It was empty. The top of her dresser was bare except for a runner that hung over each side. There were no sheets on the bed. He picked up the pillow closest to the nightstand and held it between his hands.

Pictures flashed through his mind, a slide show on overdrive. He struggled to slow it down, to grab an image and freeze it. He saw her in the kitchen, putting a lid on a pot at the stove, standing in the doorway of the kitchen, caught in still frame her left leg raised as she ran through the dining room.

Then he saw her lying on the rug, blood trailed down the side her forehead and caked in her hair, her face a mask of terror. He saw the broad back of a man in black, the back of a woolen ski mask covering the man's head and neck, bloody knife gleaming in his left hand.

He saw the room he'd seen before in Alex's dining room, every wall filled with macabre charcoal renderings of his various victims. Jace focused on the room, frozen in time as it was. In each of the drawings the women's faces were portrayed in exquisite detail, yet he had drawn them in soft shadow. They appeared almost ethereal, as though he revered them. Their bodies, however, were drawn in harsh strokes of charcoal, an eerie carbon copy of their appearance after he had finished with them, throats slashed, nipples gone, blood trailing from copious cuts on their torsos.

He tried to memorize the faces. The slide show continued. He saw a huge house with a stone façade, columns on either side of a porch with arched double doors, then a flash of a dock with a large boat hoist next to it. He saw a man's body. He hadn't been in the water very long. There was no bloating, and the body and clothes were still in good shape, his eyes wide in death, his hair floating up from his scalp. Several ropes were tied around his body. Something underneath the man kept him weighted down. Jace couldn't see what it was.

The slide changed again. In the middle of a river, Jace saw a massive oak tree. And then as suddenly as it had begun, the slide show ended. He felt the pervading weakness that always followed the "seeing." He let go of the pillow and stood there for a minute, reorienting himself to his surroundings.

Mike put a hand on his back. "You okay, buddy?"

Jace forced his rubbery legs to move. "Yeah, just give me a minute." He retraced his steps as far as the dining room and sat down heavily on one of the chairs. Alex dug into her giant purse and pulled out a small bottle of water, handing it to Jace.

"Ah, bless you," he said. He opened it and sucked it down.

"Okay, I'm trying to be patient, but did you see anything useful?" Detective Stone asked.

"To tell you the truth I'm not quite sure what I saw." Setting down the empty bottle, he looked up at Stone. "You were right in your assessment of how it happened. I saw her cooking, and then running through the dining room. Then I saw her on the floor in the living room, he was on top of her, but his back was to me."

"Shi-i-i-t! I was hoping we'd get something," Stone said.

"Something weird happened though. Usually when I'm holding a personal item, I only get impressions from the person who's been in contact with the item. I might see things related to their disappearance, a street sign or something like that. But this time I got impressions from the killer too."

Stone nodded. "Actually, we're not sure why, but we think the killer laid down on the bed at some point before he left the house. That's why the sheets are missing. We found black fibers on the pillow case and on the bedspread."

"That explains it then. I saw a room," Jace made eye contact with Alex, "the same one I saw at your house. It was filled with charcoal drawings of his victims."

"Do you think you'd be able to remember any of their faces?" Stone asked. "It might help us with some of the unsolved missing persons cases."

"I tend to remember everything I see while I'm under quite vividly, sometimes a little too clearly as far as I'm concerned. Of course I'll help with that. But I don't think his only victims are women."

"What!" Amazement and rage warred for dominance in Stone's expression.

"I saw a man. He was dead and in a lake or river, weighted down with something, I don't know what. I also saw a house and a dock with a boat launch. I didn't recognize the area."

"So we come here hoping to solve a murder, and we find out there's been another one. This is just crazy!" Mike Stone paced the floor anger in every step. After a moment he calmed down. "Anything else?"

"I don't see how this will help, but I saw a tree in the middle of a river."

"A tree... floating? On the bottom? A dead tree? What?"

"No, I saw a live tree complete with leaves and it was sticking out of the river. It was an oak tree."

"So we're looking for a river with an oak tree growing in the middle of it?" Stone asked.

"I told you, I don't know what it means yet. Sometimes what I see are symbols. I need to think about it."

"My turn," Alexandra said walking toward the living room.

"Hold on, Lexi. Let me get in there before you grab hold of anything," Jace said.

She ignored him. She walked directly to the hole where the carpet had been cut away and knelt on the edge of the carpet. After taking a deep breath, she pressed her palm onto the bloodstained floor.

The familiar pain sizzled through her brain and then she was humming a tune she'd never heard before. She stirred a small pot with boiling water and rice in it and then put a cover over it, turning down the burner. In a pan on the opposite burner, she flipped a burger carefully so that it wouldn't break apart. The smell made her mouth water.

Her head came up. What was that noise? Had it come from the bedroom? The cat must have knocked something over. She walked through the arched doorway and saw a man walking down the hallway. His face was covered with a woolen ski mask. She was momentarily paralyzed with fear. She'd gone too far into the dining room to turn around. He was right there!

That mobilized her. She ran through the dining room. She had to get to the front door. Then there was a hard blow to her back pushing her forward. As she fell, her head hit the edge of the glass coffee table. She didn't have time to dwell on the pain. She crawled on hands and knees toward the front door. Blood ran from her forehead.

Her neck snapped back as the man grabbed her hair and pulled her around, pushing her roughly down onto the carpet.

He whispered to her, "Why did you make me do that to you? Your face was so beautiful. Don't worry. After I kill you, I'll make you perfect again." The woman whimpered. His hand tightened in her hair.

"Please," she pleaded, "please don't kill me."

"You look like an angel, but you aren't, are you? You're just like her. You make me want you and then you cry and beg me to leave you alone. I love the fear in your eyes. It makes me hard. Can you feel that?" He raised his left hand. "You will soon." The polished blade snaked down the front of her. Alex watched the blade slice through her t-shirt and bra. The funny thing was that she didn't even feel it until she watched him part the cloth with the tip of his knife.

A line of fire burned its way from her chest to her stomach. She screamed.

"Shut up!" His harsh whisper sounded in her ear, the hiss of a snake. "You think that hurt? Well that was nothing, Ann. Do you remember the last time?" He was breathing hard now, his erection pushing against her. She thought she might be sick.

He cut her pants in one cruel slice, pushing them down and out of his way. He opened his fly and roughly rammed into her. She screamed again. He brought his right hand up, covered in latex, pressing it over her mouth and nose. She fought for breath as he continued to buck and grind against her. Her distress served only to heighten his excitement. His breath rasped harshly in her ear.

Black dots appeared in front of her eyes. She tried frantically to bring her hands up to push his hand away from her mouth and nose so that she could get a breath, but she found that they were trapped beneath her. She heard him groan loudly as he finished and then she blacked out.

Chapter 19

Alex heard Jace calling her from far away and then somewhere closer, demanding that she wake up. She opened her eyes. Jace and Detective Stone were both on their knees beside her where she lay on the carpet. She saw Jace first, his face set in a worried frown, which softened in relief as she watched.

"You okay?" he asked.

"Yeah, I'm okay."

"You scared the hell out of me. You acted like you couldn't breathe and then you just passed out," There was something dangerous in his expression, she thought, something savage.

"You both scared the hell out of me," Stone said. "It's like watching science fiction. If I had to go through that all the time to get at the truth, I think I'd close up shop and move to a deserted island." He shook his head. "Are you really all right, Alexandra?"

She held out her hand for some help getting up. Jace grabbed it and pulled her up, keeping an arm around her for support. She did feel a little shaky, so she stayed in the circle of his arm. "He loves their beauty, but he hates them. They are all Ann to him. He called the victim Ann. He wanted her so much and thought that she was so beautiful. He believes that she enticed him and then rejected him.

"In the course of things he found that he liked the fear. He feeds on it. It makes him feel powerful; it's an aphrodisiac to him. He sees the cutting and the murder as the ultimate conclusion to his masterpiece. To him it's not only perverted sex, it's performance art. It's also vengeance. He knows at the beginning that none of them are Ann, but once he has them in his power, they become Ann. He's never going to stop the killing. It's a compulsion, and it's the only way he can find sexual satisfaction."

"As with most serial killers," Stone said, grim determination in both his tone and face. "I don't remember anyone named Ann in the database. I printed them all out and I've examined them about a thousand times."

"No one's found her body yet. She's his first victim," Alex said.

"We think," Jace said. "We're working on finding her."

"We're done here. Let's get the hell out of here," the detective said.

They followed him out to where the cars were parked. He turned to them. "Tell me everything you know about the first victim." They told him everything they had gleaned from Alex's vision. He asked several pertinent questions and wrote everything down in a pad he produced from his shirt pocket. He thanked them and said goodnight.

"If we think of anything else, we'll let you know," Jace told him.

"Okay, and keep me posted on the other thing you're working on, hopefully sooner rather than later." He nodded in Alex's direction. "Good to meet you, Alexandra."

"You too, Mike, and call me Alex."

"Okay then, Alex."

"Goodnight, Mike," Jace said. "I'll be in touch soon."

They drove to Jace's house in strained silence. The radio volume was set too low to actually hear the songs playing. All Alex could hear were low, throbbing beats. As she tapped her foot in time to the beat, her knee bounced up and down. She wished he'd say something, anything that would tell her what he was thinking.

Finally, he pulled into the driveway, hit the remote and drove into the garage. Getting out of the car, still without saying a word he opened the door leading into the kitchen.

That did it. Now she was officially pissed. She leaned over and hit the trunk button. After grabbing her bag, she stalked after him. She tried to slam the door as she let herself into the kitchen, but the seal was tight and the effect was totally unsatisfactory.

He stood at the sink, staring moodily out into the darkness of the back yard.

"What is your problem? You don't say a word to me all the way home and then you just leave me in the garage. You're acting like an immature jerk!"

He turned to face her, but still didn't speak. She advanced on him, belligerence in every step. "What the hell is going on with you?"

He laughed at that, a tight little laugh that held no humor. "I'll tell you what's going on. I just stood by and watched while you almost died back there in that house."

She let out an impatient breath. "But I didn't die. I passed out, Jace. That's all that happened back there."

He shook her slightly by the shoulders. "That's not all that happened. You were choking, gasping for air. I could see the blood vessels in your eyes bursting. You were being smothered."

"What are you talking about?" Alex said, her tone defensive. "My eyes are fine."

"They weren't when you passed out. But by the time you opened your eyes, they were clear again."

"Oh my God!" she said. The hair stood up on her arms. No wonder Detective Stone had mentioned science fiction. "He was holding her down, and she was begging him not to kill her. Then she screamed. He put his hand over her mouth and nose. He was so strong and he had her arms trapped. I could feel her struggling to breathe and then everything went black and we passed out. I mean she passed out."

"No, you don't," Jace said. He gazed down at her, his lips pressed into a grim line. "You mean you both passed out. Lexi, you can't do this anymore. You've blocked it before. You have to start doing it again."

"Don't tell me what I can and can't do, Jace!"

"I'll tell you anything I damn well please if I think it will save your life. Or don't you care about your life anymore? Why'd you come back if you don't care?" Alex winced as his grip on her shoulders tightened. Seeing that, he dropped his arms. He snapped his fingers. "Oh, that's right. You did it because John asked you to. Otherwise you'd be happily dead right now."

She punched him in the chest hard. "You bastard! You can go straight to hell." She turned on her heel and stalked to the door. After picking up the bag she'd set down by the door, she turned the doorknob. The door swung open. Jace's hand reached over her shoulder pushing the door shut again.

"What are you doing? There's no way you're going back to your house." He sighed wearily. "Look, I'm sorry." His body was pressed against her back, his breath warm in her ear. "I've seen people die horribly. I've seen things that no one should ever see and as hard as it is to admit, most of the time it's just my job. But I've seen your death once. I don't think I can do it again." She started in surprise, looking at him over her shoulder.

"Yeah, that's right. I went to the scene of the accident. I couldn't believe John was gone and that you might not make it. I saw you go and then come back, but not all the way. From there I went straight to the hospital. After your surgeries, your dad sneaked me into intensive care a couple of times. I tried talking to you," he told her, his face stark with pain, "but I didn't know what to say. I hated seeing you that way. And I hated seeing you with the life half-choked out of you tonight."

Alex turned around and leaned back against the door, though she was far from relaxed. "I had no idea that you'd done all that. I don't remember anything from the first few days. I know it must have been a really bad time for everyone, but don't you see? I can't stand by while these women are murdered. It's a huge part of the reason I forced myself back to the land of the conscious and breathing.

I'm sorry that I spoke my fears out loud at the restaurant. But you have to stop treating me like I'm made of glass." She was still angry, and it came through in every word that she uttered. "I know it may be dangerous, but it's something that I have to do, something I'm meant to do. And I don't want to have to fight you every step of the way. If that's the way it's going to be then I should leave now. Maybe I've been leaning on you too much. I like to think that the things I've been through have made me stronger. I can do this Jace. If it's too hard for you to watch, then I'll leave now and do this on my own. Otherwise, you're just going have to bite the bullet and let me do what I have to."

Pushing back from the door, Jace said, "John said you were a stubborn woman and that you always called him on his shit! I see what he meant now. And I do see your point. I'll try to back off, but don't expect me to be happy about it. And I still reserve the right to try to talk you out of something if I think it's going to get you killed. Take it or leave it?" He stood gazing down at her, his eyes blazing with determination.

She shrugged one slim shoulder in an arrogant way that caused his temper to flare up once again. He managed to clamp down on it. She said, "I guess I'll take it."

He picked up her bag. "C'mon, it's late and we've both had a long day." She followed him up the stairs. He put her bag just inside the door of the same room she'd stayed in before. "You know where everything is. There are clean towels in the bathroom."

He left her standing there. He crossed the hall and went into his room, closing the door. Perversely, it ticked her off that he had just walked away from her like that. She set her bag on the bed and got out what she needed before taking a long hot shower. She was happy to wash away any remnants of the dead woman's house. She hated sleeping with wet hair, so she blew her hair dry. She padded barefoot back into the bedroom and lay down in bed. She thought about Jace in bed in the room right across the hall.

Where she'd felt drained and exhausted earlier, suddenly she was wired, hot and restless lying there in the dark. She always ended up feeling that way when she was near Jace. Even losing her temper had felt good somehow, the adrenaline rushing through her veins. She wanted to hold on to it. She wanted more. She wanted sex.

Was it wrong to think of John's best friend at the same time she thought about having sex? She knew that it was only natural that Jace would bring up John in conversation. He'd been a big part of both of their lives, but whenever it happened, it was like a big old bucket of cold water thrown in her face.

She didn't want John to be there in the room with her and Jace. She wanted to fling the covers off and rush into the bedroom across the hall. She wanted to climb into bed and lose herself in great sex, to forget everything for a few glorious minutes. It wasn't that she exclusively wanted Jace, she told herself. It was all about the sex and forgetting. It was natural to think of him when they were in such close proximity lately. She really missed sex. She sighed. After punching her pillow, she turned onto her side.

Chapter 20

Jace closed his cell phone and set it on the kitchen table. John Smith had proved to be a man with an excellent memory. It seemed he not only remembered where he had bought the dining room set, but he'd been able to recall the house in great detail. As he'd described it, Jace had no doubt that it was the same one he'd seen in his vision.

He had asked Smith if the house was near a river or if there were a lot of oak trees around the house. "So you know the house then?" Smith had replied.

"No, just asking."

"Huh. Well, the property did have some acreage and it was on a river. There were a group of trees down by the water. I didn't really notice whether they were oak trees or not."

"Do you know if there was a dock on the property?" Jace asked.

"Oh yeah, there was a dock with a boat hoist."

"Did you meet the owners?"

"No, I didn't. It was an estate sale."

Jace sat forward in his chair. "Do you know what happened to the family that lived there?"

"Apparently the whole family went out one day in the family boat for one last ride before they put it up for the season. That's how I knew there was a dock. I took a look at it after I heard the story. Word has it that a big storm came up while they were out there. They never found the boat until several days later. By the time they found it, there was no one on board. I talked to one of the guys at the sale. He had a friend in the sheriff's department and he told me that they thought the bodies were probably carried out on the current. I guess it had been storming for several days before they could even get out there and search."

"If they never found any of the bodies, why were they having an estate sale?"

"Oh, it had been over a year since the accident. I asked the guy I was talking to if they had ever found the family. He said that they had closed the case and declared them dead a few months before. A lawyer for the estate was wrapping things up."

"Who was the attorney handling the estate?"

"I don't have a clue. It wasn't important to me, so I didn't ask," Smith said. "I know that a local auction house handled the actual estate sale. I think the name was... Doyle or Dobson or something like that."

"Do you remember the name of the family?"

"No, but it should be easy enough to find that information. They were a rich family, and it was a pretty big deal at the time. I'm sure it was all over the local papers."

"One more thing," Jace asked. "Do you remember when this happened? What year?"

"Let's see." Smith deliberated. "I was still married and in the antique business, but it was one of my last trips. So that had to be the fall of 1997, late November I think. I remember that it was cold as sin that day. So the boating accident must have happened in late September or early October of 1996."

"Thanks, John. You've been a big help."

"Hey, no problem. Glad to help. I wish everything were that easy."

Jace chuckled. "Yeah, I hear you." Jace ended the call and got up to pour himself another cup of coffee. He took a few sips, then picked up his phone again and dialed Eli at the office.

"Yo, talk to me," Eli said.

"No wonder you work behind a computer all day. No communication skills whatsoever."

"So teach me. Communicate."

"Eli, can you access newspaper archives online?"

"Please. Don't make yourself look any more ignorant than you already do."

Jace laughed. "I'll take that as a yes. Okay this is what I need. There was a boating accident in Ruston, Ohio. It happened in September or October of 1996. This family went out in their boat. Big storm. They never found them, only the boat. I need to find out everything I can about the family... and the accident."

"What's this about? Did you find out something last night?"

"I saw something that I'm pretty sure is connected to the killer."

Jace was hungry. He grabbed a bagel from the bag on the counter. It was a little hard, but he managed to find a knife sharp enough to cut it. He popped it into the toaster.

"Tell me."

Jace told Eli what he'd seen.

"Man, how do you sleep at night? If I saw stuff like that, I'd walk around with a coffee IV hooked up to my arm twenty-four seven."

"I've seen stuff like that all my life."

"That's just wrong, bro."

"Don't worry about it, Eli. I'm used to it."

"I got news for you buddy, nobody could ever get used to that. In any case, I'll be happy to apply my superior skills to this search."

Jace snorted. He opened the fridge. Damn, he was out of cream cheese. He found a jar of almond butter on the door and set it on the counter.

"Seriously, I'll get on this right away. You working out of the house today? Is your laptop at the house?"

"Yeah, it's here."

"Okay, give me an hour, two tops and I'll send you whatever I find. I just have one more question, bro."

"What?"

"Who's gonna meet with the Anderson's later today?"

"Shit, I forgot about that. That's at two o'clock, right?" He held the phone to his ear as he buttered the bagel.

"Yup. Please don't make me do it. You know I'm not good with people."

"No. I'll be there for the meeting. Let Mattie know what's going on, will you? And Eli, thanks a lot."

"Jace, you gotta stop thanking me for doing my job. You'll make me feel guilty about that big fat paycheck I keep cashing."

"Okay fine. I'll talk to you later. Oh and let Mattie know that I'll probably be going to Ohio. Ask her politely not to schedule anything for tomorrow or the next day. I know I'm behind on my paperwork, but tell her not to stress about it. I'll catch up on things when I get back." He closed his phone. He sat down at the table, biting into the bagel.

He looked up. Alex was standing in the doorway of the kitchen in black shorts and a light blue tank top. Her face was scrubbed clean of make-up. He smiled.

"What?" she said.

"You look really young, that's all. How long have you been standing there?"

"Long enough to hear the tail end of your conversation with Eli." She walked over to the coffee maker and helped herself to a mug of coffee.

"I talked to John Smith and he gave me some interesting stuff. Eli is doing some digging for me now. Sit down and I'll tell you what I found out."

When he was finished, Alex said, "But if they're all dead, why are we even bothering? They can't be the ones, right? Maybe John Smith was remembering another dining room set."

"I don't think so. I'm not convinced that they're dead. That body I saw weighted down wasn't there by chance. No, I don't think it was an accident, and if I'm right then that means that someone did some pretty intense planning in order to stage the 'accident.'"

Alex grimaced. She couldn't even imagine the kind of person who would calmly make plans to kill an entire family. She took a seat at the breakfast bar, sipping her coffee. "Where do we go from here?"

Jace finished the last of his bagel and got up to put the plate in the dishwasher. "After Eli sends us what he's found, we'll look it over and then decide on our next course of action. I'm gonna go for a short run while we're waiting."

"Wait for me. I'll come too."

An hour and a half later they sat freshly showered in front of Jace's computer pouring over the information Eli had sent. The first thing was a newspaper article from the Ruston Times dated November 5, 1996.

FAMILY MISSING AFTER BOATING ACCIDENT – David Hensley, 59, his wife Ann, 41, and David's twin sons Nathan and Noah, 18, left on a boat ride late Friday afternoon. A storm came through the area several hours later. They never returned home. Strong winds, rain, and hail delayed the search for several days. A fisherman spotted the boat early Monday morning drifting near Duffy's Landing. There was no one in the boat. According to Sheriff Tom Shaffer, no bodies have been recovered. The Coast Guard is continuing the search.

"Twins! I wonder if they're identical. If they are and one of them is the killer, how will we know which one it is?" Alex asked.

"As if this wasn't complicated enough. Keep your fingers crossed that they are fraternal or that one of them really is dead." Jace grimaced. "Sorry, that was a rotten thing to hope for."

There was another article dated November the tenth.

SEARCH FOR HENSLEYS CALLED OFF – Dozens of agencies aided in the search both by air and sea, however, there has been no sign of the Hensleys. Sheriff Tom Shaffer says the investigation is still ongoing even though the search has been called off. Anyone with information is asked to call the Ruston Police Department at 555-0999.

Jace pulled up the next file. It was a business certificate for the state of Ohio. The business was listed as Hensley & Drake, LLC, and the owners were David Hensley and Paul Drake. It was dated May 13, 1991, and it had been filed in Columbus, Ohio. There were also two company stock reports that were sent to all the stockholders in the company on a yearly basis. One was dated September 30, 1994. The other was dated September 30, 2008. The numbers both then and now were impressive. Whatever they sold they were doing well.

"So it looks like the business partner is still there running the business. At least his name is still listed as CEO," Jace said. "I think I'll call and see if I can get an appointment to talk to him. He must've known the Hensleys well if he was Mr. Hensley's business partner. I wonder if the sheriff is still there? I'd like to talk to him too."

"You mean we, right?"

"Can you get the time off of work? You haven't been there very long."

"Fortunately Paulie says I'm the biggest star they've ever had there and he thinks I can do no wrong. I think he'll be fine with it. I'll call him as soon as we check everything out."

Jace scrolled down. "Okay, fine. We can leave today if my meeting goes well with my two o'clock appointment. No pictures of the family. I'm a little disappointed."

The next thing in the file was a picture of the Hensleys' house. It was a real estate photo. "Damn, that's the place," Jace said, excitement in his voice. "There are the columns and the two arched doors. We're definitely on the right track."

"Just a little million dollar shack, huh?" Alex said, looking over the stats on the page. "The taxes alone are high enough to give me a nose bleed. I think I'm depressed now."

"Yeah, money may not buy happiness, but at least you can be miserable in a nice place."

They moved on to a small article in the local newspaper announcing the graduation of Nathan and Noah Hensley from Ruston Central High School. According to the article, both boys had graduated with honors. Both were college bound, Noah had a scholarship to Harvard and Nathan had been accepted at Princeton.

"So if they were both in college, what were they doing home on a Friday afternoon?" Alex asked.

"Good question. We'll have to try to find the answer to that one."

There were copies of two marriage certificates. The first one was from David Hensley's first marriage to Lailah Moreland. It was dated January 11, 1975. The other one was to Ann Singleton. It was dated June 5, 1993. There's also a death certificate for Lailah Moreland dated September 13, 1992.

"Wow," Alex said. "Nine months from the time his first wife died, he married Ann. He didn't waste any time did he? I wonder how his sons felt about that?"

They were at the end of the file. Alex sat back in her chair. "I wonder who owns the house now? Could you have Eli run a title search? I'd really like to see if it's possible to get in and check it out while we're there. You know, if one of them is the killer, and they're identical twins then I may already know what the killer looks like. Or what he looked like when he was around eighteen."

"And if that's the case, and we find a picture in Ohio, then Eli could do an age-progressed picture so that we'll know what he looks like now. But we're really jumping the gun here. We need to get there and find some proof that the killer is really one of these men.

"Listen, why don't you make the call to your boss and if your boss is okay with the time off, I'll make some calls to Ruston and see if the people we want to talk to are still there and willing to talk to us. If so, we'll stop by your house so you can pack a few things. Then you can come back to the office with me while I talk to my clients. Mattie can book us hotel rooms and then we'll take off. It's only about a six-hour drive."

Chapter 21

Jace opened the door to his office. "Help yourself to some coffee or some water if you're thirsty. I'm just gonna straighten up my desk a little." He picked up several piles of papers and stacking them in a bin marked "IN BOX."

"As you can see, paperwork is not my favorite thing." He grinned at her. "The Andersons will be here in a few minutes. You can either sit in Eli's office while I see them, or you're welcome to sit in. I'll tell them you're a colleague of mine."

"Oh no, I don't want to get in the way. It's hard enough to talk to someone you don't know about your private life. I don't want to make things harder for them."

"Actually you might be able to help with their problem. You have the same senses that I do."

"Only different," she said.

"Right. Anyway, you're welcome to stay. It might put Mrs. Anderson more at ease to have a woman in the room."

"Okay, if they agree, I'd love to stay and learn more about what you do in the office." She took a seat in a chair by the wall, tucking one foot up underneath her.

He picked up random pens, paper clips, and sticky notes and slid them into his top drawer, dusting the top of his desk with his sleeve. Then he rubbed his hand up and down his sleeve. "Don't tell Mattie that I did that. It's our little secret." He threw her a wink. She chuckled.

"Hey, it did the job." Her cell phone rang. She checked the display. "It's the police, probably about the break-in at my house. Hello?"

"Mrs. Pope?"

"Yes?"

"This is Detective Richard Hogan. I was at your house the other day."

"Uh-huh. Were you able to find anything? Any prints?"

"Well, we found lots of prints. Unfortunately, most of them were yours. We found a few others. One set belongs to Olivia Stanton. She says she's a friend of yours."

"Yes, she is."

"The other two were from Jace Moseley and his brother Eli. I know both of them, so I'm assuming that neither of them is the man who broke into your house. However, if you want me to question them and find out where they were at the time of the incident, I will certainly do that."

"No, that won't be necessary," Alex said.

"We also found a smudge on your dresser, but we weren't able to get anything from it, not enough to ID it. Nothing on the emails, they've all been a dead end so far."

"Thanks for trying, Detective. I'm also wondering about the 'gift' the stalker left on my bed? Did that tell you anything? Actually, can you tell me what was in it?"

"It was a necklace, a very nice-sized diamond on a silver chain. It looks like it's worth a pretty penny, but then I don't know squat about jewelry. I'm sorry, but there was nothing on it as far as evidence. It had been cleaned recently."

"We checked with all the neighbors. Apparently no one has seen anything suspicious. We've been running patrols by there several times a day. Haven't seen anything weird. No strange vehicles parking on the street, no strangers in the neighborhood. Sorry we didn't come up with anything helpful. You can come down and pick up the necklace whenever it's convenient. Just go the front desk and ask for me. If I'm not there, I'll leave word with them to expect you. If anything else happens give me a call. Hopefully, now that you have the security system, things will quiet down."

Maybe she could get something off the necklace. "Thank you for getting back to me, Detective."

The Andersons walked into the room.

Alex said a hasty good-bye and hung up.

Jace introduced himself and Alex. He indicated two seats in front of the desk and the couple sat down.

"My secretary says that you have a problem, and that the police have been unable to help you. What can we do to help?"

The couple looked at each other and then they both turned to Jace. Mr. Anderson cleared his throat, but seemed unable to figure out how to begin.

Mrs. Anderson played with a tissue she held between her hands. "Our son is missing, and no one will help us find him. They say that because he's eighteen, he isn't considered a missing person or a runaway. The officer we spoke with told us that since he left of his own free will, there was nothing he could do for us." White lint from the tortured tissue collected in her lap as she tightened her grip on it. "We just need to know that he's all right."

The father spoke up this time. "He and I had a big fight. He was always a great kid. An A student, great at sports, lots of friends. Then he started screwing up, first at school and then at work. I got so mad that I said some terrible things to him, things that I didn't mean.

"We lost his sister to cancer a little over a year ago. He'd been so great, never seemed to mind that we had to spend so much time and energy on Kara. But afterwards, he seemed so remote, so angry all the time. We tried to talk to him, but he would just walk away. He spent hours alone in his room. He wouldn't talk to any of his friends. He stopped doing homework and began showing up late for work, if he showed up at all.

"His soccer coach called to say that he hadn't shown up for practice and that he was afraid that Chad was doing drugs. Of course we didn't believe that. We were so sure that he would never do drugs. He'd seen his sister after her chemo treatments and he was always so upset about what the drugs did to her. He finally managed to graduate high school, but wouldn't talk about college, or anything else for that matter. That last day when he came home, he smelled like marijuana. I accused him of doing drugs."

Mrs. Anderson was crying softly into the tissue now.

Mr. Anderson sighed sadly. "I said a lot of other things too. There's no excuse, I know, but we've all been wrung dry by the experience with Kara. I hadn't been sleeping well. I felt so damn guilty about not being able to do anything to save our little girl. And now I've driven my son away. I need to make things right with him. We've already lost our daughter, we can't lose our son as well." He looked at Jace, pain and hope in his eyes. "Will you help us?"

"We'll do our best. Do you know who saw him last? Was he in contact with any of his friends?"

This time Mrs. Anderson answered. "He's lost touch with most of his friends. We've called everyone we could think of. No one has talked to him. They all said that he'd been keeping to himself. They all tried after the funeral, but he wouldn't talk to any of them. I guess they just got tired of trying and finally gave up." She sighed, a sadly poignant sound, as if her heart were breaking all over again.

"I was the last person who saw Chad. After we fought, he went to his room and locked the door. He left sometime during the night," Mr. Anderson said.

Jace came around his desk. "You said on the phone that John Butler referred you to our agency. Did he tell you how I work?"

"Yes," Mr. Anderson said.

"And you're both all right with that?"

"John told us that you have a near perfect record for getting information using your method. So we're fine with it. We brought one of Chad's favorite shirts. John said you needed something of his." Mrs. Anderson retrieved her purse from the floor next to her chair and pulled out a plastic bag. She took the shirt out, cradling it to her chest for a few seconds and then she held it out to Jace.

Taking the shirt, Jace said, "This may be a little scary to watch so if you'd rather wait in the lounge, feel free to do that. It may seem like I'm not here for a few minutes. That's okay. Are you two ready for me to do this?"

"Yes, please," Mrs. Anderson said. "We can't wait any longer to know. We've spent seven months not knowing."

Jace took a deep breath, closed his eyes and then held the shirt between both of his hands, focusing on it and nothing else. The slide show began. Chad in his bedroom, on the bed, pacing the room, pulling clothes out of his dresser. Chad sitting on a sidewalk waiting, then sitting in a chair in front of a desk talking to a man in uniform. Chad getting off a bus with a group of other young men. Chad wearing a uniform, standing in front of a sign. Jace read, Camp LeJeune, Home of Expeditionary Forces in Readiness. The slides stopped coming. Show over.

Jace came back slowly. He sat back on his desk. He could see the Andersons watching him in an agony of waiting. Jace knew that what had seemed like seconds to him, was in reality probably more like five minutes. "He's fine. He's at Camp LeJeune, in North Carolina. He's joined the Marines."

"Oh thank God," Chad's mother said through a sob. Her husband reached over and took her in his arms. They stood, laughing and crying at the same time. Jace picked up the phone and talked to someone on the other end. Then he hung up and sat quietly, letting the Andersons deal with what they'd heard. After a few minutes, they broke apart. "Why hasn't he called us?" Chad's father asked. "Is he still so angry?"

"I'm sorry. I don't know that. All I see are clips of events and how they happen."

Alex stood then and came over to Mrs. Anderson. She pointed to the shirt. "May I?"

"You're psychic too?" Mrs. Anderson said.

"Sometimes I can see what people were feeling when something significant happens."

Mrs. Anderson handed her the shirt. Alex rubbed the shirt between her hands. She stood still, waiting. There was the jagged trail of heat in her head and then she was inside his.

He was so angry, furious in fact. It was a raging blaze burning its way through him. The blood pumped through his veins at such velocity that he sometimes feared that the veins in his head would pop. It was a runaway train, and he had no idea how to stop it. But he'd rather be suspended in this state of anger than be back at Kara's bedside listening to her take that last gurgling breath. Or live again the hopeless empty pull of standing in front of the silk-draped coffin gazing down at Kara, so white, so small and silent in death.

His eyes misted for the millionth time remembering her little giggle and the way she used to twist her curly hair around her index finger... back when she still had her hair. And most of all he remembered her eyes brimming with happiness. How she could always make his parents smile and laugh.

They never laughed anymore, or ate, or slept. Every night he could hear his mother crying softly in her room and his dad pacing the floor in the living room. He didn't know how they could stand it. The pain must be even worse for them. He wanted to do something, anything to help them heal. He couldn't help them, though. He couldn't even help himself lately.

It was funny, but even with the fiery rage that was with him all the time, the inside of him was the planet Mars: distant, stark, and cold. The only thing that filled the cold emptiness was the red-hot anger. And it was all eating him up inside.

He'd alienated every one of his friends. He'd done it on purpose. Every time he saw the sympathy in their eyes he wanted to either cry like a baby or hit something really, really hard. He'd done so many stupid things lately. He was becoming someone he didn't even like. He couldn't let that happen. He was all they had now. His parents were already the walking wounded and he was causing them so much more pain.

He had to get away. Somewhere where he could take a full breath, somewhere far away from his sister's death and his father's disgust and his mother's grief.

He knew where he was going. He'd already decided.

He'd make himself into a person he could recognize. Someone he could be at peace with. Someone his sister would have been proud of, and most of all, someone his parents would be proud to call a son. He vowed then and there not to hurt his parents again. If that meant not talking to them until he was the son they deserved to have, then that's what he would do, however long it took. He picked up his duffel bag and quietly let himself out of the house.

Alex sank down in the chair she'd sat in earlier. Everyone was watching her expectantly. She turned to the Andersons.

"Chad doesn't hate you. He was so angry and sad. He was grieving for his sister, and he was grieving for you two as well. He was holding on to the anger as a way of dealing with things, but it was changing him. He hated what he was doing to you and to himself. He made a pact with himself not to contact you until he was sure he wouldn't hurt you anymore. Until he was the son you two deserve."

A gasping sob broke from Mrs. Anderson. "He's always been a son to be proud of. My God, he's been a grownup since he was little. He never even got to be a child, with everything going on with his sister. If he needed to act out a little now, who could blame him?"

"I could," Mr. Anderson said. "I did. Not in my heart, but through my angry words to him. I drove him away."

"No," Alex said, "You didn't. He never blamed you for saying the things you did. He knew you were speaking the truth. It was the only way he could stop the cycle. He did it for himself as much as for the two of you."

Mr. Anderson raised his eyes to hers. "You're not just saying that? He really felt that way? Do you think he's okay?"

"I'm not just saying that to make you feel better. It's the truth," Alex told him.

Then Jace said, "The Chad I saw was better. I think he's made peace with himself, or he's well on the way."

The couple sat quietly for a minute, pondering what they had heard. They wanted to believe that everything they'd heard was the truth, but Jace could see they were struggling with the method of discovering it. There was a knock on the door, and Mattie entered with a piece of paper in her hand. "That's everything they'll need," she said. Jace thanked her and she left the room.

Squatting down in front of Chad's mother, he took her hand. "This is the number to call at Camp LeJeune. They can get you in touch with your son. I really think he's ready to hear from you. Call him." He pressed the piece of paper into her palm. She gazed at the paper in her hand. A tear splashed onto his thumb.

"I'm almost afraid to hope. We've been disappointed so many times lately."

"Would you like to make the call right now?" Jace asked her.

"Oh, could we?"

"Sure. Why waste any more time?" Jace replied.

She looked over at her husband beseechingly. He said, "Let's do it."

Jace dialed the phone and talked to the person at the other end of the line, explaining the situation and then listening while the Anderson's sat in an agony of waiting and hoping. Jace hung up the phone. He looked across at them. "He's on the base right now. They are going to locate him and have him call you here. I know it's tough to wait like this, but they said to give it ten minutes."

"It's been seven months." Chad's father said. "Ten minutes will be nothing."

In less than five minutes, the phone rang. Jace answered it. "Hi Chad. Yeah, just a second. Let me get them for you." He hit the button to put the phone on speaker so that they could both talk. "We'll leave you alone to talk to him. Just hang up the receiver when you're done... and take your time." He led Alex out of the office.

They went into the room next door to his office and shut the door.

Alex blew out a breath. "Whew! So that's what you do for a living. I can see why. Those people look at least ten years younger than when they came in this afternoon. It's incredible that you can do that for people."

"You did it too, you know. And this was one of the good ones. For every couple that comes out looking ten years younger, there are three or four that go out looking ten years older. But what keeps me going is the fact that they all come out of it with something that they needed, one way or another."

"It felt really good to help them. I'm glad that you do this for people. That's what we're doing by finding this killer, aren't we? Giving the victims and all their loved ones closure."

"Yeah, we are. And don't forget the part about saving the lives of other potential victims. It's important work. A way to use our talents in a positive way."

"Way better than telling fortunes and performing party tricks," Alex said. "Thanks for letting me in on that."

He smiled at her. "You're welcome."

Eventually, the door to Jace's office opened. They went out to meet the Andersons. Alex barely recognized them. The beaten and grieving couple who'd entered the office an hour or so earlier had been replaced by two vibrant parents beaming with love and joy.

"I see that it went well. How is he?" Jace asked.

"He's doing wonderfully. He loves what he's doing and he seems to be happy for the first time in years. He was so glad to hear from us that he broke down and cried. I didn't even see him cry at the funeral. How can we ever thank you?" Mr. Anderson said.

Jace smiled. "Hey, this is what I do. The best payment is seeing your smiling, happy faces now. Of course, my secretary may disagree with that." He grinned at his own joke.

"It's well worth it, whatever you charge." Mrs. Anderson said. "You gave us back our son. We'll be singing your praises high and low."

Mr. Anderson shook his head. "You know, I always thought that this stuff was a bunch of hooey, but you've made a believer out of me. Whatever it is, you two clearly both have it and it's different for each of you, isn't it? It's kind of spooky, but if you can help every client the way you helped us, then you should have a line a mile long out the door."

Mrs. Anderson leaned forward and hugged Jace. "There aren't words enough to thank you." Then she turned and hugged Alex. The woman's love and joy flowed through Alex's body, a warm wave of sensation that brought tears to her eyes.

"You're very welcome," Alex whispered into her ear. The woman stepped back and then they made their way out to the reception desk.

Jace smiled at her. "A very good day so far. Let's get your stuff and get on the road."

Chapter 22

Alex blew into the small hole in the plastic lid of her coffee and then took a cautious sip. It still burned the tip of her tongue and she struggled to swallow it quickly before it did any more damage. "Holy shit!" she mumbled.

Jace glanced her way. "Hot?"

"Volcanic."

"Thanks for the warning." He lowered the cup he'd been in the act of raising to his mouth, resting it on his leg instead.

A man with rumpled brown hair and an equally rumpled white shirt, top button unbuttoned, poked his head out of a door to their right. "Jace Moseley?"

"Yup."

"Come on in. Sorry to make you wait. I finally got hold of someone I needed to talk to."

"No problem." Jace put a hand on Alex's shoulder. "This is Alexandra Pope. Alex, this is Sheriff Tom Schaffer." They shook hands and then the sheriff indicated two seats across from his desk and they sat down.

Tom Schaffer rounded his desk and took a seat. "I'll admit your call piqued my interest. I haven't heard anyone mention the Hensley case in quite a while. It's always been a thorn in my side, to tell you the truth." Schaffer ran a hand through his hair. "I have a fairly impressive record for closing difficult cases, but I've spent countless hours beating my head against a brick wall with that one. Every possible lead came to zip. Very frustrating. Mike Stone filled me in on what's going on in your neck of the woods, but I'm not sure how it relates to the Hensley case. It happened thirteen years ago. If they're all dead, how can any of this possibly help you?"

He looked at the two of them questioningly.

Jace glanced over at Alex and then returned his gaze to the sheriff. "Would you mind if we ask a few questions first, and then I'll try to explain?"

"Sure, what would you like to know?"

"I understand that the boat was found. Were you able to get anything off of it? Prints, blood, fibers?"

Schaffer leaned forward in his seat. "Yeah, we got a whole bunch of prints off the boat. Mostly David Hensley's and his two sons, Paul Drake's, that was David's business partner, some from another guy they worked with. They sometimes went fishing together. Along with a couple of partials that we couldn't identify."

Alex uncrossed her legs, dropping her foot to the floor. One of them could be the killer! But she knew that Ann wasn't killed on the boat. "None were Ann's?" Alex asked.

"We found a partial print that may have been hers, but there weren't enough points of identification to confirm that. The only blood we found was fish blood on a fillet knife. We found some fibers on the seats. A couple of them were from a sweater that one of the boys kept on the boat. We found a thread from an old fishing net that we found underneath one of the seats. A few more that were consistent with fibers from a blanket, but we never found the blanket, so we couldn't verify that."

"Any shoe prints?" Jace asked.

"No, but remember that it rained for almost three days before the boat was found. There were a couple of inches of water in the bottom of the boat."

"Did anyone see them leaving their house in the boat?" Alex asked.

"No, there were no witnesses, but Nathan had mentioned to several people that the family was going out in the boat that night for a last run before they put the boat up for the season and someone saw Noah stop in town on his way home and buy something... at least they thought it was him." Schaffer shrugged his shoulders. "We were never able to definitely confirm that, though. Word was that they'd come home especially for the outing. Both boys loved being out in that boat. They went out all the time by themselves, sometimes for days at a time."

Jace and Alex looked at each other.

"Have you seen many other drownings where the bodies were never recovered?"

"We had a father and son drown a few years ago. We didn't find the bodies until the next spring, but other than that the Hensleys are the only ones that I know of from around here who have never been found. Why? You don't think they drowned?"

"No, not necessarily. Not all of them, at any rate."

"You mind telling me how you came to that conclusion."

"Oh boy, that's not an easy question to answer. What did Mike Stone tell you?"

"He said that there've been several women murdered up your way and that you think there may be a connection to this case. I can't for the life of me see how these two cases could possibly have anything to do with each other." He waited.

"We think that Ann Hensley was killed by the same serial killer who killed the women in New York," Alex said.

"And you think this because...?" He looked back and forth between Jace and Alex.

"I think that because I saw her death in a psychic vision," Alex said.

Jace groaned, turning to look at her. "I can't believe you just said that."

"Why not? It's the truth."

In a split second Schaffer's body language changed completely. Jace had seen it happen a thousand times. "Okay then," Sheriff Schaffer said. He pushed back from his desk and stood up. "Thanks for coming by. Sorry, but that's all I can tell you. I have another appointment now, but if I find anything that I think is pertinent, I'll be sure to let you know."

"We are not a couple of nuts! You can't just dismiss us like this," Alex said.

Jace took Alex's elbow. "Alex, let's go." He stood up then, forcing her to rise also.

"No," she said. "I will not be dismissed as a crackpot."

Jace took a firmer grip on her upper arm. "Thank you for your time, Sheriff. We'll find our way out."

She turned back to the sheriff. "You shouldn't have had the watch engraved. She's planning on dumping you."

With that Jace dragged her out of the office and down the hall. She struggled for a few seconds and then walked stiffly by his side until they stood outside on the steps of the station.

She turned on him. "Damn you, why did you pull me out of there?"

"Alex, I'm been through just this scenario too many times to count. It was all over as soon as he heard the word psychic. Believe me when I tell you that revealing that up front was the kiss of death as far as Sheriff Schaffer is concerned. Unless we find some physical evidence to use as proof of our theory, he's going to avoid us like the plague from now on. I do admire your style though."

Her defiance deflated like air from a balloon. "So what do we now?"

"We go see Paul Drake."

"David Hensley's business partner? Were you able to make an appointment with him?"

"Unfortunately no. But if he and David Hensley spent time on the boat fishing, then chances are they were friends. He probably knows a lot about the family. I wrote down his address before we left the hotel this morning. Let's go anyway and take our chances."

****

Paul Drake was a very busy man. They sat in the waiting room for over two hours before he had a few minutes to spare. When he appeared at the door, Alex looked over at Jace in surprise. Paul Drake was significantly younger than his business partner. In fact, he couldn't be much older than David's sons, maybe six or seven years. He came around the desk as they entered his office. "My secretary tells me that you're here to see me about the Hensleys. I don't have much time, but I admit to being curious. Has the case been reopened?"

"Not yet, Mr. Drake, but we're hoping that we can change that. I'm Jace Moseley and this is Alexandra Pope."

"Are you police officers?"

"Private detectives," Jace said. Alex wisely remained silent. She forced herself to focus on the framed photographs on the wall behind Paul Drake's desk.

"And you've found something new?"

"We believe that we may have, but it's too soon to say," Jace said. "We'd like to talk to you about the Hensley family, ask you a few questions."

"I'm sorry, but I only have about five minutes. I suffer from low blood sugar and if I don't eat at certain times, my blood sugar goes crazy."

"Listen, we'd be glad to buy you lunch. That would give us more time to talk," Jace offered.

Drake deliberated for a minute. "Sure. I have to eat anyway. We can eat upstairs in the company cafeteria."

After they were seated and had served themselves from the lunch line, Drake said, "Okay, shoot. What can I help you with?"

"What can you tell us about the Hensley family? What were they like?"

"Wow, a tall order. Well," he broke a roll in two, spreading butter on each half, "David was a great business partner and a good friend. He was so sharp in business that it was scary. He could conceptualize things most people couldn't even see when they were put down on paper. And he could troubleshoot anything from production problems to labor relations. I wish you could have seen him in action. There isn't a day that passes that there isn't something I wish he were here to handle."

"Yet your business has done well without him."

"Not as well as it would have done with him here." He cut a piece of chicken, popping it into his mouth and chewing slowly.

"What about his family life? Did you know him when he was married to his first wife?"

"Yes. She died about two years after we went into business together."

"What was his first wife like?"

"Beautiful, young, fragile. She seemed fine when I first met her. In fact, she was the most vibrant person I'd ever met. At first I was secretly jealous of David, until I realized that her highs were just one side of the coin. The other side of it was pure and utter hell for Dave and the boys.

"She clung to them so desperately when she was depressed. She even homeschooled Noah and Nathan for a while before she died so that they would be near her all the time. She had this phobic dread of losing them. When she was like that she'd accuse David of cheating on her and she'd sleep in the guest room for weeks on end. Then all of a sudden, she'd come out of it and then she'd be madly in love with David again. That was the only time those poor boys had any semblance of a normal life."

"Why didn't David divorce her?" Jace asked.

"Because he was also madly in love with her. He indulged her every whim and when she was in a manic slump, he was beside himself. It was a terrible relationship for all of them. I hate to say it, but it was a blessing for all of them when she died."

"She was still a young woman. How did she die?" Alex asked.

"She fell down the stairs one night and hit her head. David was away on a business trip. The poor twins tried to help her, tried to get her to go to the hospital. But she insisted that she was fine and refused to go. What none of them knew was that she was hemorrhaging in her brain. She died in her sleep."

"How did the boys react to her death?"

"They were devastated by her death, but I think Noah took it the hardest. He never seemed quite the same after her death. And when his father married again he was angry and bitter for quite some time. Nathan was less vocal, but no less upset by his mother's death and his father's remarriage I think. He'd always been pretty outgoing, but he became much quieter, more subdued after his dad remarried."

"What did you think of Ann?" Alex asked.

"Now there was a wonderful woman. She was quite a bit younger then David. So was his first wife come to think of it. But she didn't care about that. Anyone could see that she was in love with David and he with her. Dave was a great guy."

"How about Nathan and Noah? How did they feel about Ann?"

Drake speared a green bean and took a bite. "As you might imagine, they felt that their father had married too soon and they resented Ann, Noah more so than Nathan I think. He was so angry all the time. He barely talked to his father for a while. David didn't see it as much as I did, maybe he was too close to it, but the way Noah treated Ann bordered on contempt."

"How about Nathan?"

"He had what I would call a perpetual poker face. No one ever knew what was going on in his head. I always told Dave we should send him to Vegas with as much money as we could spare. But I don't remember him ever being rude to her, at least when I was around."

"Where the twins identical?" Jace asked.

"Yes, they were. David told me that when they were young no one but Lailah was able to tell them apart, not even David. As they got older though, I guess it was easier to tell them apart. Their personalities were very different. And for a while one of them, I forget which one, dyed his hair brown."

"Were they blond?" Alex asked.

"Yes, blond hair and blue eyes, just like their mother. That Nordic influence I guess."

"Did the twins get along?"

"Oh yeah. They were extremely close. Frankly, I was surprised that they agreed to go to different schools for college."

Jace swallowed the last bite of his club sandwich. "Did you know that the family was going out on the boat the day of the accident?"

"The boys both had the day off of school. David told me that they were very excited about the outing. David had just gotten back from a business trip that day and he stopped at the office a little after two that afternoon to touch base with me. I could tell that he was really happy that the boys had planned the boat ride and that they had included Ann."

He put his coffee cup on top of his empty plate. "He told me that the twins had finally come around. I do know that the three of them had spent a lot of time together during the summer. He'd been trying to mend the relationship for years. Apparently, even Ann had agreed to go with them, which was nothing short of a miracle."

"Why do you say that?" Alex asked.

"One day while Dave and I were out in the boat, he confided in me that Ann didn't like being on the water. She couldn't swim, and she had a fear of the water. She only went out on the water a couple of times that I know of. After that she absolutely refused to go out in the boat. So, yeah, I was very surprised to hear that she was going. Pretty ironic, don't you think? That she was afraid of drowning and that's how she ended up dying."

Ironic indeed, if it were really true.

"How long had Mr. Hensley been gone on the business trip?"

"He'd been overseeing the opening of our first overseas plant. He'd been gone for ten days."

Alexandra drained the last of her iced tea. "When was the last time you saw Ann, do you remember?"

"She dropped David off at the office the day he left for his trip."

"Can you tell us where she worked?"

"She was a senior tax attorney with Lucas, Markham, and Stephens."

"Is that a local firm?" Alex asked.

"Kind of, their office is in Cleveland. It's not a bad drive from here. A lot of people live in this area and commute to Cleveland."

"With such a high-power job, and the commute, Ann must have needed someone to help in managing that big house. Did they have a housekeeper?"

"That would be Theresa Alvarez. Best cook in Ohio. I tried to steal her away plenty of times, but she was happy where she was."

"What happened to her after the accident?"

"She never liked the cold weather here. I tried to talk her into staying, but she took a job in New Mexico to be near her son, I think." He glanced at his watch. "Look, I hate to be rude, but I have to get back. I have a meeting in about five minutes."

"No problem. Thanks for taking the time to talk to us."

"Certainly, and thanks for lunch. You'll let me know if you find out anything more about David and his family, won't you?"

"Absolutely, just one more question. Do you know who lives in the Hensleys' house now?"

"No, I'm sorry, I don't."

Chapter 23

Jace sat back in a chair in his hotel room, his feet propped up on a chair across from him. He flipped his cell phone closed. They'd decided to go back to the hotel to regroup after lunch. Alex sat with her back against the headboard of Jace's bed, remote in hand, flipping through the channels.

"Was that Eli?"

"Yeah. I had him google the housekeeper. Surprise, surprise… she died six months ago, so that's a dead end. But he says he caught up on everything and he was bored to death so he did some research on the Hensley place. Guess what?"

"What?"

"It's empty right now. The present owner's in the slammer."

"You're kidding? What for?"

"Eli says he was in the import/export business. Come to find out he was importing more than just coffee and bananas."

"Drugs?" Alex asked.

"Uh huh, big time… worth millions on the streets. In fact, this was his summer home."

Alex stopped flipping through channels. "His summer home! No wonder people sell drugs. Didn't you say this house was on the market for a million dollars?"

"Yeah, I did. But Eli says that he got a real bargain on the place. Records show that he only paid eight hundred, ninety-five thou and some change for the house."

"Oh is that all?" she said, sarcasm dripping from her tongue. "How long is he in jail for?"

"You'll love this. He's serving a hundred and eight years."

"Wow! That's crazy, who gets a sentence of a hundred and eight years?"

"Drug dealers, apparently," Jace said.

Alex resumed her channel surfing. "You know, if this ends up being the killer's house, then I'd have to say that this place has some really bad karma."

"No kidding and that was a very spiritual thing to say."

She pointedly ignored him. He couldn't help but smile.

"Eli also told me that the property has been seized by the DEA and the U.S. Attorney's Office."

"Shit. If the house has been seized by the government then we have zero chance of getting inside."

"Did I mention that Eli has been really bored? He called Ray Jeffers. He's a guy we used to hang out with when we were teenagers. He's an FBI agent now. Eli waved the serial killings in front of his nose and he started salivating. He called Mike Stone and they talked at length. Now Ray wants in on the case. I don't know what Mike told him, but he convinced Ray to contact a guy in the Columbus office." Jace checked his watch. "The local guy's gonna meet us there in about an hour and a half."

"I think I'm impressed."

He smiled over at her. "You mean I've finally managed to impress you?"

"Not you. Eli. I'm thinking he might really be as good as he believes he is."

Jace laughed. "Do me a favor and don't tell him that."

Alex smiled at that. She sobered, saying, "It's been a long time since the murder. I'm afraid that even if we see the killer, we won't recognize him."

"The FBI has facial recognition software and they can do age progression too."

"The funny thing is though, that so far we haven't seen any pictures of the family. They were wealthy. David Hensley was an important businessman. They must have been somewhat in the public eye, right? It would really help if we could see pictures of the four of them and maybe even Lailah, too."

"You're right. I'm surprised that there weren't any in the papers when they disappeared. Let's look for some right now." He grabbed his laptop. Stacking some pillows against the headboard, he joined her on the bed, leaning back against the pillows. He settled his computer in his lap.

His arm brushed against hers as he opened his computer. A shiver of awareness ran through her and settled in her stomach, a flutter of butterflies that she hadn't felt since high school. He smelled good, like soap and the cinnamon gum she'd given him on the way back to the hotel. His head was bent over the computer and she silently savored the feeling of being close to him. What was it about him?

His hands moved over the keyboard for a few minutes. "Ah ha! Pay dirt."

She leaned in closer to see the picture on the screen. It was a picture of David and Ann Hensley at a charity auction. Alex sucked in a breath. "Oh my God! It's her. I never realized what a shock it would be to see a picture of her like this." She gazed down at the picture sadly. "They really were a beautiful couple, weren't they?"

"Yeah, they were." When she lifted her head, she realized that he was watching her. He ran the back of one finger gently down her cheek. "Your eyes are incredibly blue right now... and way too sad. You didn't even know them."

"But I was there, in their lives for a few minutes. I sat with them intimately in their own home. I felt Ann's fear and pain. I feel like I know her a little." She sighed. "I wish I could have saved her."

"I know you do, and it sucks that you couldn't. Let's work on saving some other women." Looking back at the screen, Jace said, "He's the one."

"The one? The one what?"

"David Hensley. He's the man I saw tied to the bottom of the lake."

She stiffened in surprise, tilting her head to look up at him. "Damn. For sure?"

"Yeah," he said, his tone grim. "For sure. So now we know what happened to David and Ann Hensley. Let's see if we can find Noah and Nathan." He clicked on another picture. His eyebrows rose in surprise. "Holy Shit, Drake was right. It's pretty damn freaky how much they look alike."

"Yikes, I guess so. That's definitely the young man who was sitting across from me at the dinner table. At least one of them is. They look like the quintessential Ivy League candidates, don't they?"

"Yeah, they do." Jace began typing again and then clicked enter. There were quite a few pictures of the different family members. They even found a picture of David and Lailah at their wedding. They both looked young and beautiful.

Jace clicked on a new picture. The caption read, "David Hensley and Paul Drake spend time with family at the company picnic." Someone had taken a random picture of Ann, David, Noah, Nathan, Paul Drake, and one other man. It was a candid shot. Only David and the unidentified man were aware of the camera. The twins were standing close, obviously having a private conversation, and they were both looking at Paul Drake. Drake was standing with Ann. He was focused on her and from the expression on her face, she was not happy.

"Hmm, that's an interesting picture," Jace said. "No one looks very happy do they?"

"No they don't. And Paul Drake is definitely invading Ann's personal space. The only one who's oblivious seems to be David Hensley. Makes you wonder, doesn't it?"

"It certainly does. It looks like Drake may have had more than a casual interest in his partner's wife."

They checked out more photos but didn't learn much else. Jace closed the laptop and set it on the chair nearest him. He sat back in the bed and looked down at Alex. She gripped the remote tightly between both hands, suddenly nervous, but unable to look away.

"I've finally got you where I want you," Jace said, running his hand through her hair, pulling her in closer. He bent his head, touching his lips to hers. Alex dropped the remote and lifted a hand to his shoulder. She leaned in, pressing her lips more firmly to his. His warmth spread through her body, quickly followed by a wash of pure desire. His, hers, both; she couldn't tell; she didn't care. She brought her arms up and around his neck, brushing the soft hair at the back of his neck with her fingertips. He turned his head to take the kiss deeper. She parted her lips for his tongue.

They kissed for what seemed like hours, and then reluctantly pulled back, coming up for air. He ran his hand down her arm and then up under the hem of her shirt, his fingers leaving trails of heat wherever he touched. Her stomach muscles jumped as he lightly caressed her abdomen. Leisurely, he made his way up to cup her breast. She arched to meet his touch. He circled a taut nipple with his thumb. She groaned softly in his ear.

"God," he said, "You're so damn responsive. When you make those little sounds, it drives me nuts."

She laughed softly. "I'm glad. It's only fair that I return the favor." She ran her hands up his back underneath his shirt, reveling in the feel of warm skin covering hard muscle. Tilting her head, she kissed his neck, and then slid her tongue lightly along the hollow of his collarbone. The arm around her back tightened and he sucked in a breath. She tilted her head up and met his lips in another searing kiss. When they ended the kiss, he rested his forehead on hers.

"Damn. Our timing stinks," Jace said. "We don't have time for this right now."

"We could make time if we hurry," Alex murmured, her voice low and sexy.

"Believe me when I say that we couldn't. We're going to need a lot more time than this. And we need to leave here in about ten minutes if we're going to get to the house in time to meet the FBI agent."

She sat back, pulling her t-shirt back down around her waist. Jace climbed off the bed and offered her a hand up. "You might want to do a quick check in the mirror before we go," he said, smiling.

"Oh," she said, raising a hand to the back of her hair. She could feel it sticking straight up. After taking his offered hand, she hoisted herself off the bed. He pulled her close for a minute, kissing her lingeringly and then turned her towards the bathroom.

Chapter 24

"So, does your FBI friend Ray know about your investigative techniques?" Alex asked from the passenger seat.

Jace glanced over at her and then returned his eyes to the road. "He knows that I used to zone out sometimes and that I seemed to know things other people didn't, so I think he has some clue. We never talked about it though."

"Do you think Stone filled him in? Is this local guy gonna think we're a couple of nuts like Sheriff Shaffer did?"

"Maybe... do you care?"

"Not as long as we can get into that house and do whatever we need to do. If this guy gets freaked out and thinks we've come here direct from the Psychic Fair, it may not go well."

"I talked to Mike while you were getting ready. He said that he told them that he's worked with me for years and gotten amazing results. Plus at this point they're willing to do whatever it takes to catch this guy. Mike really believes that they'll give us free rein in there. After all it's not a crime scene, as far as they know. It's not like we're gonna go in there and mess with their case. Besides, according to Eli, this guy owes Ray for something in a big way, so I think we can stop worrying."

They drove for a few minutes in silence and then Jace made a right into the long winding driveway that led to the house. There was a government car parked in the front circle of the drive by the double doors. Jace pulled up in back of the car. The door to the car in front of them opened. A man unfolded his tall, tree trunk body out of the driver's seat and stood facing them.

They approached him and introduced themselves. He shook their hands. "I'm Jim Barber. Ray tells me that you need to get inside and look around. He says to just let you have at it. I hope there are no hard feelings, but I checked you out anyway. What I saw impressed me. You've been very successful in solving some pretty tough cases. I hope that this will be one of them."

"Thanks. We really appreciate your help here. We kind of alienated the lead detective on the case locally, so..." Jace left the sentence unfinished.

"I've alienated a few people in my time for the good of a case, so no big deal. Well, you ready?" Barber asked. They both nodded. "Okay, then let's go." After taking a key ring out of his pocket, he led the way to the front door.

They entered the foyer and Alex closed the doors behind them. The ceiling was high and their feet echoed on the Italian marble tiles. The musty air held the damp chill usually associated with properties with water frontage. In front of them was a huge staircase leading to the next level. Alex remembered that Lailah had supposedly fallen down these stairs, which had led to her death.

Turning to the two men, she said, "Why don't you two go ahead and explore? I'm going to stay here for just a minute."

Jace understood immediately, and he led Barber farther into the house. Alex moved to the staircase. She laid her hand on the railing. She closed her eyes and felt the familiar flash. When her eyes opened, she stood gazing up at the top of the landing.

She knew immediately she wasn't inside the killer's head. This person's brain was different, more organized. Right now though, he was extremely apprehensive. She could see why. A beautiful blond woman, Lailah she assumed, stood at the top of the landing. She was clinging heavily to a younger version of one of the twins. "Please don't leave me, you know I can't be by myself right now. I love you so much. I need you to stay with me. Please don't leave me alone. You know I'll die, if you do."

He was struggling to disengage her hands from around him. "Leave me alone! I'm sick of trying to make you feel better. When you're like this, you suck the life out of all of us. I can't take it anymore. I can't even breathe when I'm around you."

The head Alex was inside of seemed to be echoing the same thoughts, filled with resentment all mixed up with guilt and a feeling of sadness and futility. Alex was 'with' the other twin son. "Careful," she/he shouted.

As he did, the young boy at the top of the landing freed himself from the hands still desperately grasping his arms. He pushed her away from him, determined to be free of her. Lailah stepped back, crying hysterically now, "Please, please… I need you. Don't leave me."

The young man next to her cried angrily, "Leave me alone. Stay away from me." She recoiled as if in pain, stepping back as if he'd struck her. Her foot slipped and she lost her balance.

"No," they shouted from the bottom of the stairs. The woman grabbed for the railing but couldn't reach it. The young man next to her realized in that instant that she was going to fall, and he moved forward, frantically trying to reach her.

Alex watched in frozen horror as the woman tumbled down the stairs towards her. Belatedly, she launched herself up the stairs in an effort to stop the fall, but Lailah was falling with such force that she hit their knees, and they and Lailah tumbled down the remaining stairs. Alex was powerless to stop the events unfolding in front of her. Lailah landed with a sickening crack of her head against the marble floor. And then she lay still. The young man on the landing continued down the stairs at a dead run. "Mom!" He knelt down beside her, checking her pulse. "Thank God! Mom, can you hear me?" Alex knelt on the other side of their mother.

"Is she okay?" she/the other twin said.

"I don't know. She's unconscious. Call 9-1-1." As Alex got up to make the call, Lailah's eyes fluttered open.

"No," she said. "I'll be fine in a minute. Just let me lie here for a second." They argued with her, but she insisted she was fine and after a few minutes, she sat up and asked them to help her to her room.

They settled her in her bed and brought her some water and Tylenol. She insisted once again that she was fine, just a little headache. "I'm very tired. Just stay with me for a few minutes until I fall asleep." Both the boys stood by the bed, anxiously wondering what was the right thing to do. Alex let go of the railing. So it had happened just the way they'd been told.

Alex could hear the two men talking. After a minute, she followed the sound of their voices until she stood outside of what must have been the new owner's home office. They were talking about a case that Jace had solved. Apparently the FBI had been on the case too, but hadn't had a clue. Barber was quizzing Jace on his methodology, while Jace was slickly avoiding telling him how he'd actually found the evidence.

Alex continued on down the hall, peering into each room as she found a new doorway. The house was huge. Each room was richly appointed and furnished mostly with dark traditional furniture. She finally found the kitchen, which was the most modern of all the rooms she'd seen. She figured that the dining room must be the room just beyond the white six-paneled door on the other side of the kitchen. She crossed the room and pushed through the door. The room was dominated by a massive maple dining room set. Alex tried to picture the room from her visions, but realized she hadn't seen much of it. The light from the windows looked to be the same however and the floor was covered in the same hardwood.

She walked around the table and stood in the spot where she thought Ann's body had been. Instead of getting on her knees to touch the area, she slipped off her clogs and stepped onto the cool wood floor in her bare feet. She felt the connection and then she was looking at Ann through the killer's eyes. Dark uncontrollable anger and lust swept through her. Her blood pulsed wildly with the need for violence.

"I said leave," Ann said, her voice coldly angry and impersonal. Ann tried to pull free from where they held her wrist with their right hand. "How many times do I have to tell you that I don't want you here? I want you to leave me alone."

Alex said, "Leave you alone, Ann? There's only one way I can do that. The only way you'll be free of me is if you're dead." At the sheer terror on Ann's face, a sharp spike of sexual pleasure filled Alex's body. It surged through her. She felt the absolute power of it take over their body. And then she realized that there was a knife in her left hand and she raised it, cutting Ann's shirt down the front until the two halves parted. Her hand, holding the knife moved to further part the fabric and then the blade caressed Ann's nipple. Ann shivered.

"You like that?" Alex said. "How about this?" He ran the sharp blade around her nipple.

She screamed in pain and then looked up at him with a mix of terror and begging. "Please don't."

"You're not so detached now, are you? Now you're going to beg me not to hurt you? Well, you didn't mind hurting me did you? Trying to brush me off like I was some bug on your arm or something."

Ann whimpered in pain as he raised his right hand, twisting the bleeding nipple between his finger and thumb. Again Alex felt the surge of hot desire. "Oh baby, this is so good. Better than anything we've done before." And with that they pulled her nipple out and cut it off. Ann screamed in agony.

Alex had to get away. She stepped back and felt around with her foot until she found a clog. She slipped it on, placing her bare foot on top of the foot with the clog. The scene faded. She was back in the present. She weakly gripped the edge of the table and found her other clog. She stumbled into the kitchen and turned the faucet on. Nothing came out. The water had been shut off. She leaned against the counter for a minute, clearing her dry throat and pulling herself together.

She still didn't know who the killer was, damn it! She had to go back in and try again. She should try to get inside of Ann's brain, but fear overwhelmed her. Alex had told herself a million times that there was no way she would die if she was inside someone's brain when they died, but she still wasn't convinced.

162

She was such a coward. It only made sense that she would see the killer if she did get inside of Ann, but she'd also feel her skin being cut away and the brutal rape that she felt sure was about to take place. Neither choice was attractive. The inside of the killer's head was an unspeakably ugly place to be. The fact that she also experienced his sexual arousal and the thrill he felt when he did all those things was almost impossible to reconcile.

She straightened up. She had to go back in. Even if she was still in the killer's head, she had to find out where Ann's body was, what he had done with it. She retraced her steps to the dining room. She took a deep breath, shed her clogs once again, and waited. In an instant she felt the arc and she was back, once again inside the killer's head. Mercifully for her, she saw that Ann was already dead. She had somehow missed the rape and murder.

The killer's emotions were all over the place. She felt his sexual satisfaction, the overwhelming feeling of being all-powerful, his grief, and his elation. Tears ran down Alex's cheeks, her lips were curved up into a sad smile. "I'm sorry, Ann, but it's better this way. Now I'll have you with me. They patted the bloody pocket of his shirt. You should have been mine. Now you always will be. Don't worry, no one will ever know about us."

They bent down, picking her up as if she were a precious thing, cradling the blonde head that was almost severed by the deep slash across her throat. Alex carried her through the kitchen and out the back door. She knew where they were going. The caretaker's cottage out back had been converted into a studio for the twins.

Alex opened the door and swung Ann into the room, closing the door carefully with her elbow. The room was full of drawings, clay statues in various states of completion, lumps of clay in bowls with cloth draped over them, still moist and ready for use. Shelves near the door held jars of glazes and all kinds of brushes and tools for working the clay. A layer of gray/white dust covered everything in the studio, the remnants of sanding the artwork.

She pushed everything off the table and laid Ann's body gently on top of it, pausing next to her, tenderly smoothing a few strands of Ann's hair back with bloody fingers. "I'll be right back," she said.

She walked into the brick lined area of an adjoining room. She took some heavy pieces off of a thick stone slab set on the floor and swept off the top of the slab with her bloodied hand. Back at the table, they took a moment to say good-bye to Ann, bending over her to place a last kiss on her lips. They were still warm. Another wave of sadness swept through her/him. Why couldn't she have seen that she should have been with him all along? That they belonged together?

They picked her up, carried her into the brick lined room and placed her almost reverently onto the slab. They stepped out of the room and closed the heavy metal door. A few moments passed as they adjusted the dials and prepared to push the rubberized green button that said "on." No, not just yet. There was more work to be done. There couldn't be any trace of what had happened left in the house.

They realized that in the heat of the moment, he had been careless. But if he covered his tracks well enough, no one would ever have to know what happened here. He worked it all out: e-mailed letter of resignation to work, a missing suitcase and some of her clothes, along with her purse. It was a blessing that no one but him was around this weekend.

Alex saw all that he had done after that: him on his hands and knees scrubbing every surface of the dining room that had been touched by her blood, gathering her things in the house and taking everything that would burn out to the brick enclosure. He opened the door and laid her things next to her on the slab. Only then did he close the door and press the "on" button. He stood there until he heard the whoosh of the gas firing up. He blew Ann one last kiss and left the building.

Alex walked out of the studio and sank down onto the grass. She was exhausted. Her tongue was stuck to the roof of her mouth and her head ached so badly, she thought that she was going to be sick. She lay back, closing her eyes against the light of the late afternoon sky, which seemed unbearably bright to her sensitive eyes.

He had burned her in a kiln. Even the first time, he had been smart enough to cover his tracks. Would there be any evidence left in the kiln? She had no idea. But at least it was a place to start. After a few minutes she retraced her steps into the dining room, stopping short of the place where her shoes were.

Careful not to touch the spot where she'd stood earlier, Alex got down on her knees, sliding over until she could reach her clogs. She stood, slipping into her shoes and leaned down to dust off the knees of her jeans before going in search of Jace.

"Where the hell have you been?" he asked with a frown. "I've looked everywhere in the house and all I found were your shoes. I even checked the garage."

"I've been out in the studio." She related what she'd seen.

After she was done talking, he said, "Show me."

They both crossed the lawn and went into the studio. Most of its contents had long been removed, but some ceramic dust still showed white-gray in the corners and in the cracks in the floor. Alex led him through the studio and into the brick room.

The kiln was there, the thick metal door closed. Jace grabbed the handle and pulled it open, revealing the thick slab still in place on the floor of the huge brick oven.

"So you still haven't actually seen the killer's face while he was in the act?"

"No, I was going to try to…"

"Hello? Anybody in here?"

"Yeah, Jim we're in here."

They heard his footsteps on the tile floor and then he stood in the doorway. "So you found her, huh?" He looked into the kiln. "What the hell is that?" He walked farther into the room. "That my friend is the site of our killer's first body dump. The site of Ann Hensley's cremation," Jace told him. "Any chance that you could get the FBI to send a forensics team out here to check out the kiln for evidence?

Alexandra stepped over to stand with the men. "They also should check out the floor in the dining room. That's where the victim was killed."

"If I could tell them how you arrived at these conclusions, it would really help. I'm relatively sure that they won't just take my word for it. To tell you the truth, I'm dying to know how you came up with that stuff." He looked at Jace. "You've been with me practically the whole time we've been here. I don't see how you could have investigated anything. So tell me how you know all this."

"Here we go again." Alex sighed.

"What did Mike Stone tell you about us?" Jace asked Jim.

"He said you have some really unorthodox methods of investigating, nothing illegal, just 'outside the box' I think was the term he used. Your reputation and your case resolution rates were what convinced me to go ahead with this. But I have to have something to take back to my bosses."

"Okay, Jim, I'm going to level with you. Just bear in mind that however whacked this may sound to you, the reason we're all here is because my record speaks for itself."

Jim waited.

Jace sighed. "I have certain abilities. When someone is missing, I can sometimes locate the missing person by holding an item that belongs to him or her. Alex on the other hand touches something and feels what the person is thinking and feeling."

Jim Barber shuffled his weight onto the balls of his feet, his shell-shocked gaze shifting between Jace and Alex. "So... you're both psychic."

"Yes."

"So I'm supposed to tell my boss that you had a vision. I can already tell you that one won't fly."

"Then think of something else. I don't care what you tell him, just so long as you get the forensics team to come check the place out."

"Even if you're right, the family has been gone for what? Ten years?"

Jace nodded. "Actually somewhere in the neighborhood of thirteen. But according to my sources the house was vacant for years until your guy bought it, and believe me from what I've read about him, he doesn't strike me as the artistic type. In fact, it seems more likely that he'd use this the way our killer did than to fire ceramics."

"Look, I'm on your side and I'd certainly like to help you, but my boss is a real hard-ass. I don't think he's going to agree to use agency funds for this."

Jace suppressed a low growl and dropped his head in frustration.

"Okay," Alex said, "If he won't agree to do this because it's not in his budget, then what if you allow us to hire a private forensics team to come in and collect evidence? The FBI can even screen them to make sure they're on the level and do everything by the book. We'll foot the bill. All you have to do is let them come out here. And if we find anything that will help find this guy, we'll gladly surrender it to the FBI."

"Let me run it by my boss." He shook his head. "I don't see how he could turn down that offer. I'll talk to him this afternoon and then we'll go from there."

"One more thing," Jace said. "Could I have a few minutes alone in the house? I'd like a chance to check it out on my own."

"Sure, why not? We're already here. What can it hurt?"

Alex led Jim Barber down to the dock. She wanted to take a look at it and maybe see if she could get anything. As they reached the dock, she stopped to take off her shoes. She stepped gingerly onto the wooden planks hoping for nothing and something at the same time. When nothing happened, she took a moment to enjoy the view of the lake. Or was this a river? A thought occurred to her. "Is there some place around here with oak trees and a river in the same place?"

"Probably. There are oak trees all over the place and Ohio has quite a few rivers and lakes. Oh, you must be talking about River Oaks State Park. That's over off of County Route 45, about 3 or 4 miles from here."

Bingo! Maybe they were batting a thousand here. Maybe that was the river where David's body had been dumped. Suddenly, she was impatient to talk to Jace. She wondered how he was doing in there. She forced herself to walk out further on the dock, just to see if there was anything worth "seeing" out there. Nothing came to her.

She retraced her steps. Jim Barber fell in line and they walked back to the house. Jace was waiting outside for them. She gave him a questioning look. He shook his head no.

Jace thanked Barber for helping them get into the house. They shook hands. Barber locked up the house and they headed for their cars. Jace said to Barber, "You've been looking for some of the missing drug money, right? There's a trap door in the floor of the master bathroom, under the vanity. You'll find it there."

"Holy shit! We've looked everywhere for that money. If it's there, I owe you one."

"Nah. You got us in here. Just get your boss to agree to the forensics and we'll be even."

"I'll be in touch as soon as I talk to the powers that be," Jim Barber told them. He got into his car and drove away.

Alex turned to Jace. "You didn't get anything on the murders or the family?"

"Nope. I guess there's nothing left of theirs here anymore."

"Except ashes maybe."

"Yeah. Hopefully there's something." He buckled his seat belt. "Where to now? An early dinner maybe?"

"Not yet."

"Where then?"

"River Oaks State Park."

Chapter 25

They walked through the park to the water's edge. Looking out over the expanse of the river, it seemed like an impossible task to figure out where someone might have sunk a body. There were a few boats on the west end of the river near what looked to be a marina, but the rest of the river was quiet and deserted. None of the homes dotting the banks of the river showed any signs of life.

"Maybe we could rent a boat," Alex said.

"I'm not sure that would help. My gift can be pretty frustrating sometimes. Usually I get the best results from either a personal item of the victims or from taking the same path they did somehow and getting something that way."

"Then we need to find the Hensleys' boat."

"Just like that? You think it's going to be that easy?"

Alex took out her cell phone. She dialed the phone and waited. "Hi, Mattie, is Eli around?"

"Sure, thanks."

Jace started to say something. Alex held up a finger.

"Hi, Eli, it's Alex. Yeah everything is fine. I just have a favor to ask. We need to find out who bought the Hensleys' boat at the estate sale. Can you find out and call me back?" She listened for a minute.

"Jace, did you get the name of the auction house involved in the estate sale?"

"Yeah, Smith told me it was something like... let me think a minute. Dobson or Doyle or something like that."

Alex relayed the message to Eli. "Okay, thanks. What a guy! Talk to you later."

"Let's take a quick walk around the lake just in case anything pops, and then we'll call it a day."

"Okay, sounds good. What's on the agenda for tomorrow?"

Jace took her hand and helped her up the bank.

"Thanks," Alex said. He kept her hand in his.

"I thought we'd go to the twins' high school and see what we can find there. Other than that we'll play it by ear."

They walked through an area with swings for the kids, and through a wooded picnic area adjacent to the playground. They saw a sign that read River Oaks Lodge. The structure had clearly been built with an effort to meld with the landscape. The façade was all done in natural stone and wood with massive windows on two sides. Cupping their hands to cut the glare, they peered through the windows into a very large room furnished with round tables and chairs. There was a stone fireplace at one end of the room and a doorway that showed a small kitchen at the other end.

They could see the back lawn of the building through the huge windows on the other side of the building. There was a spacious well-manicured lawn leading down to the river. They walked around the lodge to get a better look. About halfway down lay a gazebo and a stone garden with several sculptures set in strategic places throughout.

"Nice place for a wedding reception," Alex said. They walked through the gazebo and onto the stone path. "Great place for pictures. Except that some of those women in the statues are so beautiful that they're libel to eclipse the brides."

Jace had stopped in front of a statue several feet back. Alex moved to stand beside him.

"She look familiar to you?" Jace asked.

"You've got to be kidding me! She's a dead ringer for Ann, only with longer hair. Are we in the twilight zone here?" Alex took her phone out of her pocket.

"Who are you calling now?" Jace asked.

"No one." She flipped the phone open. She took a picture of the statue on her phone and then went to each statue, snapping pictures of each of them and saving it to her memory card.

When she was done she came back to where Jace was standing. "I just want to be able to check these out later. Maybe they're all modeled after local women. Who knows, maybe we can show them to someone at the high school. And maybe we can find out who did the sculptures."

"You're good, you know that? We could use you around the office."

"Thanks. I'll keep that in mind just in case deejaying doesn't work out."

"Let's get out of here," Jace said. "This place gives me the creeps. I feel as if all these women are watching me."

Alex laughed. "Let's go get something to eat. I'm starving." As they passed the statue with Ann's face, Alex reached out and touched it but got nothing from it. She couldn't have been happier.

They found a restaurant with the help of the GPS and took their time eating. In the car on the way back to the hotel, Alex laid her head back on the headrest and drifted in a happy wine-induced fog. She wondered what would happen when they got back to the hotel. She nibbled her bottom lip, sneaking glances at Jace in the darkness of the car. Would they continue where they'd left off earlier? Had that only been five hours ago? It seemed like much longer. It had already been quite a day. She sighed.

"Tired?" Jace flicked a glance at her.

"I think it's more a case of wine catatonia. Let's just say I feel very relaxed right now."

"That's good. We'll be back to the hotel in a few minutes."

Jace walked with her to her door. She didn't feel relaxed any more. She stuck the keycard into the slot and strolled inside after swinging the door open. Jace followed her in. She set her purse and keycard on the dresser and turned to face him. He was very close.

Raising his hands to her shoulders, he said, "You were fantastic today, you know that. You did all the work. It was killing me not to be there while you went under, but I'm sure that Jim would probably have freaked out if he were to see that."

"I hate to say it, but it seems to be getting a little bit easier. I feel like a coward though. I was going to try to get inside Ann's head, but I was too afraid of what might happen. And then I figured that if I was inside the killer's head I could find out where the body was buried. That really helped a lot, didn't it?" She frowned. "That's the first time I've actually traveled while I was having a vision."

"Damn, Alex, I can't believe that you even considered getting inside of Ann's head! I thought we'd already talked about that!" He took a calming breath. "You did exactly right by channeling the killer. You found out where the body was. It just wasn't buried, that's all. And I'd hardly call it cowardly to recognize danger and decide to stay away from it. That's just self-preservation. Anyway, we know a lot more now than we did and it's all due to you, Alex."

"We still don't know for sure who the killer is, damn it. The other night I even got up the nerve to sit in every one of the chairs in my dining room set. I didn't get anything. Why can't I see him?"

"I don't know, but we're getting closer all the time. All things seem to point to one of the twins, with the exception of the fact that they may have drowned years ago." He dropped his hands and sat against the back of the bed, flipping on the bedside lamp. "The killer was at the dinner table with the family. She was killed right there in the house. The kiln is right on the property. We know the killer knew how to work the kiln."

"The killer draws in charcoal. Some of the drawings I saw were done in pencil. You saw a room full of charcoal drawings, not a room full of ceramics," Alex said. "But you're right, the rest of it seems to point very strongly to one of the twins. Even if that's true the question is, which one?"

"So where the hell are they now? Assuming they really aren't at the bottom of the river."

"If one of them is the killer, then I think we can both agree that right now at least, he's somewhere in New York, somewhere very close to where we live." Alex moved to the chair by the bed and slipped off her clogs. Her laptop sat on the table. She picked it up, opened it, and waited for it to go online so she could check her messages.

She had twenty-two emails. One was from Olivia "Oh my God, I don't believe it! Olivia is thinking of opening her own practice. She's thinking of moving closer to me. She says she really liked the area and she can't stand her boss or the firm."

"Wow, that would be great for you. Has she mentioned this before?"

"She's been talking about leaving for years, but the timing has never been right. I guess it is now. She's coming to visit and check out the area."

"Eli will be happy."

"Huh?"

Jace grinned. "He won't admit it, but he's hot for her."

"You're kidding. He didn't act like it. And he's never said a word to me about her."

He smiled across the bed at her. "This isn't high school Alex. Besides, Eli tends to play his cards pretty close to his chest."

"Then how do you know he's hot for her?"

"Because I grew up with him and I know him. He's said a few things to me about her. Please don't say anything to Olivia, though. He'd be very upset."

"Who's in high school now, Moseley? Anyway, she's coming into town in a couple of days. She'll be here for a few days at least. I can't wait to see her again. Maybe we can all go out again. It was fun last time."

"You're not matchmaking are you Alex?"

"No way. Olivia and I made a pact when we were teenagers that we would never try to fix each other up. And we never have. Besides, Olivia's gorgeous. She doesn't need my help." She continued checking her emails while they talked, deleting the junk mail and reading the work related emails.

"Shit!"

"What?"

"Another email from the stalker."

"Effing A! Read it to me."

Alexandra,

I can't believe that you went away… and with your husband's best friend. Shame on you! I know that I can trust you… that nothing will happen because I know that you are waiting for me, just like I'm waiting for you. But you know it doesn't look good. Your fans would be so disappointed in you. I promise I won't tell, but hurry back to me, Angel. Is it as hard for you to be away from me as it is for me? You pretend that you haven't figured it out, but I know that you know me and long for me too. I miss your voice. You need to come home soon. I'm waiting.

Jace smashed a fist into the mattress. "How does the bastard know all this stuff? Alex, he's really delusional. We've got to find out who this guy is. I'm calling Eli. Send him that email now. We're gonna have to get tougher with this."

"You think I don't know that this guy is a nut? I don't know what else to do. I've got a security system, I get the creeps now whenever I'm in my house that I used to love, and this freak knows every move I make. What am I supposed to do? I just don't know."

"I'm sorry. I wasn't yelling at you. I'm mad at myself because we haven't found this guy. When we get back, we'll pick up the necklace and see if we can get anything from it. I'm gonna give this guy the full court press when we get home."

She shut down her computer and set it on the table. She was sick to death of dealing with monsters and deviants and dead people. She hadn't come back from the dead only to spend all her time being terrified and stressed out. She wanted to relax, blow off some steam. She wanted to have some fun. She gazed over at Jace reclining on her bed. How did he manage to look like sin itself in an ordinary pair of faded jeans and a long sleeved t-shirt?

"I don't want to talk about any of this right now. Distract me."

Jace looked at her for a minute and she could see the wheels turning. He smiled.

"What?" she said.

"I was just thinking about the first time I saw you."

"When John introduced us?"

"No, that wasn't the first time. I'd seen you plenty of times before that. I saw you at the freshman orientation. You were so intense," he said, his grin widening. "You were checking out all the brochures on the tables as if they were the Holy Grail. And you were wearing that short Catholic school skirt and a white blouse."

"I didn't think you even noticed me. You actually remember what I was wearing?"

"Every guy there remembers what you were wearing. You were a walking sexual fantasy. Right down to the black bra that showed right through your white shirt."

She smiled. "Oh my God, I remember that day. I looked everywhere for my white bra, and I couldn't find it. I was panicked that I was going to be late so I finally just wore the black one. Wow, every guy's fantasy? If I'd only known."

"I kept watching you, trying to catch your eye. I was hoping you would join my group. But you looked at me standing there with all the girls and I saw you roll your eyes. Then you just turned your little self around and ignored me. My ego took a little hit, let me tell you."

She snorted. "Your ego was bigger than all of us there put together."

He laughed. "Yeah you're probably right. I was pretty cocky back then. But you made quite an impression. I had a few dreams about you in that outfit and out of it too." His eyes slowly perused her from head to toe. Alex felt the heat of his gaze and her body answered in kind. He wanted her. It was there on his face. And she wanted him.

She walked over to the bed. Grasping the bottom of her t-shirt in both hands, she pulled it up and over her head. She reached around and unfastened her bra, letting it drop to the floor. "I don't have that little skirt anymore, but let's work on a new fantasy." She knelt on the bed. Jace reached for her and took hold of her arms, pulling her down on top of him.

His lips met hers in a scorching kiss. He caressed the bare skin of her arms, running his hands slowly up and down. He took his time exploring every inch of skin with his hands and his mouth. He was driving her crazy. He had too many clothes on. She murmured, "Take off your shirt. I want to feel your skin against mine." Jace struggled to get his shirt off without moving away from her. When he couldn't get the shirt past his elbow, Alex pulled it free and tossed it over the side of the bed.

"Thanks." He laid her back on the bed so that he was on top of her. He gazed down at her, his eyes heavy with lust. "God, you're even more beautiful than I imagined you would be."

"So are you," she said. The familiar sizzle moved through her, fanning the flames of her hunger for him, only now the charge was so much greater than she'd ever experienced before. So this was what it felt like to be struck by lightning. Her bare breasts pressed so closely against his warm hard chest it was hard to tell where she ended and he began. He worked his magic on her again. His talented mouth traveled from her earlobe to the sensitive nape of her neck and then down to pay homage to first one breast and then the other.

After bringing his mouth to her nipple, he lapped at it with his tongue, and then applied gentle suction. Alex felt the erotic tug all the way to her toes! Moisture pooled between her legs. She arched her back in an effort to get closer. Her nails dug into his back. He moaned, his hoarse growl sending shock waves through her.

She felt so much… his desire, hers, theirs, all mixed up. Suddenly, she was petrified. She wasn't sure she could stand such exquisite torture. His hand trailed slowly down her stomach beneath her jeans and panties into the thatch of blonde hair and beyond.

"Oh my God!" She tightened her legs around his hand. If he touched her there, she thought she might shatter. She closed her eyes, grinding the back of her head into the pillow. So good, too much! Maybe if she blocked it just a little.

"No, Lexi, baby, don't shut me out, not now. We need to feel this. Just relax and let it happen."

"I can't. I feel too much. It's too intense."

"Lexi, you're so strong." He moved up to kiss her tenderly on the lips. "If you could stand all the pain you been through, then surely you can stand this much pleasure. God knows you deserve it. Let me give it to you. Take it for yourself." He ran the back of his knuckles gently down her cheek.

She did deserve it. And what's more, she wanted it, all of it. She forced herself to relax and she closed her eyes. He slowed, pressing soft kisses into the sensitive spot just below her ear and then down her neck to her shoulder, giving her time to settle. He moved to her lips again and she told herself not to think, just to feel. She deepened the kiss, slipping her tongue inside to mingle with his. He pulled her tighter against him, his erection hard against her stomach.

She wanted to touch him, to feel all of him against her. She pulled back slightly, her hands going to the snap of his jeans. He was so stiff that his jeans were tight and she had trouble with the zipper.

"Here, let me," he said. In no time, his jeans joined had her bra on the floor. He whispered in her ear. "Your turn." She turned slightly, unzipping her jeans and pushing them down her legs. She kicked them away and they tumbled off the end of the bed.

He gathered her close again, pressing the length of his body against hers. He was so hard. It felt so good. She responded, sliding up and down, enjoying the friction.

He sucked in a breath. "If you keep doing that I'm not going to last long."

"That's okay," she said, wrapping a warm hand around him. "We've got all night."

He jerked at the contact. With the pad of her thumb, she collected the bead of moisture from the head of his penis and rubbed it in a circle over the head. His head dropped back and he moaned her name. His hand drifted between her legs and into the moist heat there. He found her swollen bud and brushed his finger lightly over it. She moaned, arching up to meet his hand. "Ah, Jace, yes… please." Her grip tightened on his penis.

"Please what, Alex? Tell me what you want."

She moved her head from side to side. "Don't stop," she said. "It feels so good." She was so sensitive. Her breath came in gasps. "Oh my God, I think I'm going to…"

"Go ahead, baby, come for me," he said, pushing his finger inside her just slightly, still using his thumb. Rubbing, even as he moved his finger erotically in and out. She threw back her head and let out a prolonged high-pitched cry as she dropped over the edge. He didn't leave her until he felt her go limp and she lay panting, her eyes closed. He smiled down at her. Then he scooted down the bed.

"Where are you going?"

"Nowhere. Just getting something." He reached for his jeans and fumbled in the pocket, coming up with a foil packet. After ripping it open with his teeth, he rolled the condom over his erection.

Alex watched him make his way back up the bed. An instant ago, she'd felt languid and boneless. But watching Jace, her body began to hum again, as it had since the day she'd first met him. Only now it was so much more. She held out her arms. Smiling, she said, "Come here, big boy." He smiled, leaning down to kiss her. "Big, huh?"

"I was gonna say huge, but it didn't sound right." She teased. "Need any help?"

"No, I think I can find my way," he said settling between her legs. She was slick and hot and he slipped inside of her, sighing in pleasure. The depth of his desire washed over her, bringing moisture to her eyes. She tightened around him and he moaned. "I'm sorry, I was going to try to go slowly, but you're so hot and tight. You feel so good that I can't." He rose up and then pushed into her again.

"Thank God!" she said, rising to meet his thrusts. It was a rough ride, both of them raw with wanting, wishing it could go on forever, but desperately galloping toward the finish. Alex felt the rising wave for the second time that night. She could tell that he was holding back.

"Ahhhh, I can't hold on any longer."

"Don't then."

She felt him swell inside her and suddenly she was inundated, wave after wave of pleasure rolling through her. The blood sang in her veins. Her eyes were closed and still she saw vivid colors behind her lids. As he felt her tumble, Jace bucked wildly and he let himself go. He collapsed against her and then rolled to his side, bringing her with him, pulling her close as they waited for their breathing to return to normal.

After a few minutes, Jace looked down at her. "Are you all right?"

"Much better than all right. In fact, I was thinking that I maybe I'll go back and buy that bumper sticker I saw the other day.

At the time I thought it was trite and stupid, but I'm definitely rethinking that now."

"What did it say?"

She smiled up at him. "It said, 'Psychics do it better.'"

He burst out laughing.

Chapter 26

"I haven't been to the principal's office since my senior year in high school. Let's hope this will be a more fruitful experience." Jace grinned over at Alex.

"What'd you do?"

"Made an ass out of my physics teacher." He smiled down at her. God, he's gorgeous, Alex thought, watching him.

"We never did get along," Jace continued. "He was constantly on my case in class. He'd single me out and make me look like an idiot. So finally I got sick of it. I'm not saying what I did, but I embarrassed the hell out of him in class. He was really pissed and so was the principal, Mrs. Betts. She really reamed me a new one. After that I made sure that whenever I decided to make a statement I was much more subtle about it." He chuckled, still thinking about it. "I bet you were never sent to the principal's office," he said still smiling. "I bet you were too much of a goodie two shoes."

"Well, you'd lose that bet," Alex said. "When I was in fourth grade, I told Carol Timmons that her cat hadn't really run away. I told her that her mom got rid of it because it kept peeing on the rug. She didn't take it well. Neither did my teacher. I was so scared when she sent me to the principal that I started crying. But when I told the principal what had happened, she couldn't keep a straight face. So it didn't turn out as badly as I'd imagined it would."

Jace chuckled.

The door opened and they stood up. A bored looking teenaged boy walked out of the office, followed by the Principal. She came over to meet them.

"Hello, I'm Mrs. Bergen. Sorry to keep you waiting. Come on into my office where we're less likely to be interrupted." They all sat down and she said, "You mentioned on the phone that you wanted to talk about the Hensley twins. It's been a long time, but I'll help you in any way that I can."

"So you remember them?" Jace asked.

"Oh yes. Noah and Nathan definitely stood out among the students. They were both taking college level classes from their sophomore year on. We really had to scramble to keep them from becoming bored. And on top of that they were both extremely gifted artists."

"Can you tell us what media they dealt in?"

"At first Noah painted in acrylics and Nathan liked using ink and charcoals mostly. A few of their pieces are still hanging in the Ruston Public Library, I think. But then they met this sculptor and they both became interested in working with clay. The guy even helped them build a kiln on their property. It's such a shame, what happened to them. They seemed to be so blessed. Everything they tried, they excelled at and their work with clay was no exception. I know that they sold a few pieces before they died, and from what I heard the price tag on them was pretty substantial."

"Were they popular? Well liked?" Alex asked.

"Well, at first Nathan was fairly outgoing and seemed to have a lot of friends, whereas Noah always seemed to be kind of quiet, pretty much of a loner, except of course for his brother.

Then after their mother died and their father remarried, Noah started getting rough with some of the kids and he started getting into fights, even with a couple of his teachers I remember. Nathan on the other hand became quieter, more withdrawn. At the beginning of his senior year, he stopped hanging out with his friends. From that time on until shortly before they graduated the only people they hung out with seemed to be each other."

"Who was their mentor, the sculptor who influenced them so greatly?"

"I never heard his name. He was from out of state… somewhere in New York, I think."

Alex and Jace exchanged a look. Alex asked, "Have you been to River Oaks Park?"

"Yes, I have. There are some great hiking trails around the park. I go there a lot on the weekends."

"So you've seen the statues around the lodge?"

"Sure, they've been there for years. Why do you ask?"

"Do you have any idea who the artist was?"

"No, I don't. But you might want to ask David Hensley's business partner."

Jace started in surprise. "Why would we want to do that?"

"Well, as far as I know the lodge and everything in that section of the park was developed with an endowment from Hensley and Drake's company. I would assume that they contracted for the art work as well."

"That's interesting. Tell me, were the statues in place before the Hensleys disappeared?"

Mrs. Bergen thought for a minute. "I'm not sure, to tell you the truth. I know they've been there for quite a while. I can't even remember whether the project was completed before or after the Hensleys' accident." She thought a minute and shook her head. "No, I don't think it was finished until several years later, because I remember the DOT was working on the road and the opening of the lodge was postponed until they had completed the project. I remember that well because we had just bought a house and we had to detour to move everything."

"Has anyone ever mentioned that the one statue looks remarkably like Ann Hensley?"

"God yes! Just about everyone, along with the statue that's in the grouping closer the water. Everyone is always speculating on what the one woman is pointing to."

"The ones by the water? I didn't even notice them, did you Alex?"

"No, I didn't see them. Were they in the same area?"

"They're easy to miss unless you go down to the water's edge. They're off to the side, near a stand of trees. You should take a look before you leave."

"Do any of the other statues bear any resemblance to any one you recognize?"

"I've always thought that the woman who's pointing at the lake looks something like a woman who used to live here."

"Used to?"

"Yes, she only lived here a short time."

"Did you know her?"

"Not really. I met her through a mutual friend, and we did a cancer run together. I was surprised when she moved. She seemed to really like it here." The principal shrugged. "I guess she changed her mind."

"Do you remember her name?" Alex asked.

"Sure. It was Sue McGruder."

"Thanks."

Jace changed the subject. "With the twins being so close, I'm surprised that they chose different colleges."

"I think that was Noah's choice. I know that Nathan was very unhappy about it. In fact, they had a huge fight about it one day in school, and they both ended up in my office. It's a good thing Nathan was as strong as Noah, because the teachers who pulled them apart had quite a battle getting Noah under control." She picked up a pencil and played with it while she talked.

"After the fight they didn't talk for several weeks, but then they seemed to mend things and by the end of school, they seemed as close as ever. I really don't know what happened with them after graduation. Unfortunately, with all but a few students, I pretty much lose touch with them after they leave us." She tapped the pencil on her desk blotter. "I did hear that they both went off to their respective colleges. And then of course there was the accident."

"Well, thank you for seeing us on such short notice."

"I admit to being curious about the reason behind all your questions."

"We're interested in the accident and just trying to gather more facts about the family and their history here. You've been a big help. We really appreciate it," Jace said, and they got up to leave. Mrs. Bergen walked them out.

"Where to next?" Alex asked, opening the passenger door.

"Let's head back to the park and check out the other statues," Jace replied, starting the engine. "I'd love to try to catch Paul Drake again and see what we can find out about the sculptor, but I know you have to get back today and Mattie will have a fit if I don't get back to the office soon. We don't have time to sit around and wait another two hours for him, so I'll call his office later."

"Sounds like a plan," Alex said through a yawn.

Jace smiled over at her. "I'd say I'm sorry for keeping you up last night, but I'm not."
She grinned at him. "Me neither. I'm feeling a few muscles I haven't in a while, like I just started a new workout at the gym." He chuckled, running a hand up and down her thigh before returning it to the wheel.

****

He pulled into the entrance of the park nearest the Lodge and they walked down to the water's edge. To their right they saw a group of oak trees, and there stood the three statues. They approached the statues. Alex again took out her phone and took pictures of each of the women. Jace stood to the side of the pointing woman and looked out at the lake. He reached out with his hand and laid it on the statue. His eyes glazed over and he became as still as the statue.

Alex stood and waited for him to come back. After a few minutes, Jace blinked and then he turned to Alex. "I know what she's pointing at. He's out there." Jace pointed in the same direction as the statue. "I saw him again. I have to talk to Sheriff Shaffer before we leave, even though it's doubtful he'll believe me."

"Did you get anything else?"

"Nothing useful. Just the impression that whoever created the pointing woman doubted whether anyone was sharp enough to figure out what she was telling them," Jace said grimly. "This just keeps getting better and better."

They left and drove straight to the sheriff's office. Jace told the officer at the desk that he had information on a prior crime and that he would only talk to Shaffer. When Shaffer saw who was waiting he hesitated for a second before coming to talk to them.

Alexandra hung back, knowing that the detective thought she was a tarot card-carrying kook. As Jace started talking, Shaffer moved closer to the counter, dipping his head and leaning in to listen to what Jace was saying. After Jace finished, Shaffer nodded and held out his hand. Jace shook hands with him. They talked for a few minutes more and then Jace joined Alex and they left the Police Department.

"How'd you do it?" Alex asked as they got into the car.

He knew what she was asking. "I didn't. Mike Stone did. Shaffer called him to tell him not to waste his time with carnival sideshow freaks, and Mike ripped him a new asshole. Told him that we had uncovered more evidence in a major homicide case in a few months than Law Enforcement in three states had in over ten years. He not only apologized but hung on my every word." He grinned over at her. "I have to tell you, it was really satisfying."

"Jace, you need to stay here. You need to help them find David Hensley's body," Alex said. "You know, the airport is only about a half hour or so from here. Why don't we grab my stuff from the hotel, you can drop me at the airport and I can catch a flight home."

"I don't want to do that. I don't want you to go back there alone."

"I'll be fine. How about if you call Eli and ask him to pick me up from the airport? Then he can check out the house when I get home."

"I guess that would work, but why don't you stay at my place until I get home?"

"Because I don't live there, that's why. Besides, I have a brand spanking new security system that I'm not taking advantage of. I'll be at work most of the time anyway. Paulie was grousing about me leaving him in the lurch, so I told him I'd do a double tomorrow. And by the time I get out of work, Olivia should be there. So I'll be fine."

"Are you sure? Shaffer did ask me to join them, but I didn't want to leave you stranded at the hotel."

"It's fine. Let's go so you can get out there and find David Hensley."

Chapter 27

Alex set down the book she'd been trying to read for the past hour. Her flight hadn't gotten in until almost midnight. Eli had been there to pick her up and he'd checked the house for her, but the truth was that she had been so exhausted by the time she'd gotten home that she'd just fallen into bed and slept straight through until morning.

She showered, trying not to feel creeped-out the whole time and ate some cookies she'd stashed in the freezer several days ago. Then she settled in on the couch with a book and a cup of tea. But she'd read the same page about ten times. She was restless wondering what was going on with Jace, wondering if they'd found the body, waiting for the phone to ring. Maybe he'd called while she was in the shower.

She got up to get her cell phone and check her answering machine. Three hang-ups on her answering machine. She shivered, wondering if her stalker was the caller. Could the police trace hang-ups? She doubted it. She'd mention it to them the next time she talked to them. It felt like she was running out of time and it scared the hell out of her.

She had a voicemail on her cell phone from her Mom. There was nothing from Jace.

She pulled out her laptop. She would check her email and then maybe play some games before work. She answered some emails from work and added some comments to her profile on the work website. While she was playing a game, she heard her email ding.

Hoping it was Eli or Jace, she clicked on her email.

Dear Alexandra,

I'm glad you hurried home and didn't wait for Moseley. Do you know how much I missed you? Can you feel my presence? Can you feel my loving eyes on you? I can't wait to hold you. I hope you aren't worried about the scars. They're as much a part of you now as that birthmark on your arm. Your body is just as beautiful as it was before the accident, and I can't wait to be with you. It's finally here, my angel. Our time has come. I can't wait to make you mine. Are you ready for me? Here I come.

"He can see me! And he's coming for me." Her first impulse was to get up and run out of the house. She grabbed her purse, digging through it until she found the business card for the security company. Her hands were shaking so badly that she had to dial the number three times before she got it right.

"TK Security. How may I help you?"

"This is Alexandra Pope. I need to talk to Tom Knight. It's very important."

"Can I tell him why you're calling?"

"Yes, you can tell him that his damn security system is not working and that I need help."

"Let me connect you with the security floor."

"NO!" Alexandra enunciated every word. "I need to talk to Tom Knight."

"Okay, Mrs. Pope. Please hold for a moment."

"No..." The woman put her on hold. She waited impatiently, her eyelid twitching.

"Tom Knight."

"Hello, Mr. Knight. This is Alexandra Pope. You put a security system in my house, and now I have some nut watching my every move and telling me how I look with my clothes off. I need you to come to my house and take the damn thing out. Is someone there getting a good show?"

"Alexandra, I can assure you that none of my people are watching you undress. We don't place cameras in client's bathrooms or bedrooms, even if they ask us to."

"Well somebody placed them there, and one of your guys was in my bedroom and my bathroom. Look, right now I just want you to come over here and get whatever it is the hell out of here, okay? I've been weirded-out in my house for too long. The whole reason I had the system put in is because I have a stalker who keeps visiting my house and now he's telling me that he's ready to be together and he's coming to get me!"

"Alexandra, do you have a neighbor you could go to until we can get there?"

"I'm not running away this time. I'm sick of doing that. Please just get over here. And I want just you. I don't know if I trust anyone else in your company right now, but it's your business so I'm going to trust you. I'm warning you, I intend to go everywhere you go and watch everything you do."

"I understand how you feel and that's fine. I'll be there in twenty minutes."

"Fine." She ended the call and dialed Jace's office. When Mattie answered, Alex asked for Eli.

"Eli, hi. It's Alex. Have you had any luck finding my stalker?"

"Well, I've found him in about six different places now, but I don't think any of the IP addresses that he's using are his. I'm trying something different now. I've called in a few favors and I'm waiting for access to some server data. It should finally tell us who this guy is."

"Eli, time's up. The guy sent me another one. He says he's ready and he's coming to 'be' with me. And he's been watching me in my house."

"Well, shit Alex, get the hell out of there!"

"I can't. I called Tom Knight and he's on his way over to go through the house, but I'm going to send you the newest email. And don't you dare call Jace. He's got enough on his plate right now. Please, please find this guy, Eli. I'm really getting scared."

"I'm coming over. I can do the search from your house. I'll be there in five minutes. Hang in there."

"You don't need to come over. I'll be fine. Right now I'm mad as hell. If anyone comes in here right now I'll probably kick the living shit out of him."

"I'll take my chances. Be there in a few. Bye."

Two minutes later, her phone rang. It was still in her hand and she flipped it open.

"Hello."

"Alex, are you all right?" It was Jace.

"Damn it! I told Eli not to call you. I'm fine, just nervous… and pissed off. How are things going there?"

"Don't try to change the subject. What did the psycho say this time?"

"You don't want to know."

"Yeah, I do. Look, Alex, I'm on a boat in the middle of the lake and we're about to pull a body out of the water. I don't have time to bully you right now, so just tell me what he said this time."

"Oh, you found him," she said softly. "I don't know whether to say I'm sorry or congratulations."

"I'm sorry. I was a little rough on you there. I always get this way during these things. I hate this so much sometimes, you know. And I hate not being there when you need me."

"I'm fine. Besides, Eli insists on coming over. But if it weren't for you, David Hensley would probably have been stuck at the bottom of that lake forever. That strikes me as a very cold and lonely place to be. I think he'd be grateful."

"So what's happened there? Eli said the guy has been watching you? How do you know? Have you seen anyone around?"

"No, he's been watching me inside the house, in the shower."

"What! How?"

"I don't know yet, but he told me not to worry about my scars, that he sees them as being just like the birthmark on my arm."

"Fucking A. I'm gonna kill the bastard! Alex, come back to Ohio, now, today. Just get in your car and drive back."

"That's ridiculous! I have to work in a few hours. Besides, I'm tired of running away. I'm going to find a way to nail this bastard. I want my life back."

"Damn, Alex, I need to be there."

"No, you don't. You need to finish what you're doing there first. I'll be fine; I'm a big girl. Eli will be here in a minute and so will Tom Knight. He's going to search the house for whatever the stalker left here. Then I'm on the air for a double. Olivia is meeting me at the station when I get out. I won't be alone at all, so you don't have to worry."

"I'm coming home tomorrow no matter what happens here Alex. Don't take any crazy chances while I'm gone. In fact, why don't you and Olivia stay at my place tonight?"

"Stop! Go find David Hensley and let me handle things here."

"Listen," Jace said, "I've gotta go. But I mean it! Do not take any chances, you hear me. Take care of that cute little ass of yours till I get home. That's an order."

"I'm not good at taking orders, but that one I'm okay with. Good luck out there, Jace. Hopefully I'll see you tomorrow. Bye."

"Bye, Lex," he said softly, hanging up.

Alex went to put some coffee on. She was just finishing up when the doorbell rang. It was Eli.

"How you doing, kiddo?"

Impulsively, she hugged him. "Thanks for coming right over here. I'm fine." She smiled. "Even though I should be mad at you for calling Jace and getting him all worried."

"Better to deal with your wrath than his. Besides, you feel better now that you've talked to him, admit it."

"I'm not admitting to anything." Alex smiled. "Want some coffee?"

"That would be great! Mattie's mad at me so she made tea this morning instead of coffee."

"Really, what did you do?"

Eli began setting up his workstation on her coffee table. "It's what I haven't done," he said, bending to plug in his power cord. "Paper work will be the death of me! I'm working on computerizing all the forms and reports in the office so that I won't have to sit and fill out endless forms, but I haven't gotten very far with that yet. Too busy." He straightened up. "Okay, lead me to the coffee. I'm getting a high from the fumes."

Alex laughed. "I'm glad you came over. I feel so much better now." Alex got two mugs out of the cupboard and poured the coffee. Eli leaned over one, inhaling deeply. "Ahhhh, life's blood." Alex rolled her eyes, crossing to the fridge for some creamer. "There's sugar in the cupboard right in front of you. Do you want hazelnut, French Vanilla or regular flavor creamer?"

"I know my manhood's at stake here, but I think I'll take the hazelnut. Just so you know, I usually drink regular."

She laughed. "You're such a guy," she said, pouring the creamer into his coffee.

"Thanks." He took a big gulp. "Oh yeah, that's good stuff. All right, show me that new email."

She sat down at her laptop and pulled the email up. She went to forward it to Eli but clicked on the one above it by mistake.

He opened it. "This isn't... wow, Olivia's thinking of moving here? Um... sorry, you sent me the wrong email Alex."

"Oh, sorry. She clicked on the stalker's email and sent it. He read it. Whistling through his teeth, he looked up at Alex. She blushed bright red. "This asshole is goin' down. This time I'm not stopping until I find out who he is. I should have access to that data sometime today. That should give us everything we need to finally get this sicko."

"I hope you're right," Alex said, closing her email. "I feel like I'm living with a ticking time bomb and time is definitely running out." Eli started clicking away furiously on the keyboard. She sipped her coffee, comforted by Eli's company. She wondered if her life would ever be anything approaching normal again. Her night with Jace had certainly been anything but 'normal," more like mind-blowing. She smiled.

"You look like the cat that swallowed the canary."

"Just thinking about something."

"Must have been pretty good."

"It was." The doorbell rang.

Alex went to open the door. It was Tom Knight. "Hello, Alexandra." He shook her hand. "Sorry, it took me longer than I thought. I decided to take the 90 because it's so much faster and then there was a roll-over accident, and I got stuck in traffic anyway."

"Thanks for coming right over, Tom. I've calmed down a bit since our phone conversation, so I won't bite your head off."

"Hey, I don't blame you for being upset." He walked in, taking his coat off and hanging in on a hook by the door. "Oh hi, Eli. How you doing?"

"Fine, Tom. I came over to check out the email from the guy who's been stalking Alex and from the sound of it, you'd better start looking for some hidden cameras."

"That's what I'm here for. So," he said turning to Alex, "let's get started. We'll start in the most likely places and then work our way through the house. Which way to your bedroom?"

She led him down the hall and into the bedroom. He walked through the bedroom to the bathroom. After setting his tool belt down, he stepped into the tub and looked up at the overhead combination fan and light fixture. He reached up and found the screws on either side. "Hand me a Phillips head screw driver, will you?" She located one and handed it to him. He unscrewed the cover and pulled it off. A small black wire dangled down. "Hand me a piece of toilet paper." She ripped some off and handed it to him. He lifted the wire using the toilet paper so that she could see the little fisheye lens on the very end.

"There it is. This isn't one of ours."

"So you don't think it was one of the guys who put in the system? I found the one guy coming out of this bathroom." She was relieved to hear that he was so sure that it wasn't one of his men. Tom shook his head.

"Both Devon and Hank have worked for me for years. Every employee goes through a pretty intense background check before they're hired. After we talked though, I pulled their personnel files. They're never had any complaints filed against them. I'll sit down with each of them separately until I'm satisfied that they're both on the level, but my gut feeling is that it's not one of them. Someone spent some time in this house, but I don't think it was one of my men." He indicated the camera. "I'd bet that this is spliced into the cable down in the cellar somewhere. I'll take care of it after we check out the rest of the house. That way if there are others, I can take care of all of them at the same time."

"Others…" She felt sick to her stomach, but she took a deep breath. "Okay, let's do this."

Chapter 28

Alex stepped out of the car and leaned in the window to talk to Eli. "Thanks for the ride. I can't believe that on top of everything my car wouldn't start. Olivia left right after work today, so she's picking me up when she gets here and we're going somewhere to eat. Actually, I think she secretly wants to see what the DJ booth looks like."

Eli chuckled. "No problem. I needed a little break from the office anyway. I don't know what's taking my guy so long. I'll check on it again as soon as I get back to the office. Tom told me about the cameras. He's on his way to talk to the officer who investigated your last 'home invasion.' They're going to see what they can find. Who knows, maybe we'll get lucky."

"I hope so." She frowned.

"I promise you, Alex, I'm making this my first priority. We're going to find this guy… and soon. So you're sure that Olivia is going to be here to pick you up?"

"Yup. She texted me just before we left the house. It'll be great to see her."

"Yes, it will. I mean, I'm sure it will do you good."

She smiled. "I told Jace we'll all have to go out one night while she's here like we did before. You okay with that?"

"Sure. I'm up for whatever."

"Okay, I gotta get in there and get to work. Thanks for everything. Text me if you find out anything new, okay?"

"You bet. Now get your butt in there."

She walked through reception and into the back. Opening the bottom drawer of her desk, she dumped her purse and sat down to check her schedule for the day.

"Hey, nice of you to come in, princess. I thought we were gonna have to go off the air."

She turned at the sound of the voice. "Hey, Paulie. Still can't find anyone with a voice like mine, huh?"

"That's right, babe. The voice of an angel."

The color drained from her face. "What did you just say?"

He snorted. "I said you had the voice of an angel, but you're really a pain in the ass. Taking time off at the drop of a hat like that." He noticed that she'd gone pale. "Hey, are you okay? I was only joking. You know the other guys all jump at the chance for more air time."

"Sorry, Paulie, it's just that there's a lot going on right now. Now get lost so I can get some work done."

"You sure you're okay?"

"Yeah, the drama's over." Paulie looked her over for a minute and then walked back into the production booth.

She shook her head. She was really losing it! There was a lot of work to get through. She read through everything in her in-box and made a few notes and a few phone calls. Then she went into the booth. She went on the air and then recorded a few commercial spots during her afternoon show.

Between shifts she went into the break room to grab a quick snack. She wanted to call Jace and find out how things were going there, but she didn't want to bother him. She ate some

196

yogurt from the vending machine and then went to get her phone out of her desk. Maybe Jace had called and left a message. She picked it up. Nothing! She sighed. After putting it on vibrate, she stuck her phone in the pocket of her jeans and headed back into the booth.

The time seemed to drag, but finally it was time to leave. Olivia had sent her a text saying she was just a few minutes from the station. When Alex came out of the booth, the workroom floor was all but deserted. It was after eight and most of the support staff had gone home for the day. She figured she had just enough time to grab her purse and touch up her make up before Olivia got there. As she approached the desk, she felt her phone vibrate in her pocket. She opened it. It was Jace. She sat down at her desk, opening the bottom drawer and propping her feet on it.

"Hey, how's it goin'?" she said.

"Hey," Jace said. "Well, we found David and we got him out of the lake."

"Wow, they've already made a positive ID? That was fast."

"Luckily when they went missing, the family dentist decided to keep the dental x-rays in case they were needed at some point. Another good thing is that it was in a fairly sedentary point in the lake, so we found all but a few of the bones. And guess what it was weighted down with?"

"Tell me."

"A huge ceramic urn. We couldn't tell at first. It was completely covered with Zebra Mussels. Damn, those things are sharp. We had a hell of a time getting it into the boat. Anyway, I think I've answered every conceivable question. I'm sure a few of the investigators are keeping their handcuffs handy. The looks they're giving me are making me very uncomfortable.

"At least Shaffer's a convert. After I led them right to the body, he had to admit that there might be something there. I guess Stone really got to him." He paused a minute and then he said, his tone intimate, "Okay, I'm gonna get some sleep now, that is if I can stop thinking about the way you looked when I was inside you."

Her breath caught. "Wow!" Alex said. "Are we having phone sex?"

"No, just a little foreplay. I can't wait to get back. It's been tough to stay focused, even on something this important. I feel like a horny teenager again. You pack a powerful punch, Lex."

Alex answered, her voice husky with wanting, "I feel the same way, Jace. There've been a lot of things going on here but every so often during the day, I find myself remembering something from our night together and wanting it to happen all over again."

"Damn, I'm dying here. Listen, I'm leaving early tomorrow morning, so I should be home by lunchtime. I'll call you when I get back. Maybe we can grab some lunch before you go into work. "

"I'd really love that, but you know Olivia is here, so it depends on what she's got planned."

"No problem. Sorry, but I have to go. Shaffer is waiting for me. I just came outside to call you before you left work. Have fun with Olivia and I'll see you tomorrow. And Alex... just be careful, okay?"

"Okay, I will, I promise. I'll see you, and Jace... I'm so glad that you were able to find David and bring him home."

"Me too. Thanks, Alex. Bye."

"Bye." As Alex hung up the phone, she heard a noise behind her. She swiveled her chair around quickly, but there was no one there. She went down the hall, checking all the offices. The only people there were the night DJ and the older woman who cleaned the offices. Alex caught up with the cleaning woman. "Excuse me, did you just come from the main office area?"

The woman turned toward Alex. "No, I've been in there for the last ten minutes or so." She pointed to the office she'd just walked out of.

"Oh, okay thanks. I'm leaving now, so have a good night."

"Thanks, you too."

After returning to her desk, Alex took another quick survey of the empty room and then grabbed her purse and went through to the reception area. Olivia was probably waiting outside for her by this time. As she came around the reception area, she saw Olivia's grey Mercedes in front of the building. After pushing through the door, Alex hurried to the car and slid into the passenger seat.

"Hi. Hope I didn't keep you waiting. Jace called just as I was getting ready to leave and I wanted to find out how he made out."

"No problem, I just drove up," Olivia said. "I know you'll find this hard to believe, but I got a little turned around for a few minutes."

"You? No way!" Alex kidded. "So, what's up?"

"First tell me where we're going."

"I'll do better than that." Alex took Olivia's GPS out of the holder and found the restaurant. After keying it in, she set the unit back on the dash. Olivia listened for a minute and then pulled away from the curb and turned out of the parking lot.

"So," Olivia tilted her head in Alex's direction for a second. "I hate my boss, and I'm sick of working with slime balls like Harvey and Stanton. Now that the divorce is final, I've decided that it's the right time to make the changes I've been talking about for a couple of years now. I've got the money from the sale of the condo." She glanced over at Alex again. "There's nothing for me there anymore, Alex. I'm really unhappy there."

"Well then," Alex said, "you're right. It's time to make the move. I've been nagging you to leave that firm for ages anyway. They're a bunch of stuffy, unprincipled asses. Wow, do you have the heat on? It's really hot in here." Alex pushed the button to open the window a few inches.

Olivia laughed. "Tell me how you really feel, and yeah, the heat is stuck in the on position. I have to take it in to the dealer when I get back home."

Olivia turned at the urging of the GPS unit. She kept glancing in her rear view mirror.

She sped up a little and took a look in her mirror again. "Damn!"

"What's wrong?" Alex asked.

"This guy in back of me is right on my bumper. When I speed up, he does too."

Alex checked in her side view mirror. The car was awfully close.

The GPS told them to turn again. Olivia turned. So did the car in back of her.

"It's like he's following us," Olivia said. "I noticed him behind us almost as soon as we left your parking lot. Every time we turn, so does he."

Alex's heart sped up. "Maybe if we pull over, he'll go by us."

"I don't think we should stop, Alex. It's dark and we're alone out here."

"Well, maybe if you slow down and put your flashers on he'll pass us."

"Yeah, that's a good idea." Olivia turned her flashers on and tapped the brake. The driver in back of them kept coming. They were both jerked back as the car rammed their bumper.

"Holy shit! That asshole just rammed us!" Olivia screamed, speeding up again. The car stayed right on them. Alex got out her cell phone and dialed 9-1-1. The car rammed them again, harder this time. They both screamed and then Alex said quickly into the phone. "We're on 73 North and a car is following us and ramming into the back of us. Please send help."

"Where are you on 73, ma'am?"

"I don't know!" Alex said, "A few miles from Chatham according to the GPS." She listened. "Okay, I'll hang on, but please hurry." She screamed as the car rammed them again.

"What should I do, Alex? I can't keep speeding up. I'll get us both killed."

Alex laughed a little hysterically at that. "I know. You're doing great. Just keep us on the road until the cops get here." Olivia drove a little faster. For several miles the car kept pace with them advancing periodically, ramming them several more times.

"Do you hear a siren?" Alex asked.

"Maybe," Olivia said, but she was totally focused on her driving, hands white on the wheel, her face taut with fear and tension.

"It is a siren! They're coming, Liv." The car in back of them must have heard it too because suddenly it swung out into the other lane, moving up on the side of them. Alex got a glimpse of a man, behind the wheel and then the car veered sharply into their lane, ramming them in the driver's side door.

Olivia's car swerved onto the shoulder of the road. Olivia tried to brake, but the front wheel was off the shoulder. The car skidded across loose gravel. Alex had a sudden horrifying flashback of the other accident, of skidding unchecked off the road, helpless to control the outcome. In a split second, the tires sunk into the soft moist soil and the thick brush on the side of the road and the car continued down into a gully before coming to a jarring halt against the roots of a huge tree stump.

In the passenger seat Alex's head connected with the half-opened passenger side window just before the airbag exploded. Blood ran down her face from a gash on her forehead. She wiped the blood out of her eye and turned to see if Olivia was okay. Waves of dizziness and nausea washed over her, and she froze, closing her eyes until it passed. The siren was very close now, and the other car sped away into the night.

"Alex, are you okay?" Olivia said, her voice weak.

"Yeah, I think so. How about you?"

"Everything hurts right now, but I think I'm still in one piece."

The wailing of the siren came to an abrupt halt and then they saw the flashing lights of the police cars. In the space of maybe half a minute there were several cop cars lining the side of the road. Two men and a woman came running down the embankment.

"Everyone okay in here?"

"Yeah, I think so," Olivia said. She peered through the red and white strobe of light and saw that Alex had her head back and was holding the sleeve of her blouse on her forehead. The side of her face was red with blood, as was the sleeve of her blouse. "Oh my God, Alex. Help her, she's bleeding."

"It's okay, Olivia. Head wounds bleed a lot. It looks worse than it is."

"Sit tight. Help is on the way." One of the officers said. He opened the driver's side door and reached in to unbuckle Olivia's seat belt. "Don't try to move yet. The EMTs will be here before you know it.

After that, it was all a blur. Fire trucks arrived, sirens screaming followed by one ambulance and then another.

Chapter 29

Eli charged through the automatic doors of the entrance to the emergency department. He scanned the waiting room seats for Olivia. When he didn't see her, he approached the desk. "I'm looking for a patient, Olivia Stanton."

"Eli!"

He turned. Olivia was coming through a set of doors at the far end of the room, her right arm thickly bandaged and in a sling. He crossed the room. "Are you all right? Where is Alex? What the hell happened?"

"Calm down," Olivia said, "I'm okay. I have a broken wrist. They gave me some good medicine though and I'm feeling fine. I have to go to an orthopedist on Monday and have a cast put on it. Alex cracked her head on the window and she's got a good-sized gash on her forehead. They're almost done stitching it up.

They wanted to keep her overnight for observation, but she refuses to stay. She says she's fine."

Eli reached out, gently running his knuckles down Olivia's cheek. "I'm glad you're okay. Can you tell me what happened?"

"It was crazy. This bastard was following us and he kept ramming us from behind. I sped up, but he just kept dogging us. Alex called 9-1-1, and then we just tried to stay on the road. As soon as the guy behind us heard the sirens, he pulled out and rammed us from the side and then took off like a shot. I tried to stay on the road, but the car went off the shoulder and I couldn't get the wheel out of the gravel. We ended up off in a gully on the side of 73."

"Oh my God, you could have been killed." He shook his head in disbelief. "Since the day I arrived in New York, everything here has been nuts! Stalkers, killers, peeping Toms, people running you off the road. What's next?" Eli took in Olivia's white face, the bruise on her neck from the shoulder harness, the ace bandage and sling on her arm. "This shit has got to end... tonight. I know who the stalker is now, and he's going down! I was just gonna call the police in on it. I picked up my phone to call them and that's when I got your call. I just grabbed my keys and raced over here." His hands were balled into fists at his sides. "If I find out that he's the one who ran you off the road... the asshole is mine. The hell with police justice."

"Eli, don't go after this guy alone. He's a pretty twisted individual. Don't do anything that's going to come back on you. Let's do things right so we can put him away where he belongs."

"I don't want to do things right. Right now I want to beat him to a bloody pulp."

"Eli," Olivia said, resting her good hand on his arm, "take a deep breath and calm down. Alex will be out in a minute and she doesn't need to hear about any of this right now. She's pretty banged up. She's got the mother of all headaches. It's been a very long night. I need you to get us home and stay with us till morning. The doctor thinks she has a slight concussion. He says that the only way he'll let Alex go home is if someone will be there to wake her up every two hours and make sure she's okay. The stuff they gave me is really starting to work on me." She grimaced. "I doubt that I'll be able to stay awake. Jace isn't back yet, so that only leaves you. I'm sorry."

Eli dropped his head down for a second, making a conscious effort to calm down. "No, that's fine just let me go call Detective Hogan so he can get this freak off the streets and then I'll be right back."

"After you make the call why don't you pull the car around to the sliding doors. Alex should be out in a few minutes. We'll meet you at the car."

"Okay, fine." He raked a hand angrily through his hair. Then he stalked out through the glass doors, digging his cell phone out of his pocket. His first call was to Jace.

"Hey."

"How is she? Is she all right?"

"Yeah. She's a little banged up, but she's going be fine. I'm going to bring them home and stay with them tonight. Where are you?"

"About three hours away. I'll meet you at her house. You sure they're both okay?"

"Yeah, I'm sure. How'd you know?"

"She left something in my room. When I picked it up I got a flash of her with blood running down her face and lights flashing into the car. I really freaked out. When I checked out of the hotel, the girl at the front desk thought I was a maniac. Tell me what happened."

Eli filled him in quickly. "Did they get the guy?"

"No, but listen man, I finally tracked down the stalker. I was just on my way to go after him when Olivia called. I'm calling Detective Hogan right after I get off the phone with you."

"Who is the bastard?"

Eli told him.

"The fucking Wizard of Oz! I should have known. She told me, damn it!"

"Jace, we're gonna get him."

"Not if I get there first."

"Look, I gotta go. They're coming out in a minute and I've gotta bring the car around. I'm calling the police. If they can't find him, I promise you we'll personally track the piece of shit down and make him pay."

"Just don't let Alex and Olivia out of your sight. I'll be there as soon as I can."

"I won't. Don't do anything crazy, man. See you in a couple of hours."

Eli hung up and dialed the number he had for Detective Hogan. He quickly filled him in on the situation and Detective Hogan promised to get an arrest warrant and pick the guy up. "Check out the guy's car while you're there. Someone ran Alex and her friend off the road earlier tonight," he said, getting into his car and starting the engine. "Call me as soon as you know anything." He pulled the car up to the doors.

****

Olivia came out of Alex's bedroom, shutting off the light as she left. "She's out. I don't think she's had a lot of sleep in the last forty-eight hours."

Eli walked over to her. Gently tracing the dark circle under one eye with his thumb, he said, "You look like you could use some sleep yourself."

"Yeah." She leaned into the warmth of the palm resting on the side of her face. "I'm beat. But I'm not going anywhere until you spill about the stalker. Who is he? Does Alex know him?"

"Yeah," Eli said grimly. "She does. It's her good buddy at the station, Paulie. Turns out he's been keeping tabs on her for a long time, since she worked at the other radio station, even before the accident. Detective Hogan says that his apartment is plastered with pictures of her, some of them dating back several years. And it gets better…the right front section of his car is really smashed up."

"Oh my God, he was the one who ran us off the road?" Olivia said. "If he was so obsessed with Alex, why would he do that?"

"Apparently he heard her talking on the phone to Jace at the office and he heard some stuff he didn't like. We found another email he'd sent to Alex. The time stamp showed it was sent right around the time she left the station. He called her a slut, ranting about how she'd betrayed their sacred bond and so on. The guy is a total whack job."

"Yeah he is! If the police hadn't have gotten there when they did, I don't like to think about what would have happened to us out there on that highway."

"Luckily we've got a ton of solid evidence against him. It turns out that the necklace that he left on Alex's bed belonged to a woman who was recently raped over in Dayton, and they have DNA evidence from the rape to back it up. They also got a DNA hit on another unsolved rape case. He's definitely going away for a long time. Right now though, you need to get some sleep. Jace should be here by the time Alex needs to be woken up again, but if not I'll make sure she's okay." Turning her around, he gave her a little push toward the guest room.

She looked over her shoulder at him. "If I were feeling better, maybe I'd invite you to tuck me in." A dimple appeared on her cheek.

"If you were feeling better, maybe I'd take you up on that offer." He smiled. "Now get to bed before you fall flat on that gorgeous face of yours."

"Wow, gorgeous! Now I'll have sweet dreams." She winked. Then the smile was gone. "Seriously, Eli, thanks for coming to our rescue... and for catching the bad guy. You really are a prince. 'Night.'"

"Night, Olivia."

Eli searched the kitchen for something to eat. He hadn't eaten since lunch. He settled on a bag of chips and plopped down on the couch. He found the remote and turned on the television. He navigated his way through a sea of infomercials and finally found an old movie to watch. He was just finishing the last of the chips when he heard a car pull into the driveway. A minute later the doorbell rang. Eli got up and let Jace in.

"Hey, Eli. How's Alex doing?"

"She's fine. Due to be woken up in about..." he looked at the clock near the TV, "ten minutes. I checked on her a while ago and she seems to be sleeping fine."

"Thanks for the text. Catch me up on everything."

After Eli was done, Jace said, "I don't know whether I'm glad they got the bastard or not. I'd like to tear the guy apart." He paced around the living room. "They could have been killed, God damn it!" he ground out.

"But they weren't. Alex has a bandage on her head and a slight concussion. Olivia has a broken wrist. But they're both doing all right, Jace."

"Have you told Alex yet?"

"No. Tomorrow is soon enough. She'd had it by the time we got out of the ER. Olivia asked me not to tell her and I agreed." Eli looked Jace over. "You know, you look all in too. Why don't you go wake up Alex and check on her and then set the alarm for two hours from now and get some sleep? Now that you're here I'm gonna hit the sack. You'll have to bunk in with Alex or sleep on the couch, 'cause she gave me the third bedroom."

"Okay, see you in the morning." As Eli passed Jace, Jace said, "Thanks, man… for everything. You're the best."

Eli grinned. "Yeah I am, aren't I? G'night."

The minute Eli left the room, Jace made his way into Alex's bedroom. He had to see for himself that she was okay. He approached the bed, taking a minute to set the alarm on his cell phone. He set it on the nightstand. Alex was sleeping with her back to him, and he sat down carefully on the bed, not yet ready to wake her. He could see her back moving and he could hear the slow puffs of air as she exhaled. He hated to wake her. He stood, taking off his clothes and then slid under the cool sheets, spooning his body against her warmth.

He curled his hand over her hip and laid it on her flat stomach. Her hair smelled of almonds and Betadine. The bandage on her forehead stood out, starkly white in the otherwise dark room. He nudged the collar of her shirt over with his chin, planting a soft kiss on her collarbone. "Mmmmm… am I dreaming?" Alex murmured sleepily.

He kissed her shoulder once more. "No, I'm here. Wake up and let me make sure you're okay." He moved back and she rolled to her side, groaning as her sore muscles protested.

"Poor baby."

She opened her eyes, smiling when she saw him leaning over her.

"Your eyes look good," he said. "How're you feeling otherwise?"

"Like I've been chewed up and spit out," she said, "but better now that you're here."

"I'd kiss it and make it all better if I could." He kissed her softly on the lips. "But for now, let's get some sleep… at least a couple more hours' worth."

Alex turned onto her side again and Jace curled into her. "I'm glad you're here," she said as she drifted back to sleep.

Chapter 30

Alex turned onto her side and moaned, bringing a hand to the bandage on her forehead. Everything came back to her in a rush. The man behind them, the car jerking as they were rammed from behind, the frantic call to 9-1-1, then the crash and the police arriving. Everything after had been a painful blur of nurses, doctors and tests. She sat up carefully, every muscle screaming as she slid her legs over the edge of the bed. Her head throbbed with a dull ache.

She was alone, she realized. Had she only dreamed Jace climbing into bed with her? No. She shook her head and then regretted it immediately. It seemed that every time she'd fallen back to sleep, he'd been there, insisting that she wake up and open her eyes. She stood up, stuffing her feet into a pair of ratty slippers.

She shuffled carefully to the kitchen, following the scent of freshly brewed coffee.

"Hey sleepyhead, how you doin'?" Eli said as she appeared in the doorway.

"What time is it?" she asked, heading straight to the coffee pot. She poured herself a mug and then opened the cupboard next to her and took out a bottle of ibuprofen. She shook out four of them and then carried them along with her mug to the table.

"2:10."

"Holy crap, that late? Where is everyone?"

"Olivia had an appointment to see some office space. She looked like hell, but according to her it's 'prime space' and dirt cheap, so she insisted on going to see it. Jace had to go out anyway and his car was in back of mine so he took her to see it. He just called. They're on their way back. How you doing?"

"Every teeny tiny little muscle in my body hurts," she shrugged, grimacing as her muscles protested. "But it could have been a lot worse. I'm fine. I just feel so badly that Olivia got caught in the middle of this and now she's got a broken wrist and her car is smashed to hell." She sighed.

Eli smiled over at her. "I think you'll feel better once you see Olivia. She insists that she's getting a blue cast. Apparently her little sister broke her arm when she was younger and she had a green cast. Olivia said she was very jealous and wished at the time that she had broken hers so she could've had a blue one." He chuckled. "She told me that she's actually always been a bit of a princess. That she's always had to have her way… and that now she will."

Alex smiled, taking a sip of her coffee. "Ah, nectar of the Gods. You know, half the stuff Olivia spouts is bull. She calls herself a princess, but her life hasn't been easy by any means. Her father died of a heart attack when she was in high school. She worked her ass off to get scholarships and she just finished paying off her college loans a couple of years ago."

"Her sister was diagnosed with cancer while she was in college. Then, right about the time that she found out that her husband was cheating on her, my husband John and I were in a car accident. He died and I was in a coma for a couple of months. Basically she's been through hell and back. I shouldn't be telling you all of this, but Olivia's my best friend in the world and I don't want to see her hurt again. "Although I seem to be doing a fairly good job of that myself."

"Alex, Olivia's fine. She doesn't blame you. She blames the bastard who ran you off the road."

"God! He could have killed us, Eli. If the police hadn't gotten there when they did... "

"Jace wanted to talk to you about this himself."

"About what?" She leaned forward in her chair. "Did they find the guy?"

Just as he was about to answer, the front door opened. They heard Olivia's laugh and then she and Jace walked into the kitchen.

"Hey, you're awake." Jace knelt down in front of her chair. "Wow, nice shiner. How you feeling?" Leaning forward he kissed her.

"I'm good. Thanks for taking over for Eli and keeping watch on me all night." She looked over at Olivia just as she was taking off her sunglasses. "Oh shit. You've got a black eye too."

Olivia smiled. "Yup, we have matching shiners. But I'm gonna have a great blue cast and you only have a boring white bandage." She came and sat in the chair next to Alex. "Really, though, how are you doing? How's your head?"

"It's fine, just a little headache and I just took something to take care of that. Olivia, I'm so sorry about all this... your arm, your beautiful car!"

"You have nothing to be sorry for. I'm gonna love my cast and as far as my car goes, Eli's already on that. My insurance company is sending someone to check out the car today and then they'll cut me a check. I'll have a new car in no time. I need a new one anyway. Eddie drove this car. It has cooties. I want one of my own."

"You sure."

"Absolutely."

Alex turned to Jace. "I was just talking to Eli about the guy who rammed us. Did you find out anything?"

Jace stood up, taking Alex's hand. "Let's go into the living room and get comfortable."

She got up, wincing only slightly. As soon as they were out of the room, she said, "So tell me."

He pulled her gently down onto the couch. "The man who ran you down was your stalker."

"Oh my God! How do you know that?"

"Eli finally was able to track him through his IP address." He took her hand again. "I'm sorry, Alex, but it's Paulie."

"What?" She recoiled as if he'd slapped her. "No, that's not possible. He's been there for years. He's helped me every step of the way since the day I arrived."

"When the police went to his house to pick him up, they found pictures and video of you dating back from before your accident right up to a week ago."

She fought to hold back the tears. Her head throbbed with the pressure. "So you're saying that not only was he stalking me, but that he's the one who followed us last night?"

"When they checked out his car, the whole front right side was smashed in," Jace told her. "When we talked on the phone at the station, he was listening. What he heard sent him over the edge."

"I thought I heard someone. After I hung up with you I looked around, but I didn't see anyone but the woman who cleans the station."

"Apparently he was so snapped out that he fired off an email to you and then got into his car and followed you." When he told her about the necklace, she blanched. "And the rest is history."

She leaned her aching head back against the cushion. "I can't believe this! That poor woman! I should be relieved that it's over, but I just feel kind of numb right now."

"Come here." He pulled her gently into his arms, offering her what comfort he could. They sat there like that for a while. Alex pulled away, looking up at Jace. Alex could hear the soft murmur of voices coming from the kitchen. "Let's go back out to the kitchen," she said. "I have some things I want to say and I might as well tell all of you at once."

After they were seated around the kitchen table, Alex announced, "I've made a decision." She took a deep breath and then continued. "I'm not going back to the radio station. It's not what I want anymore. It's a great job and I love it, but I feel like it's really a part of my past.

"From the moment I came back from wherever I was, in that time following the accident, I've struggled to feel comfortable with myself. The more I think about it, I consider coming out on the other side of that as something of a rebirth; things that I've rejected or refused to see in the past... the abilities that I inherited from my mother's side of the family, my confusion and frustrations about my feelings for Jace. I've confronted them and have begun to reconcile them in regards to the new me. Between John's insurance money, the sale of the house, and the savings from our past investments, I'm in a position to take a little time and figure out where to go from here. So that's what I'm going to do."

"That's wonderful!" Olivia said. "And while you're thinking about what you want to do, you can help me get my new practice up and running." She grinned. "I put down a deposit on the office space I was telling you about. I meet with the realtor in a few hours to draw up the contract of sale. The best thing about it is that it's a two-story building and the upstairs has two apartments. I'm going to make it into one great big living space for myself. I can't wait." Her face was alight with excitement. "And now you can help me decorate it."

"Olivia, that's wonderful! I'm so happy that we're going to be living so close again. Your emails are fun, but it's always better in person," Alex said.

"Wow." Eli smiled. "You women are just full of surprises. This calls for a celebration sometime in the near future, as soon as we can all go out without Jace and I being publicly harangued for knocking you two around."

Alex laughed at the thought. "We'll definitely have to do that." She kept her gaze on Eli. "How can I thank you for everything you've done, for tracking down my stalker and coming to our rescue last night?"

"Hey, just doing my job, ma'am," Eli said with a cocky little smile.

"Which you do very well," Alex said.

"Thanks. I love a woman who appreciates my talents." He grinned widely.

Jace groaned and the women laughed.

Olivia said, "I'm going to go lie down for a while, just get in a little nap before I meet with the realtor." With that she left the room.

"Well, I've got to call and talk to the station manager since I'm supposed to be to work in—" she checked the clock on the stove, "—an hour."

"You're not going back there!" Jace's voice was explosive. "Look at you! You can't even move without moaning and groaning."

"I will if they can't get anyone to cover. I'm not going to leave them in the lurch. But I'm hoping under the circumstances that he won't insist." She left to make the call.

Eli tipped back on his chair. "So fill me in on what happened in Ohio, bro. Alex said that you found David Hensley. How the hell did you do that? He's been missing for a long time."

"You won't believe how I found him." Jace told him about the statue. "They were all pissed because I made them start right in that spot and I kept making them steer the boat one way and then the other because I had to follow the exact path, or I couldn't see the slide show. It took us a while to get out there, and they were all laughing behind their hands."

Jace shook his head, his lips turning up in a mocking smile. "They all thought I was a joke. But when the first diver came up with his digital camera everyone shut right up. David Hensley was right where I'd said he was… well most of him anyway."

"How'd they act after that?"

"My personal space got considerably larger after that. Everyone gave me a wide berth for the rest of the day. It would have been funny, if it weren't for the reason we were all out there. I wish I could have been on the dive team."

"Don't want to take the chance again, huh? Smart man."

"Yeah, slide shows are dangerous underwater. Can't do much of anything while I'm 'seeing.'"

"So the artist sculpts the statue and then purposely points it at Hensley. Not a big leap to conclude that it's highly likely that the dude killed Hensley or at least was involved. It even makes sense that the guy's ego is so huge that he points his statue right toward the dumpsite. It seems like it should be easy enough to find out who the guy was, right?"

Alex walked back into the room. "Well, I'm officially off the hook," she told them. "The station manager was very understanding and told me not to worry about coming in today or about giving my two weeks' notice. I must say, I'm very glad I don't have to go back there. So were you telling Eli about Ohio?"

"Yeah, I was."

Eli told her, "I was asking him about the artist who did the sculptures."

"When I got back to my hotel room, I called Paul Drake's office again." Jace told them. "He was out of town, but he called me back. I asked him about the artist. He told me that he had absolutely no idea who the artist was. It seems that other than discussing the financials with David, he had no involvement in the project. A guy in their research and development office handled everything to do with planning and fulfilling the terms of the endowment, along with David Hensley."

"The bad news is that the guy died of cancer about three years ago. I asked him if they still had any of the paperwork. He promised to check it out as soon as he gets back to Ohio and let me know."

"You know," Alex mused, "The endowment went to a state park, right? So wouldn't the information be a matter of public record?"

"I'm not sure," Eli chimed in, "but give me a little quality time with your laptop I'll find out."

"It's all yours. It's where it always is, on the coffee table." Eli got up and walked out of the room. Alex lifted a hand to her head, massaging her forehead.

"Head still aching?" Jace said in her ear. He hugged her from behind, wrapping his arms around her and clasping his hands across her stomach.

"That and everything else."

"Come on. I'll give you a back and neck rub." He led her into the bedroom. "I'll be right back." He walked into the living room. "Eli, Alex and I are going to lie down for a while. Why don't you think about sacking out for a while too? None of us got much sleep last night and you were up pretty early. When we all wake up we'll get some take-out. Now that you've taken care of that bastard Paulie, we'll get to work first thing tomorrow on finding us a serial killer."

"One asshole down, one to go. Seems like there's always one more asshole to take care of doesn't it? Come to think of it, a nap does sound good." Eli closed the laptop and got up from the couch, stretching like a large cat. "Later, bro."

Jace went back into Alex's bedroom and through to the bathroom. He opened the closet door and took out a bottle of lotion and a towel. Alex was sitting with her back against the headboard. Jace approached the bed. He leaned over and carefully pulled her t-shirt over her head and then reached around and unhooked her bra, pulling it free as he stood. She tried to cover herself, but he bent and planted a soft kiss on her breast, taking her nipple gently into his mouth and sucking lightly. For the first time that day, she moaned in pleasure.

"Go on and lay down on your stomach," he said. "You need a back rub more than you need this."

She turned over and lay down on her stomach, but murmured, "Maybe, but I could be persuaded otherwise."

"Tease," he said with a smile. Straddling her hips, he squirted lotion into his hands and rubbed them together to warm it. Then he rubbed it into her neck and shoulders, working it in with a gentle but firm touch.

"Oh God." She sighed. "That feels so good."

"That's the idea. Just relax." Jace leaned down, moving the hair off her neck. He kissed a spot just behind her ear. Then he sat up again, working his way down her back, taking his time. After a while he could hear by her slow steady breathing that she had fallen asleep. Carefully he moved away from her, sitting on the edge of the bed to wipe his hands on the towel. Alex stirred beside him. "Don't leave. Stay with me."

He shed his jeans and climbed into bed, wrapping one arm around her. "I'm not going anywhere.

Chapter 31

"So, the very nature of an endowment is to provide a permanent source of funding for use by the receiver, in this case River Oaks State Park." Eli continued tapping on the keyboard while he talked. "David Hensley and Samuel Jacobsen, head of Research and Development at H & D, set up a foundation and selected a top-notch board of directors. Hensley's company made the initial outlay of funds to the endowment. Then Jacobsen and a few of the members of the board set up a portfolio of stocks and mutual funds to help manage the money and ensure future funding for the foundation."

"Hensley had the contacts." Eli shook his head, smiling in appreciation. "I gotta hand it to the guy. He convinced quite a few big money companies to fund the endowment as well. The planning and development was a joint effort between Hensley, his man Jacobsen, the Director of State Parks, and the board of directors of the foundation."

"Eli," Jace cut in, "can you get us a list of the people involved in the planning and development? Somebody contracted for those sculptures. Someone knows who the artist is." Jace leaned over Eli's shoulder, checking out the computer screen.

"No problem." Eli immediately began another search. A few minutes later he pushed the print button and the printer across the room sprang to life. "Alex, have I told you how much I love your wireless printer?"

"Only a few dozen times." She smiled.

"It's almost as nice as mine." He continued tapping the keys.

"Well, I think it's pretty weird that Paul Drake knew nothing at all about such a huge undertaking in his own business." Olivia sat with her legs pulled up under her. "He's a partner, for Pete's sake. If I were a partner, I'd sure as hell have my finger on the pulse of the business."

"That's not necessarily true," Eli said a little defensively. "One of the reasons that people go into partnerships is that they each have different strengths to bring to the table. It stands to reason that each partner would handle the part of the business that they have the aptitude for. The guy is sharp. While I'm sure that he had a good grasp on the financial impact on the company, I can totally see why he might not be involved in the other end of it."

"I'm sorry, Eli, you're right. I never thought of it that way, but there are a lot of people who are essential to the law firm and I sure don't want to know everything about what they do every day. I sometimes forget that not everyone is a freak about detail. Being a lawyer does that to a person."

"I wouldn't actually call you a freak, but then I don't know you that well yet," Eli said.

She lifted an eyebrow at him. "And at this rate you never will."

Eli chuckled.

Jace and Alex looked over the list. "I'll make some calls and see if any of these guys will talk to me," Jace said. "Then we'll go from there."

"Sounds good," Alexandra said. "After she gets her cast on, and assuming she feels well enough, Olivia and I are going to go see her new office today and do some planning."

"I'm going into the office," Jace said, "Mattie called me this morning and told me that if I don't come in today she can predict my future, and it won't be worth a damn."

"Yeah, she sent me a text," Eli grumbled. "If I don't get in there and finish my paperwork, my ass is grass, whatever that means." He lifted his arms in a defensive move, "I'm not messing with her. Even I know my limitations." He logged off of the Internet and closed the laptop.

Jace crossed to where Alex was sitting, holding out a hand to help her up. "How about we meet back here later? Maybe we can do that Mexican place tonight."

"That sounds great. I could use a margarita or two right about now." She turned to Olivia. "Does that sound okay to you?"

"Right up my alley," she said. "Eli, how about you? You game for that?"

"I don't want to make a pest of myself."

"Don't even think of leaving me to be the fifth wheel here. They'll start getting all cutesy and I'll be sitting there like an idiot."

"Well, in that case… I haven't had any good Mexican food since I left California. My third favorite thing is eating so sure, count me in."

"What are your first and second?" Olivia wanted to know.

"I'll tell you later. It'll give us something to talk about at dinner." He winked. "In the meantime, will you two women please stay out of trouble? I don't think any of us can take much more." He grinned.

"Amen!" Alex said, walking with Jace to the door.

"See you later," Jace said to Alex. "Be careful and have a good day." Taking her in his arms he gave her a kiss that promised much more. "Later," he said roughly.

"I look forward to it," she said softly next to his ear. As she brought her arm down, Jace jerked sharply, grabbing her wrist and holding her arm between them. Rubbing his thumb along the watch on her wrist, he said, "Where'd you get this? I've never seen you wear it before."

"I've had it for years. It was an anniversary gift from John."
She searched his face. "Why?"

"No reason," he said. "I thought maybe it was new. What
do you call that black design?"

"It's Marcasite," she said smiling. "Since when have you
been interested in jewelry?" She planted another kiss on his lips.

Eli cleared his throat loudly from behind them. "Okay,
then. Time to go." Jace and Alex broke apart. Eli pushed Jace out
the door, pulling it closed as he left.

"Whew!" Olivia waved a hand in front of her face. "Is it
hot in here?"

Alex smiled. "Shut up and go get ready. We've got to get
you to your appointment and I'm dying to see your new office."

"And I'm dying for you to see it. Alex, I'm so excited about
this! All of those hundred hour weeks are finally going to pay off."
She threw her good arm around Alex, awkwardly dancing her
around the living room. When they got to the hallway, Olivia let
Alex go and danced her way to the doorway of her room. "Give
me ten minutes. Then we're outta here."

****

Jace hung up the phone and swiveled around in his chair,
growling in frustration. How was it possible that no one knew the
name of the sculptor? Someone had hired him, arranged for
shipment of the statues, and paid the commission. So why was it
that no one knew the artist's name?

He'd managed to talk with five of the nine board members.
The only one of them who seemed to know anything about the
artist at all, actually told Jace that he thought the guy had insisted
on anonymity. "Someone had to have approached the artist in the
first place," Jace had said. "Any idea who it was that originally
found the guy?"

"I'm almost certain that one or both of the Hensley boys
knew him, or of him anyway. The truth is that there were so many
details we were taking care of at the time that it's hard to keep
everything straight. I know that the board looked at about nine or
ten different portfolios and we all agreed that he was really talented
and that his pieces were the best fit for the park, but I never even
looked at the names."

Jace took a drink from his cup, making a face at the coffee, now bitter and cold. "So you don't remember any of the artists' names?"

"No, sorry. It was a long time ago and I wasn't working closely on that aspect of the foundation. I was on the finance committee. All I know about it was that his work didn't come cheaply."

Jace's pulse picked up. "Then the committee must have cut him a check, right? If so, then you would have a record of his name and address."

"Every expense involved in the project went through the finance committee for initial approval, but after that each committee handled whatever funds were allocated to them. You have to understand, it was a huge project. Each group handled its own budget."

"Right." Jace sighed. Another road to nowhere! Everything led back to Jacobsen. "Let me ask you one more question. Do you know how the statues were transported? The pieces were large and heavy. They would have to have come by truck and placed with a crane, wouldn't they?"

"I would guess so, but I wasn't there for the placement. By the time we had the dedication ceremony, everything was already in place."

Jace tossed the pen he'd been holding down on his desk. His chair creaked as he turned it one way, then the other. "It would really help me if you could remember which of the members of the board was in charge of the acquisition and placement of the statues."

The man on the other end of the line was quiet for so long that Jace thought maybe he'd lost the connection. "Greg, are you still there?"

"Sorry, I was trying to think. I'm pretty sure that Jacobsen handled the acquisitions. I don't think anyone else was involved in the process, but I'm not one hundred percent sure. Maybe Paul Drake would be able to shed more light on that. After all, Jacobsen was on his payroll."

"Okay, Greg thanks for talking to me. If you think of anything else helpful, please give me a call."

"Will do. I've got your number." And he disconnected.

Jace hung up the phone. "Damn it!" No matter which direction he took, it always seemed to lead to a dead end. Why would an artist choose to keep his identity a secret? Wouldn't any artist want to stamp his name on his work, so to speak? Unless, of course, the artist was also a murderer! He hadn't seen that when he touched the statue, but how else would the sculptor have known to point the statue in the direction of the body.

He had to find this guy and fast! He strode over to Eli's office. He rapped on the doorframe then walked in.

Eli turned in his chair. "What's up?"

"I can't find this guy and I have to!" Jace said, dragging a hand through his hair. "Everything I try leads nowhere." He paced the office. "How are we going to catch this guy when I keep hitting a brick wall? I'm better than this Eli! I've found hundreds of missing people. I've tracked down so much human garbage, that I could fill a frigging landfill with it. Why can't I find this guy?"

"Wow," Eli said, shaking his head, "and I thought I was the one with the ego problem. This is probably the guy that law enforcement in three different states has been trying for, what, ten years, to track down… and you wonder why you can't find him in a couple of months? What the hell is wrong with you? Ever since we left the house you've been acting like a maniac. You seriously need to get a grip, bro."

In a split second Jace was across the room. Leaning over Eli, his hands tightly gripping the rubber arms of the chair Eli sat in Jace snarled, "You're telling me to get a grip? Tell me, how am I supposed to do that?" His eyes blazing with rage and impatience, he said, "Eli, he's coming after Alex."

"What? What are you talking about? How could you possibly know that?"

"The watch she was wearing this morning, that's how I know."

Eli tensed, throwing his hands out, frustrated with the conversation. "Okay, I'm not like you. I can't read minds. So, you're going to have to spell it out for me."

"Remember how when I put my hand on her dining room table, I saw the arm of a woman, only one arm, with blood running down it and dripping onto her wooden floor? The watch she was wearing this morning was the one I saw on that arm."

Eli swore. "Are you sure?"

"Yes, damn it, I'm sure!" He turned away to pace the floor once again. "We've got to find him, Eli, and from where I sit, we're not even close."

"Well then, let's stop wasting time talking and get a move on." He rolled back over to his desk. "Pull up a chair." He hit a few keys and then clicked on a link. A picture came up on the screen. Jace dragged a chair over and sat down. "Who's this?"

"This is an age-progressed picture of Nathan, or Noah, or both. I got together with Stone and Ray and they let me play with their program."

"Wow!" Jace stared at the image on the screen intently. Then he turned to Eli. "That's very cool."

"Yeah, and that's not all. I talked to our new best friend, Sheriff Shaffer. He sent me a boatload of stuff from the Hensley investigation. I've been checking up on Noah and Nathan. You know, getting acquainted.

They each had bank accounts, Ohio driver's licenses, school IDs, their own credit cards, debit cards, et cetera. No action on any of the accounts after the boating weekend. No traffic stops. Nothing in the towns where they went to school."

"So," Jace said, "You're telling me you found nothing."

"Kind of. In fact, good ole Sheriff Tom and his crew came to the conclusion that the boys must have died on the lake that weekend. But I have a problem with that. I don't believe that they wouldn't have found the bodies. River Oaks Lake empties into Lake Erie. Lake Erie is the shortest of the great lakes and the shallowest. The currents aren't generally as strong as in some of the larger lakes." Eli's chair squeaked in protest as he leaned back, stretching.

"I know there were storms for a few days, but I talked to a guy at the Maritime Research Laboratory and he believes that the bodies should have bloated and surfaced after a short time in the water. He also said that the most populated area of Lake Erie is right there along the shores of Ohio. Even though it was late in the season, larger ships were still using the lake. He thinks the bodies should have been found."

"The people in the Sheriff's office, even the Police divers didn't seem to think that that was necessarily the case," Jace said.

"Hey, maybe my guy is wrong. Maybe they all drowned and maybe they didn't, but let's face it. It would be a perfect way to disappear, especially if you had just baked your step-mother like a ceramic pot and chained your father to God knows what on the bottom of the lake."

"You make a good point. But we haven't come up with one thing to suggest that the twins were alive after the accident."

Eli drummed his fingers on the edge of his desk. "Not entirely true, bro. There are a few things that I find curious. In the months before they disappeared, they both virtually dropped out of circulation. I managed to dig up a guy who was good friends with them in high school and he told me that even before the end of senior year, both of the twins had pretty much broken ties with practically everyone. They quit going to student council meetings, quit the tennis and baseball teams, stopped going to parties, stopped hanging out with everyone but each other."

"Yeah, the principal told us that, but she thought it was due to their mother's death and the father's remarriage."

"But hadn't it been a couple of years. So why wait until then to act out?"

"I agree. It doesn't make any sense. They were leaving for college in the fall anyway. Why would they need to shun everyone and quit all their activities? And Paul Drake told us that the boys had been getting along better with their father right before the accident."

"There's another thing that makes me suspicious. Both Noah and Nathan had well over forty thousand dollars in their bank accounts at the beginning of their senior year. Every month on the fifteenth there was an additional deposit of one thousand dollars from a trust fund set up by their mother. But by the time they disappeared, Noah had only thirteen hundred left in his account and Nathan had even less. They were making some pretty steep withdrawals right up until they left for college."

Jace let out a low whistle. "They were getting ready to go away to college. You'd think they'd be saving money rather than spending it. Were they buying things for college? Computers, that kind of thing?"

"Not that I could see."

"Were they making the withdrawals on a regular basis?"

224

"No, totally random as far as I can tell."

"Where they writing checks?"

"Cash withdrawals at several different branches."

"And Shaffer didn't find that suspicious?"

Eli shrugged. "They were rich kids. He said they spent a fortune on art supplies and to build the kiln in the back yard. He said they were always dropping money around town."

"What happened to the money from the trust fund after they disappeared?"

"Don't know yet. I have a call in to the lawyer who handled the trust, but he hasn't gotten back to me yet."

"Okay, let me know what you find out. I hate to admit it, but you do always seem to be one step ahead of me. Can you find me the name of the current head of R and D at Hensley and Drake? I'd like to see what he knows about the sculptures and the Park Endowment."

"Sure. Hang on a sec and I'll get it for you. Didn't Drake tell you that the guy wasn't there when all that happened though?"

"Actually he didn't say he wasn't there, he said that he's only been in R and D for a few years. I'm banking on the theory that in order to get to where he is in the company, the guy has probably been with the company for a while. And in a company that competitive, he must know his stuff. So hopefully he'll know all about the endowment."

"Makes sense. I hope you're right." Eli hit return. "Okay. Here's the guy's name." He wrote it on a post-it note and gave it to Jace. "I'll keep working on the twins, you go find the artist. We're gonna do this, Jace. We're gonna find this guy."

"Yes we are. We have to," Jace answered as he left the office.

Chapter 32

"Okay, thanks man. You've been a big help." Jace hung up the phone. "Yes, yes, yes!" Jace keyed a name and address into his laptop and followed with a Google search. Immediately he spied an article from a local newspaper in Tyler, Texas. Kevin Freeman was arrested late Friday night after he was caught fleeing the scene of an accident. Police also charged him with using fraudulent ID. He is being held on multiple charges. The article was dated two years ago.

He scrolled through the next hits until he found one dated almost a month after the first article. It was an obituary. Jace clicked on it. It was from the same local newspaper in Texas. He read, Kevin Freeman, 39 years old, was found dead in his apartment just weeks after being arrested for leaving the scene of an accident, among other charges. Sources say that Freeman had been living under an assumed name for at least ten years before his arrest. Police are calling his death suspicious. The cause of death is currently under investigation."

"I don't fucking believe this!" Jace ground out. He felt the need to punch something. Not just punch it... pulverize it. Instead, he took a deep breath and picked up the phone. He asked for the number of the sheriff's office in Tyler, Texas, writing it down on the same post-it Eli had used. He disconnected, intending to dial the number, but the phone rang in his hand.

"Jace Moseley," he answered.

"Hey, Jace, it's Mike."

"Give me some good news, will you? Everything I run down takes me exactly nowhere."

"What I have to say is not going to make you any happier. Those pictures Alex sent me of the statues... I sat down with the FBI and we checked them all out. Four of them were among the eight women in Pa and NY who were killed by our guy. Three more of them disappeared from Ohio at one point or another; none of them has ever been found. We don't know who the other woman is yet... and then there's Ann."

"Damn it! It doesn't make any sense. I finally tracked down the artist who contracted for the sculptures, and I found out that the guy's been living in Texas under an assumed name and that he died under suspicious circumstances two years ago. That means that he couldn't have killed the last two victims."

"The last three actually. Five months before Kimberly Haas, there was Janet Wicks." Detective Stone was quiet for a moment and then he said, "There is something. Since the government had already seized the Hensley's property, the FBI let us go in there. We found blood in the dining room... lots of it."

"We also found a platinum and diamond ring and a partial filling from a tooth in the kiln. Underneath the slab, the cement slopes down and there's a hole. They had rolled down into it. Luckily platinum has a really high melting temperature, or we wouldn't have that either. Let me tell you, it was a bitch moving that slab. It weighed a frigging ton. Anyway, the FBI crime lab has the evidence now. They should have something soon, hopefully."

"So we may have evidence of another murder but again no killer."

"We're closer than we've ever been, Jace."

"Not close enough. I'm almost sure that I know who his next victim is, and that cannot be allowed to happen." Jace filled him in on the latest developments.

****

Eli hung up the phone and sat back in his chair. He had to admit that it seemed like Tom Shaffer had done a pretty thorough investigation at the time of the boating accident. The problem was that there really hadn't been much to investigate. Someone thought that they might have seen Noah going into a store in town that night, but he couldn't be sure whether it really was him, Nathan, or some other guy he knew who looked kind of like the Hensley twins. No one had seen the family get onto the boat that day. The detective hadn't been able to find any other boaters who claimed to be out on the lake at any time during that weekend.

Shaffer had even gone so far as to question both Noah and Nathan's roommates at college. Reading the notes from the interview, it was clear that Noah's roommate had been seriously hung over at the time of the interview. His statement had been pretty useless. All he'd been able to tell the police was that Noah had left school on Thursday after his last class.

Nathan's roommate on the other hand, had told the investigators that while Nathan had paid to live in the dorm, he'd done it only because students were required to live in college housing during their freshman year. Nathan had shown up the first day and paid his roommate a substantial sum of money to tell people that he was living there. He'd left a few things scattered around the room and in a dresser and that was the last the roommate had ever seen of him.

The roommate wasn't even sure whether Nathan had been attending classes. Shaffer had checked with the administrative office and they had confirmed that Nathan had attended classes for the first few weeks. None of his professors had seen him after the middle of October.

Shaffer had given him the roommates' names and Eli had tracked them both down using the information Shaffer had on them, and several other sources. Eli had talked to both of them on the phone. After Eli had explained why he was asking for information, Nathan's roommate had gladly told him everything he knew. Unfortunately, all he remembered aside from what he'd told Shaffer was that Nathan had paid him five thousand dollars to keep his secret. After talking to him, Eli was convinced that he didn't know anything beyond that.

Noah's roommate, on the other hand, was a different story. As soon as Eli had mentioned why he was calling, the guy had become nervous and evasive. The guy had totally given Eli the bum's rush. He knew something that he hadn't told the police. Eli could feel it; and he was determined to find out what it was. He punched the name into his computer and began a search. He was deeply into it when Jace popped his head in the door. "Alex just called me. Olivia's office called and she had to go back to the firm and take a deposition."

Eli stopped typing and turned in his chair, disappointment clearly written on his face. "An emergency deposition? There's no such thing, bro. The wheels of justice move at a snail's pace."

"Apparently it involves a case she's been working on for almost a year. Alex says that Olivia's firm has been waiting forever for a chance to depose this guy. Anyway, the reason I'm telling you this is because there's no way I'm leaving Alex at home alone. So I'm outta here. If I can talk her into going to my place to stay, I may be back. Call me if you find anything, okay?"

"I've got something cooking here, but I'm not sure what it is yet. Eh, would it be a breach of our company's ethical code if I had to do a little discreet hacking to find what we need?"

"We have no ethical code where this killer is concerned. Do what you need to. Just don't get us arrested."

"Wouldn't think of it," Eli said already turning back to his computer. "Thanks. Tell Alex 'hi'. I'll talk to you later." An hour and a half later while he was still wading through the morass of information, his cell phone rang. He grabbed his phone off the desk. "Eli Moseley." He cradled the phone between his jaw and shoulder, and continued typing.

"Hello. This is Stephen Kaufman returning your call."

He stopped typing and sat up in his seat. "Ah, Mr. Kaufman thanks a lot for calling me back. Listen, I have some questions for you about the Hensley twins' trust." Kaufman started to say something. Eli cut him off, "I know that you don't know me from Adam, but hear me out first."

Twenty minutes later Eli hung up the phone and began the search with renewed vigor. He had to hand it to him, the kid was good, especially for an eighteen year old, but Eli was better. His fingers were flying across the keyboard, but they still weren't keeping pace with his brain. God, he really loved this job!

Chapter 33

Alex opened the door as Jace came up the front steps. She moved back to let him in. He closed the door behind him and gathered her into his arms, pushing her gently back against the wall and kissing her until they were both breathless. "Alone at last," he said into her ear. Leaning back, he checked out her black eye. "How you feeling?"

"I think I must be sick. I feel really hot and tingly all over. I feel hungry, but I don't want any food. I wonder what's wrong with me?" She smiled up at him, her eyes twinkling.

"Consider me your doctor. I know just what ails you."

"Really?" She gazed up at him innocently. "What do you think is wrong with me Doctor?"

"Have I ever told you that I'm a healer? Here's how it works. You get into bed and I'll lay my hands all over you, and I guarantee you that you'll feel better in no time."

She giggled. "Sounds good to me." She took his hand and led him into her bedroom. Turning to face him, she asked, "Should I take my clothes off for this?"

"Yeah, you definitely should and I think I can help you with that," Jace said, pulling her t-shirt over her head.

"Oh, I know you can." Alex smiled, pulling his shirt over his head and running her warm hand over his chest and down his hard abs. He sucked in a breath as she reached under the waistband of his jeans, efficiently working the button free. "Ah, God," Jace said, "I've been waiting for this from the minute you got on that plane in Ohio. You're my new addiction. I don't think I can ever get enough of you."

He ran his hands down her arms and then back up to her shoulders. He had her bra off before she knew it and then he pulled her in for a lingering kiss. She wrapped her arms around his neck kissing him back, reveling in the thrilling exchange of energy and hot desire. She felt their mutual desire so intensely that when he ended the kiss and moved to her take her nipple into his mouth she groaned, shivering with the sensation of being instantly balanced just on the edge of orgasm. Her legs threatened to give out and he moved her to the bed, gently laying her on her back.

He stripped off the rest of his clothes, then hers and stretched out next to her, slowing things down for a minute. He ran his hand over her from the tender skin under her arm to the soft swell of her hipbone. Running his thumb over the scar on her right hip, he said, "When I saw you lying in that hospital bed with tubes running everywhere and machines breathing for you, it scared the living hell out of me." He kissed her shoulder.

"I was so afraid that you were going to die. I couldn't stand even thinking about it. I stayed with you as much as they would let me for the first three days. I had it in my head that if I held your hand, if I kept touching you, then I could somehow help you heal. I thought that maybe that current that runs between us, the one that I've never felt with anyone else on Earth, would somehow transfer some of my life force into your body. And selfishly, I was afraid that if you died, I would never feel that connection with anyone else ever again."

Alex felt a swell of emotion and her eyes misted over. She said to him, "I thought that I was the only one who felt it. I hated myself for feeling that way about you when John was supposed to be everything to me." She laid her hand on his cheek. "That's why I hated being around you and why I avoided you all that time. I was confused about what it was and so afraid that it was a betrayal of John. I always thought that John was the one love of my life, but now I know that some people are luckier than others." She kissed him tenderly.

He pressed her down onto the bed, deepening the kiss, pouring all the power of his longing and love into the kiss. Suddenly he needed her with a fierceness that he hadn't known existed. He ran his hands and his mouth over every inch of her silky skin, learning every contour of her body and storing it away so that he could remember it later. She in turn, ran her hands over his strong muscled back and arms, holding on for dear life as he took her over the edge time and time again. Every time she thought she couldn't take the exquisite torture any longer, that she was too exhausted to feel anything more, he would take her up again. Using his tongue like a fine instrument, using first slow then faster strokes, he brought her to the brink once more.

"Oh no you don't. Not again." Alex bit down on his earlobe, whispering hoarsely in his ear, "This time when I come I want you inside me." Taking command of her body, she pushed him onto his back. After grabbing a condom from the drawer of the nightstand, she ripped the wrapper with her teeth throwing it aside. Quickly she rolled the condom down until it covered all of him. Then raising herself up, she sank slowly down onto his penis, every inch of it filling her, loving the friction as his penis rubbed against the inside of her.

His arms came up around her, not hurting her, but holding her still. "Don't move yet. If you move, it will be over in about two seconds and I'm not ready for that." Jace hissed out. She could feel how close he was to the edge so she resisted the urge to tighten around him. Instead, leaning down, she kissed him over and over. She relaxed against him, enjoying the head to toe contact of his warm skin against hers. How many times in the past year had she ached for this human contact and now she had it and so much more? Because it was with him, she admitted. That's what made it so incredible. Suddenly she just had to move. She couldn't hold back any longer. She rose and then sunk down slowly. "Ah Lexi, you're killing me."

"Should I stop?"

"Don't even think about it," he said, pushing even more deeply into her, causing her to gasp and tighten around him. "That's it!" he said. Flipping her over onto her back, he pulled out and then plunged into her again. She rose to meet his thrusts, suddenly as desperate as he was to find fulfillment. Sweat broke out on his forehead as he fought to hold on. "Come for me baby. I want to feel you come." As he said that he thrust into her one last time and she screamed his name as her orgasm hit her in wave after wave of pleasure. Her orgasm sent him over the edge and he rode her until they were both replete and then collapsed on top of her, gasping for breath. Reluctantly, he left her and lay next to her, giving their bodies time to recover. Sometime later, Jace raised his head up on an elbow watching her. He brushed a piece of hair off of her damp forehead. She was so beautiful, he thought, lying there all soft and satisfied. She looked so small and fragile.

His eyes swept down her body and lighted on the watch on her slim wrist. With a sudden surge of determination, he vowed that he would keep her safe. Time was running out. He didn't know how, but he felt sure of that. They had to catch the killer and it had to be soon. Jace wasn't going to lose what he'd denied himself for his whole adult life. He wanted this with Alex and he would do whatever he had to in order to make it happen.

"I hate to ruin this moment, but would you consider going to my house with me and spending the night? I need to go back to the office for a while and I'll feel better if I know you're at my house waiting for me."

"Why don't you go back to work, and I'll meet you at your house later. I want to take a shower and I've still got a load of clothes in the dryer."

"Why don't I wait until you take a shower and fold the clothes and then we'll both leave at the same time?" Jace answered.

She looked him in the eye. "You don't want me to be alone here do you?"

"No, I don't. Humor me, will you?"

"Why? Paulie's in jail. He's not getting out any time soon. The danger is passed."

"Do I have to have a reason? Don't you want to spend some time with me? Tell you what. I'll go into the office, take care of a few things and then I'll bring my laptop home along with some take-out. We'll eat dinner, then you can read or something while I get a little work done." He exaggerated a leer. "Then we can mess around all over again." He wiggled his eyebrows at her a couple of times. She laughed. When she didn't answer right away, he said, "That's not a good enough deal? All right, I'll sweeten the pot. While I'm gone you can snoop around in all my personal things and find out all my dirty little secrets."

She had already decided to go to his house. She realized that she really wanted to spend time with him, get to know all those quirky little things about him that she didn't know yet. She smiled slyly. "Well, when you put it that way, how can I refuse? Did you say all your personal things?"

"Yup, nothing's sacred."

"Okay then." She sat up, swinging her legs over the edge of the bed. "Let's get going! It's gonna take me some time to get through your whole house."

Inwardly, he sighed with relief. "You don't have to do it all in one day, you know. You can stay as long as you like. While we're waiting for the dryer let's go take a shower."

"Together?"

"Why not? I've already seen everything you've got. Besides, you need me to wash all the places you can't reach."

"How have I managed all these years on my own?" She asked, walking through to the bathroom.

"Quit grousing. You know it'll be fun."

Alex poked her head out of the doorway. "Ever heard the expression 'actions speak louder than words?'"

He was right. It was fun. An hour later Alex folded the last towel and carried the basket into the bedroom. Picking up her duffel bag, she joined Jace in the living room. He was already holding her laptop. She punched the code into the keypad by the door and they left.

He followed her to his house and waited until she was inside. Then he took off for the office.

Chapter 34

Jace walked into Eli's office. "How's it going? Any progress?"

"Oh yeah! Bow to the master." Eli preened. "Noah is alive and living just over the state line in Pennsylvania. In fact, according to Google maps, he only lives about thirty minutes from here."

"Holy shit! How did you find him?"

"It's a long story, but I'll give you the short version. I got the roommate's name from Shaffer. He interviewed him back when the twins disappeared. So anyway, I called the guy and I could tell that he was lying through his teeth, and he was all nervous and shit. So I started digging. Anyway, lady luck was smiling on me today, because the lawyer who handled their trust called me back finally and he gave me an earful."

"Get this. According to the terms of the trust, the twins got a thousand dollars a month until their eighteenth birthday. On their eighteenth birthday, which incidentally is in the beginning of July, they got the entire bulk of the trust, which amounted to a little over six million dollars."

"Six million! Their mother was worth millions? How did that happen?"

"Old family money. She got it in trust from her grandfather. So she set one up for her boys as soon as they were born. The trust only went into effect in the event of her death. As it happens, she did... die I mean."

"If they got the money from the trust, why the hell did they empty their bank accounts?"

"According to Kaufman, the estate lawyer, they were unaware of the terms of the trust, but the terms were that they weren't to be notified until the day of their eighteenth birthday and then he was supposed to help them make arrangements to receive and manage the money."

"So what happened to the money?"

"Glad you asked. Nathan had his portion transferred to an account he had opened in a little bank near Deposit, New York. Kind of ironic, don't you think?" He waited, giving Jace time to appreciate his joke.

Jace grinned. "Yeah, Deposit, I get it, it's a real laugh riot. And Noah? What did he do with his money?"

"Noah had an account set up at a bank in Tingley, Pennsylvania under the name Robert Chase."

"Who the hell is Robert Chase?"

"I don't know yet, but Noah gave it as a gift. So that means he paid the inheritance tax on it, but Robert Chase then paid a gift tax on it. That really took a large chunk of the money. I'm not sure what's going on with it yet. I've been trying to find Chase, but he doesn't have a driver's license or any credit cards. He had to have gotten a debit card from the bank, but he's never used that either. His address is a post office box in Tingley, Pa. He makes cash withdrawals from the bank, but not as often as you'd think and that's it."

"What are you thinking?" Jace asked.

"I'm thinking that Noah Hensley is now Robert Chase and that he's been a very, very careful boy. There's got to be some way that I can find him. I'm working all the angles. If all else fails we may have to go down there. It's not very far away. We could start at the bank."

Jace sat down and they tossed a few ideas around. After a few minutes, Mattie came to the door with an envelope in her hand.

They both looked up. "What are you doing here so late?" Jace asked.

"I didn't even get here until two-thirty and I won't be here tomorrow, so I stayed late to get some things done. Anyway, some young kid just dropped this off. He said it was important that I give it to the man at the computer right away. Weird, huh?" She handed the envelope to Eli and stood there waiting.

Eli smiled up at her. "You're just dying to see what's inside, right?"

"Yup. I'm planted until you read it... out loud."

He chuckled, slipping his finger under the flap and sliding it down the envelope. He pulled out the note, careful to only touch the edges, just in case. The note was written in black ink. It said,

Stop looking for me, or I'll end up like Nathan and Kevin.

"Do you even know what that means?" Mattie asked.

"Oh yeah we do!" Jace said. "It means that Nathan Hensley is dead and that Noah is alive. It also means that he's gone to a great deal of trouble to hide himself from someone."

"Or," Eli added, "he's the killer and he doesn't want to be found."

"Okay, this sounds like a soap opera. Things like this don't happen in real life," Mattie said.

"Uh, hello," Eli said. "You work for a guy who finds people with his psychic powers!"

"Hey, you of all people should know that it's only a part of what I do to find people," Jace said. "But in this case, it just might be the tool of choice. Give me the letter, Eli."

Mattie headed toward the door. "I gotta get back to the phones. I left someone on hold. Darn, I hate to miss the show." She turned back to Eli. "You let me know what happens... or else." She hurried out of the office.

"Sorry, buddy, but I'm gonna have to hold it with both hands," Jace said.

"I'll forgive you as long as you get some good stuff."

Jace took the letter in both hands. Almost immediately his eyes grew wide and glassy. Eli sat waiting impatiently for Jace to come back. Getting up he went to the mini-fridge on the other side of his office and took out a bottle of soda. He sat down popping the top and took a drink, trying to avoid looking at Jace. It still freaked him out a little to watch Jace while he was "seeing."

A few minutes later Jace closed his eyes, relaxing back into the chair. The letter dropped from his hands into his lap. Eli sprang up from his chair and crossed to Jace. "You okay, buddy?"

Jace opened his eyes. "Yeah, I'm okay. Just a little wiped. How about some water?"

"Sure thing." Eli opened the mini-fridge again and took out a bottle of water. After twisting the cap off, he handed it to Jace. Jace drank until it was empty. Then he picked up the note from his lap. He folded it and put it in his shirt pocket.

Eli sat down again and looked at Jace expectantly. "So, what'd you see?"

"He lives in a white house on a lake, not a very big house, with a porch facing the lake. He doesn't work in clay or charcoal I don't think because I saw a room with lots of oil paintings and drawings in ink. I saw a heart. I don't know what that means. He has a small boat that's tied up to a dock that's definitely seen better days. He gave the note to a kid and paid him a couple hundred dollars. The kid drove it here and delivered it to Mattie. That's what I got."

"Gee, that's all, huh? You didn't get his address and phone number? You must really be slipping." Eli turned back to his computer.

"You're really a smart ass, you know that?" Jace said, pulling his chair over to the side of Eli's.

"Okay, let's see," Eli said, his fingers moving over the keyboard. He pulled up a map of Tingley, Pa and then widened the map to see what was in the surrounding area. "Bingo. Heart Lake. That's where he lives." He started typing again. "Okay, here we are. He pulled up a satellite view of the houses on the lake. Zooming in on them he moved from house to house, giving Jace time to examine each picture."

"Wow," Jace said, "How does anyone stay hidden these days?"

"Not very easily." After twenty minutes of looking Jace said, "It's kind of hard to tell from these pictures... wait! Go back to the last one."

Eli pressed the back arrow and the previous house came up on the screen. Jace looked at it for a minute. "That's it! I'm sure of it."

Eli shook his head. "It's just damn freaky the way you do that. So, we've got us an address. When do we leave?"

"I'd like to say right this minute, but it's already almost eight o'clock and I told Alex I'd be back soon."

"Whipped already, huh?"

"Not hardly, but I don't want to leave Alex alone, even at my house. Sometimes things change when the status quo changes. I can't let anything happen to her Eli."

"I know, bro. Just jerking your chain."

"Besides," Jace said, "I have to talk to Mike Stone and Ray Jeffers. I know they'll want to go with us. I'll go call them and if they can swing it, we'll all go first thing in the morning."

"Sounds like a plan. Besides, I haven't eaten all day, not to mention the fact that I was up half the night on the phone with Olivia."

"Oh really? Olivia?"

"Shut up and get out of here, will you? Go get things set up so you can get back to Alex."

"Eli, don't do any more searching for Noah. He's got some kind of alarm set up on his computer. I don't know how he did it, but certain words or websites trigger the alarm. I hope he doesn't know that we Googled him just now, but I think he was at some kind of art show. I saw him sitting on a chair with his artwork all around him and lots of people walking around. I don't want to say anything to Alex about this until we know what's going on. If she finds out about this she'll want to go with us and I want to find out if the guy is dangerous first. She's been through enough already. Now go home and rest up. And no talking to Olivia all night."

Jace ducked as Eli sent a punch in his direction. Laughing, he walked out the door and made his way down the hall to his office. He made the calls to Mike Stone and Ray Jeffers and they both agreed to meet early in the morning at Jace's office and go from there.

He had two messages from potential clients. He called each of them, taking time to get what history he needed to decide whether or not he could help them. He decided that he could probably be helpful to both of them and he set up appointments to visit their homes in the next few days. He sat back in his seat, tiredly rubbing a hand over the back of his neck. It had been a long day, but very productive. They were getting close. He could feel it.

He just wanted to get home to Alex. He pushed away from his desk and stood up. After closing his laptop, he turned out the light and closed the door.

Chapter 34

Alex turned over in bed and nudged Jace. "Jace, the alarm is going off."

"Hmmm..." He raised his head, opening bleary eyes.

"The alarm," Alex said again. "Turn it off."

"Oh, right." He hit the snooze and then rolled over pulling her back against him.

"I would've heard it if you hadn't kept me awake half the night." He kissed the back of her neck. "You're a demanding woman, Alex Pope."

"I woke you up once and you woke me up twice. Who's the demanding one here?"

He chuckled sleepily. "I didn't hear you complaining."

"No, you sure didn't." She smiled. "I've been deprived, after all." They lay there quietly until the alarm went off again.

Jace rolled over, shutting off the alarm this time. "I've got to get going." He leaned back over, running a hand over her perfect butt, across her flat stomach and up to cup one warm breast. "More about this later?" He whispered next to her ear.

She arched against his hand. "Definitely."

"What time are you meeting your mom?" Jace asked. "I'd stay and say hi to her, but I'm meeting with some people at the office in about forty-five minutes."

"Actually, she has an appointment and it's between here and home so I'm meeting her in about two hours and we're going to have brunch. I can't wait to see her. I've been afraid to get together with her because I'm not sure I can totally block my own mother, and I don't want her to know what's going on right now. She's already worried enough about me to last a lifetime."

Reluctantly, he climbed out of bed. "You know she would have been camped out on your doorstep by now if she had any idea what's been going on here. Just enjoy your time with her and I'll meet you back here later, okay? I'll call you and let you know what time I'll be here. Have a good day. Tell your mom I said hi." He leaned down and kissed her and then strode naked into the bathroom. A minute later Alex heard the shower running. She rolled over and closed her eyes. In a minute she was asleep again.

Jace unlocked the door and walked into the silent office. He loved people and noise, but sometimes it was nice just to be alone. He sat down to enjoy the quiet. Picking up his coffee he took a healthy gulp. It burned his mouth, but he needed it. He wondered what the day would bring. How had Noah managed to stay hidden all these years, Jace wondered, when it had been so easy for them to find him? Of course, not many people could find people using the methods Jace had available to him, he admitted to himself.

Why had Noah chosen to give up everything and live the way he did? Had he helped to murder his father and left to hide it? Or was he really afraid he'd be discovered and end up dead? Did he know who the serial killer was? Or was he really the monster that they'd been looking for all this time? Jace wished the others would hurry up and get here so that they could get on the road. He wanted some answers. He only hoped that Noah hadn't pulled up stakes after Eli's search. He hoped they weren't already too late.

A few minutes later Eli came in, coffee cup in hand, looking excited and ready to go. Mike Stone and Ray Jeffers arrived right behind him. They had a brief meeting to decide on a course of action and then they all climbed into Jace's SUV and got on the road. It was only about a forty-five minute drive from the office to Heart Lake. Eli filled Stone and Jeffers in on the terms of the trust and what he had found in his search. They were impressed.

"If you ever want a job with the FBI, I'll be glad to put in a good word with the powers that be," Jeffers said to Eli.

"No way, man. I'm my own boss and I like it that way. In fact I love it. The only thing I don't like is all the paper work, and I'm working on minimizing that. Where else can I make my own hours, work anywhere I want, take the work in any direction I want to?" He smiled. "No, I'm good, but thanks."

Mike Stone said, "We found out who the other woman was, the statue we couldn't identify. She was in the country illegally, so no one had officially reported her missing. But we had the FBI techies surfing missing person's websites and one of them found her. She lived in New York City, but she was visiting some friends when she was taken. She was murdered after a concert at a college about an hour from Binghamton. Same MO as the others. We may never find some of the bodies, but at least the families will have some closure."

"Oh, and the ring we found in the kiln was Ann's. We identified it from a picture we found on the Internet," Jeffers said.

"You think this guy is our killer?" Eli asked.

Ray Jeffers shrugged. "He lives close enough to have committed the murders, but he doesn't really fit the profile. He's not married, no steady job. He's living off the grid. Usually these guys like to be where they can see and hear everything that's going on after a murder. They feed on that kind of stuff. But hey, I'm no expert in profiling. I hope it's our guy and that we can put him away forever. The things he does to those women..." He shook his head, "He is one sick bastard."

Jace turned on his right blinker. "We're almost there. I think there's a long driveway leading to the house. I'm going to park up near the road and we'll walk down. That way hopefully he won't have any warning that we're coming." The road was narrow with brush lining both sides of the road. "Look for a driveway on the right," Jace said. The road was full of holes and ruts so he drove slowly. Still, he missed the driveway.

"Shit! I think you just passed it. Go back," Eli said.

"I didn't see any driveway," Mike Stone said.

"Me neither," Ray said.

"Just go back," Eli said. "It's there."

Jace backed up slowly.

"Stop! It's right there." Eli pointed.

"Shit! No wonder no one ever found him here. If the guy went out and had a few beers, he'd never find his own way home," Mike Stone said.

Jace turned in and drove slowly through a mass of low hanging branches and brush lining the sides of the dirt drive. "This is so gonna scratch the paint on this baby, Jace," Eli said.

"I know. It sucks. But it'll be worth it if we snag a killer." Jace pulled over and parked. They all got out, quietly closing the vehicle doors. They approached the house. There was no car in the driveway. Everything was quiet. They walked to the side of the house. Jace cautiously peered in through a window into a large room, which contained a small kitchen, a tiny dining room and a larger living room. There didn't appear to be anyone there.

Jace turned to Ray Jeffers. "You do have the warrant, right?"

"Of course."

"All right then, let's go." He motioned to the others. They moved quietly around the side of the house and up onto the porch. Jace tried the door. The knob turned in his hand. The door wasn't locked. He pushed the door open and immediately the air was filled with the shrill screeching of an alarm so loud that seemed to echo off the calm lake. Mike Stone, the last one in, swiftly scooted inside, closing the door behind him. Eli rushed over to the computer, which was sitting on the dining room table. He tapped a few keys. The screeching stopped.

"Well, if he was around here somewhere, my guess is that he's not anymore," Ray Jeffers said, checking out the small bedroom off of the living room.

Chapter 35

Alex set her purse down on a chair in Jace's bedroom. She'd woken up so late that she'd just barely had time to jump in the shower, dress, and drive to meet her mother. Now she looked around. What a mess! She made the bed and then went around the room picking up the clothes they'd thrown on the floor in their haste the night before.

She folded Jace's jeans, setting them on the end of the bed. She reached down and picked up the t-shirt he'd been wearing. It was inside out and she turned it right side in. As she did, something fell out of the pocket and onto the bed. It was a note of some kind, folded into a square. She picked it up and felt the familiar zing.

She stood outside of a small house for a minute and then took the stairs two at a time on legs impossibly longer then her own. She burst through the door. "Nate, I need to talk to you. I know you're here." Oh my God! She was with Noah. She, or rather they, charged through the kitchen and into a huge room, which Alex could see was an art studio. She was shocked to see the very same statue of Ann that she'd snapped a picture of in River Oaks Park. "Nate, where the hell are you?"

"I'm back here." They went through to another room, which contained a kiln that was as big or bigger than the one at the Hensley house. "What do you want, Noah? I thought you didn't want anything to do with me anymore. I thought you were gone for good. Isn't that what you said, Robert? That's your name now, right?"

"Nathan, you've got to get away from here, away from him. He'll kill you too. He killed Ann. I know that you went out in the boat with him and Dad and now Dad's gone too. What happened out there, Nate? Is Dad dead too?" Nathan didn't say anything.

"He is, isn't he? Tell me you didn't have anything to do with it Nate."

Nathan wouldn't meet their eyes. In a voice devoid of emotion he said, "Okay, I didn't have anything to do with it."

"Oh my God, you helped him, didn't you? Nate, he's a killer. You know he killed Ann and Dad. I saw his secret room. You must know that there's a trap door under that rug in the studio." Did you see the jar with her nipples in it? How can that not bother you? The guy's a total freak. I thought we both agreed that we had to get away from him. Even Kevin agreed with us. He's crazy, Nate. Take your money and your new phony ID, and let's get the hell out of here. Leave with me now."

"Ann was a bitch. She deserved to die. He did us a favor as far as I'm concerned. And Dad, he wouldn't listen. Once he found out that Ann was dead, he went berserk. He would have killed us both if we hadn't done something."

"Look, Noah, he's not going to hurt me. He says he and I are family now, and that a man protects his family. You'd better get out of here. He's really pissed at you for running away and not going with us on the boat. He'll be back any time now. I'll be fine. Don't worry about me." Then Nathan turned away from him and began working some more clay into a partially finished statue. Nathan didn't look at them again. They turned and retraced their steps. Alex noticed that there weren't any leaves on the trees and there were Christmas decorations on the light pole at the corner.

Suddenly Alex felt warmer and Noah felt older, more solid. She looked down at Noah's arms; they were bare now, the coat he'd been wearing was gone. Noah was focused on another time now. They were still at the same house, yet it seemed different somehow. Alex decided that it seemed kind of sad now, beaten down by time and the weather. They were standing on the far side of the house and Noah was peering in the window. His heart was beating so fast that Alex felt lightheaded, which only compounded the throbbing pain radiating through her head.

They leaned a hand on the faded wood siding. She could see the studio. There was no one in there. The statues were gone. Noah turned and they went around to the back door and took a key off the top ledge of the door. Noah closed the door after them. They crossed the room and knelt down, knee on the floor next to an area rug. He moved the area rug aside and lifted the trap door that the rug had hidden.

They went down the stairs and Noah walked right over to a wood-paneled wall. He counted the lines in the paneling and then measured with three fingers and pushed in on the panel. A hidden door in the wall swung open and they stepped into a small room. The room was any woman's biggest nightmare come true. The walls were filled with graphic charcoal drawings just like the ones Jace had seen. Alex felt the blood drain from Noah's head.

He crossed to a small door in the room and flung it open… and they gasped. Inside on several shelves were jars with names on them. Each jar contained the nipples of one of the women who'd had the fatally bad luck to garner the killer's notice. They read all of the names; there were so many women. Noah squatted down to read the ones on the bottom shelf. Noah/Alex cried out his anguish as he read the name on the last bottle. The name on the bottle was Nathan Hensley. The bastard had cut off Nathan's tattoo. Nathan was dead, and the tattoo was all that was left of him. Noah picked up the bottle. Tears streamed down their face as they gazed into the bottle.

He felt sick to his soul, and then Alex felt the weight of his guilt. He was thinking that he should have told someone about Ann's murder. He'd tried. He'd called in an anonymous tip, but apparently they hadn't followed it up. And neither had he. He'd been too selfish. He'd been too afraid of being found. He'd wanted to live. So he hadn't done anything more. And now they knew where he lived. So everything was coming to a head... finally. Alex felt what she thought might almost be relief mixed with a large dose of world-weariness. No, he thought, he still didn't want to die, but he wanted to be able to live... really live and he was tired of this life. He wanted his own back. It was time to stop cowering in his little hideout and get the bastard.

Alex felt his crushing grief through a cloud of her own pain. Abruptly, she heard a ringing in her ears and she couldn't make it stop. Everything was blurring and the pressure in her head could no longer be ignored. She let go of the paper, bringing her hands to her ears. When she woke up, she was on the floor of Jace's bedroom. The note lay next to her on the carpet. She stayed where she was for a few minutes until she could summon the energy to move. Alex stood up on shaky legs. Making her way to the kitchen, she found some ibuprofen and swallowed several of them with a large glass of water. Now that she was back she was starting to feel better already.

She had to figure this out. Think, Alex, think! She sat down at the counter to sort things out.

She still didn't know who the killer was, but she knew more about who he wasn't. It wasn't Noah or Nathan, and it wasn't the artist, Kevin. But she knew that the killer had gone out in the boat with Nathan and his father, so it was someone they all knew well.

The sheriff had told them that both Paul Drake and another man from the company had frequently gone out in the boat with the Hensleys. She tried to remember. Had Paul Drake eaten with his left hand when they'd had lunch? She didn't think so. She had been sitting to his left and she was right handed. She was pretty certain that she would have noticed if they'd been practically bumping elbows. So who was the other man who'd gone out in the boat?

She grabbed her laptop out of her bag. She booted it up and found the number for Tom Shaffer. She wasn't even sure that he would take her call, but she needed information. She dialed and waited. After four rings he picked up.

"Tom Shaffer."

"Hello, this is Alex Pope. Please don't hang up," she said quickly. "I need to ask you a question and it could be important to the investigation."

"Listen," he said, "I'm sorry about the way I treated you when you were in my office, but you might want to work on your investigative techniques. I'm fairly certain that most people would respond the same way I did to the phrase 'I saw it in a psychic vision.'"

Alex smiled. "Yeah, I get that now."

"So shoot. What's your question?"

"When you took the finger prints in the Hensleys' boat, who was the other man besides Paul Drake who went out in the boat with David Hensley?"

"Hmmm. Let me dig the file out of my pile here." She could hear him shuffling papers around. He dropped something and he swore under his breath then said, "Sorry." More shuffling. She waited.

"Okay, let's see. It's right here in my notes somewhere. Ah, here it is. His name was Samuel Jacobsen. Does that help?"

"Not in the way I was hoping. Jacobsen has been dead for years. But you've helped me narrow down the field. Thanks for your help."

"Hey, keep me in the loop, okay?"

"Absolutely, and thanks again."

"And by the way, you were right. Sheryl dumped me."

"Oh, I'm sorry about that. I was really angry."

"No problem. I understand. Good luck."

She sat back in her seat for a minute. So if Jacobsen was dead and Paul Drake was right handed, then who did that leave? Everyone else was either dead or on the run. Something was bothering her, but she couldn't put her finger on it. What was it? Something she'd seen somewhere, but hadn't made the connection until now. It was just out of reach. She almost had it.

Her phone rang, and just that quickly it was gone. "Shit, shit, shit," she said reaching for her phone.

It was Olivia and she was in a very good mood. She was excited and wanted to talk, so Alex just listened. The deposition had gone even better than she planned. She'd hired a contractor to do the work on the apartment above her office. As soon as the trial was over and she settled one more case, she'd be back for good. Alex was as excited as Olivia and they talked about all the changes they were planning. Alex heard another caller beeping in. It was Eli. She clicked in and promised to call him back. She clicked back and finished her call with Olivia and then called Eli back.

Chapter 36

"Damn it!" Jace said, moving around the room. He strode to the sink and picked up a chipped coffee mug, holding it between his hands. After a minute he put it down and continued around the room, picking up objects here and there, trying to get a fix on Noah.

"Try the computer, bro. We know that he set the alarm on it. Maybe you can get something off of it."

"You're right, Eli. It's worth a try." Jace sat down in the chair and wham! The air grew still around him and the show began.

"Jesus Christ! That's just freaky man," Ray Jeffers said. "I'd almost forgotten that look he gets when he's seeing something. Man, he can have that shit! I'll take good old FBI investigation techniques any time."

"I know what you mean," Mike Stone said. "It takes a stronger man than me to go through that shit all the time. The things he sees... I don't know how he keeps doing it."

"He has no choice," Eli said. "It's a part of him. He can't turn it off. He couldn't stop it even if he wanted to, and who wouldn't want to sometimes. It's the reason he finally decided to go into this business. It was the only way he could make some sense of all the crazy things he sees. Sometimes he can change the outcome of something, catch it before it goes bad. If not, then he just has to live with giving people the comfort of knowing. It's not an easy life. He handles it as well as anyone could, as far as I can see. That's why I'm so damned determined to do everything I can to help him." He eyed both of them at once. "Don't tell him I said that."

They waited in tense silence for another few minutes and then Jace blinked and turned his head to look at them. "He's not here. He knew we were coming. He's gone to the other house, the one where Kevin Freeman lived before he disappeared."

"The one in Deposit?" Eli asked.

"Yes. The killer stays there sometimes. I saw some of his things there. I don't know where the house is though."

"I do," Eli said. "I have the address on my laptop in the truck."

"You know," Jace focused on Eli, "I saw Noah looking in a window. Then I saw him go in through the back door... and for a minute I thought I saw Alex instead of Noah. Then it was Noah again."

"What does that mean?" Eli asked him.

"I don't know." Jace stood up. "But it can't be good. We have to go. We need to get there now."

No one said anything more. They trusted his instincts. They got into the SUV, and Eli immediately opened his computer and found the address. He punched it into the GPS unit on the dash.

"Shit! Forty-nine fucking minutes to get there!" Jace backed out of the driveway and drove impatiently through the morass of potholes until he reached the main road.

"Hang on everyone! We're about to break some GPS speed records," Jace said.

Eli knew what was going through Jace's head. He dug his cell phone out of his pocket and punched in Alex's number. It rang and after a couple of rings she answered. "Eli can I call you back in a minute? I'm on the phone right now."

"Sure. No problem." He disconnected. "She's all right dude. She's on the phone, but she's calling me back. Slow down before you get us all killed."

Jace didn't slow down. "How did she sound?"

"She sounded fine. Calm down and slow down, will you?"

Jace eased up on the gas, looking over at Eli. "When she calls, put her on speaker phone."

"Fine, now watch the road, or pull over and let me drive."

They drove in silence for a few miles.

"Why isn't she calling back?"

Eli switched on the radio to fill the tense silence in the vehicle. "She will, bro. It's only been a few minutes."

Two minutes later Eli's phone rang. "It's her."

He answered, switching to speakerphone. "Hi, Alex. Where are you right now?"

"Hi Eli. I'm at Jace's house. Where are you guys? I called the office and Mattie said you'd gone somewhere and she didn't know when you'd be back. I…"

"Are you all right?" Jace interrupted.

"Jace? Yeah, I'm fine. But I just got back from a little psychic trip, thanks to the note that fell out of your shirt pocket."

"Holy Shit!" Eli said. "You weren't at some house with Noah were you?"

"You might say that. I was in his head."

"I told you I saw her there," Jace said.

"This is too just freaking weird for words! How am I ever going to write this up in my report?" Ray Jeffers said from the back seat.

"How many people are there listening to me, and just where are you anyway?" Alex asked.

Mike Stone answered for them. "Hi, Alex, there are four of us. We took a road trip to find Noah, but I guess you beat us to it. Tell us what you found out."

"I found out that neither Noah nor his twin brother are the man who's killing those women. In fact, the killer also killed

Nathan. She told them what she had learned from Noah and about the vision and her hunches that hadn't panned out."

"We're on our way to the house now. We'll probably be a while. Jeffers has already called in the crime lab. Stay at my place until we get back," Jace said.

"Don't you need a warrant to go in there?" Alex asked.

"The FBI has received a tip from a reliable source. We have probable cause."

"Wow, how'd you do that? You guys are good. Please be careful."

"Don't worry, we will. What are you going to do today?" Jace asked.

"I have some errands to run, but I'll be here when you back," Alex said.

"Alex, do me a favor, will you and don't go to your house without me," Jace said.

"Why don't you want me to be there Jace? You rushed me out of there yesterday and now you don't want me to go back to my own house without you? What aren't you telling me?"

"We'll talk about it when I get home, okay?"

"Fine," she said in a tone that implied that it wasn't fine at all.

"Alex," Mike Stone said to cut the tension in the car, "While you were inside of Noah's head, he didn't even think the killer's name?"

"No, and it was extremely frustrating. I kept trying to will him to say it, but I couldn't get through to him because I was really just seeing something that had already happened. I couldn't change it or interrupt it. I'm still looking into a few things from my end, though. I'll let you know if I come up with anything."

"Alex stop looking into things and just do your errands, will you?" Jace snapped.

"Jace, bro, you're heading into dangerous territory here," Eli said under his breath.

"Jace, for your information I stopped taking orders from men a long time ago, so you can drop the caveman act." The three other men in the car smiled. Jace wasn't amused.

"He's just worried about you, Alex," Eli said.

She sighed, softening her tone somewhat. "I know that. Look, Jace I'll be fine. I promise to be a good little girl. Call me if the crime lab comes up with anything. I think the killer's been to the house recently because his sick little room from hell was pretty clean. No dust. He's taking good care of his trophies."

"Probably visiting them to relive the murders and the sex," Ray said from the back seat.

"We're really getting close now. I can feel it," Alex said.

"Yeah we are, so relax for a couple of hours and let us handle it for now, okay? I'll call you later. Bye."

"Okay, bye Jace, bye guys."

They all said good-bye and Eli hung up the phone.

"The crime lab will be there when we get there. I told them to wait for us to go inside."

"Thanks, Ray. I'd like to get what I can from the place before everyone and their brother traipses through there," Jace said.

"I've got no problem with that. I've seen you in action too many times to doubt you."

"I appreciate that." Jace pressed down on the gas pedal, once again filled with the compulsion to get there fast.

As she ended the impromptu conference call at her end, Alex absently set her phone back down on the counter.

Why was it so important to Jace that she not go back to her house without him? Had he seen something that he hadn't told her about? A sudden chill danced across her scalp. Would they find the answers at the house she'd seen in her vision? Would they finally catch the killer and get him off the streets? God, she hoped so.

Chapter 37

He sat in his car halfway down the street, just behind another parked car. Beads of sweat dotted his forehead and he wiped away the moisture that had collected above his top lip. That had been a near miss! He'd been just about to put his blinker on in preparation for turning into the driveway when he'd seen the first police car pulling up to the house. He'd recovered almost immediately, shifting the foot hovering over the brake pedal back to the accelerator, careful not to increase his speed. He drove on past the house and continued on for a few blocks before circling back.

As he watched, several more police cars pulled up and parked. Several minutes later a van with the words FBI Mobile Crime Lab emblazoned on its side pulled into the driveway.

They'd found him! How? He'd been so careful. His beloved trophies! They would find them and take them away. He needed them. They were the only things that made his life worth living in the interim. They were all he had of Ann and Nathan, his family. What would he do without them? No more trips to his secret sanctuary. If she could see him now he knew that even his demanding bitch of a mother, yes, and Ann too, Ann the betrayer, would have to see that he had earned an oasis, a place to decompress from the pressure of business.

Not only was he a successful businessman, he was also in top physical condition. Hadn't he worked out for countless hours every week for years, just so that he could please his lovers? What were these people doing invading his domain? Rage bubbled up inside of him. He felt like going in there and killing every last one of those bastards!

No! He couldn't do that. He took a deep breath in order to calm himself. He'd figure out something. After all, hadn't he fooled everyone for all these years? Not one of them could match him in intelligence and cunning. He sat there, a thousand different disjointed thoughts flitting through his brain. He couldn't seem to focus. He watched and waited. Nothing seemed to be happening. Why weren't they doing anything? The officers had gotten out of their cars, but no one had approached the house.

He wasn't sure how long he'd been there. Along with all the law enforcement people, a crowd of maybe twenty people had gathered to watch the show. He was tempted to go and watch too, but he knew that only a stupid man would risk being seen where he shouldn't be. He knew the police would probably tape the crowd; they had at Ann's funeral. No, that wasn't right. It hadn't been Ann's funeral. It had been the teacher's. Good thing he'd stayed well out of sight.

As he watched, an SUV pulled up. An officer approached the vehicle and talked for a minute. The SUV pulled over and four men got out. He recognized one of them as Jace Moseley, the investigator who had been asking about the Hensleys, the man who had somehow known exactly where to find Hensley's body.

He'd done some research on Moseley. His reputation was that of a crackerjack investigator, but there was conjecture that he had some kind of psychic powers. Personally, he'd never really believed in that hoo doo crap, but now he experienced a flicker of fear. He watched as the men stepped aside to let Moseley go in. No one followed him in. The flicker turned into a small ripple of panic. Would Moseley be able to see into his world?

Rage filled him again, this time compounded by fear. Moseley would tarnish all of his treasures, his memories. He wouldn't know how to appreciate them. No one ever had. Not Kevin, not Noah, not even Nathan. Well, if Jace Moseley were going to destroy his world, then he would return the favor. He smiled broadly. And he would enjoy doing it.

He'd seen Jace with Alex Pope. He knew that Jace was in love with her. Let's see how you like having the woman you love taken away from you. He backed into the driveway closest to him and drove away. He knew where she lived. He'd also checked out her background. He smiled. She reminded him a little of Ann.

Chapter 38

Alex paced the floor, chewing on her thumbnail until it was so short that it hurt. Where the hell were they? What was going on? Why hadn't she heard anything? It was driving her crazy waiting like this. They should have taken her with them. She could have helped, maybe seen something that they couldn't. She'd tried to watch TV, even tried to read for a while, but she was way too restless, too churned up to sit still. Finally, she made a cup of tea and sat down on the couch to drink it, her cell phone next to her on the couch.

She'd been expecting it to ring, but when it did she jumped, fumbling for it in the crease of the couch. "Hello? What? You're kidding? No, no, that was rhetorical. Have the police checked it out? Why do I have to be there? Okay, give me ten minutes."

Alex grabbed her purse and her car keys, slipping her phone into her shirt pocket. She couldn't believe it! That house must be cursed. The security company had called to say that the alarm had gone off and the police had arrived, but they couldn't go in without her there. She didn't understand that. Wasn't that the whole point of having a security system? So other people could check things out and make sure it was safe? But she wasn't doing anything anyway, except worrying herself to a frazzle, so she agreed to meet the police there.

When she got to the house, there was a patrol car sitting outside with the engine idling. As she stepped out of her car, the officer joined her. He showed her his badge and introduced himself and together they entered the house. He had her wait by the front door while he methodically searched the house. After he'd checked the kitchen, he waited while she retrieved a bottle of water out of the fridge. She'd been so thirsty ever since her psychic fieldtrip that she couldn't seem to quench it. "I'm fine, really. Why don't you check out the rest of the house?"

"You're sure?" he asked.

She smiled at him. "I'm sure." She stood for a few minutes sipping from the bottle, enjoying the feel of the cold liquid on her parched throat. Then she went back through to the dining room. The officer was just coming into the room. She set the water on the table and met him in the entrance. He'd found nothing out of place. He filled out a one-page report and had her sign it. She thanked him for coming and walked with him to the front door.

"Are you okay to be here by yourself?" he asked.

"As long as I'm here, I'm just going to get a few things. I won't be here long, believe me. You go ahead."

"I'm sorry. Ordinarily, I'd be more than happy to wait until you're ready to leave," he said, "but I go off duty in twenty minutes and if I go into overtime again, my boss has threatened to skin me alive. You sure you'll be all right here?"

She'd only be here for a few minutes by herself. "Of course. I'll be fine. I'll set the alarm as soon as you leave. Thanks again, officer."

She closed the door behind him. She punched in the code and waited for it to beep. As long as she was here anyway, she just wanted to gather a few of her things and then she'd leave. She went to her bedroom, stepping through to the bathroom to get her shaver off of a shelf on the back of the tub. Hairy legs were definitely not a turn on. She grabbed a couple more items, tossing them into a little travel pouch she kept in the closet in the bathroom.

She stepped back into her bedroom to get a few more clothes, something to wear under that new sweater she'd bought at the mall the other day. Her head jerked up. Was that a noise coming from the living room? She froze, listening with every cell in her body. Nothing. She relaxed. Jace had her imagining things now. Nevertheless, she threw everything into a bag in about two seconds flat and moved towards the front door. As she bent to turn off the lamp on the table closest to the door, she noticed that a picture that she kept on the end table had fallen. She sighed in relief. That must have been the noise she'd heard.

She picked up the picture, settling it back on the table. All of a sudden something clicked in her head. That's what she'd been trying to remember! In the picture hanging in Paul Drake's office, he had been cutting the ribbon for the dedication of the lodge… with his left hand! She turned, planning to get the hell out of there and call Jace. The coat closet door flew open, slamming into the front door, very effectively blocking her exit. A man sprang from the closet. It was Paul Drake and in his left hand was a knife.

She screamed as he advanced on her. She shoved the bag she had hastily packed between them and then she turned and ran. She made it to the dining room before he grabbed her arm and spun her around, bending her back against the table. Her arm hit the bottle of water tipping it over. Water trickled from it and over the edge of the table onto the wood floor. She quickly blocked him so that she wouldn't get caught up in his head. "You and your pal Jace just couldn't leave things alone, could you? After all these years, you two had to stir everything up again. Well now you can find out first-hand what it feels like to gain the attention of a real man like me." He brought the knife down the front of her shirt, neatly separating it in the middle.

"Right now," Drake said, "he's at my place violating my treasures. And that's exactly what I'm going to do to him." He gazed down at her bared breasts. "I'm going to have so much fun violating his treasure." He pushed the tattered shirt from her arms.

Cool air caressed bare skin, but that wasn't what caused the chill that ran through her. He ran the side of the knife blade over her breast. "You know, you remind me of Ann in some ways."

"Why is that, I wonder?" Alex said. "Is it because both of us are totally repulsed by you?" She could see the flash of anger in his eyes, but then he smiled that sick, vile smile she'd already seen too many times.

"Did you know that I met Ann first?" Drake asked her. "She never took me seriously because of the age difference." He laughed. "Don't you find that ironic? She wouldn't see me because I was younger than she was and then she married a man who could have been her father." His eyes glazed over with the unpleasant memory.

"From the moment she saw him, I was invisible. Me! I was the person who loved her more than anyone else ever could and she didn't even see me. But I forced her to. If I couldn't have her love, then her fear was the next best thing. In fact, it was everything." He focused on Alex again. "Yes, you remind me of her." He leaned in, whispering, "C'mon, let me see your fear."

She kept silent, determined not to show him anything but contempt. He lifted the knife, running the blade up to her neck and then down over her shoulder. She felt a line of fire as the blade sliced through her tender skin, and then the painful itch as trails of blood made their way down her collarbone and then her arm, dripping off of her skin into the water that had collected on the wood floor, just as Jace had seen, she realized.

"I can't wait to see your fear, to smell it," Drake whispered to her. "And when I'm done with you, I'll go and send your friend Jace to hell as well."

"No," Alex said calmly, "you won't get Jace, because you're not going to leave here alive. I promise you that, you sick bastard."

"Names will never hurt me, Ann," he chanted, smiling in a warm manner that was obscene given the situation.

She had to make him lose his focus. She had to get away. If she gave up, Jace would be next and God only knew how many others. The nightmare would go on and on. He was smiling, but she could feel the rage building inside of him.

"I'm not Ann. I'm Alexandra. You killed Ann remember? The woman you loved. You cut her and raped her and then you burned her body. No wonder she hated you."

"She never hated me!"

"Yes, she did. She hated you. She couldn't stand to be around you."

"That's not true! She was trapped in a marriage with an old man. I knew that if he was out of the way, we'd be able to be together forever."

"But when you told her what you were planning, she was horrified, wasn't she? She looked at you like you were a monster. She said that she would never let you touch her."

"She didn't understand that I had to do it. I had to do it for us. He was an old man! He shouldn't have been touching her like that!" He was totally lost in the memory of the last time he had been with Ann. Spittle flew from his mouth as he ranted. Without the contacts that he usually wore, his eyes were the golden brown of a wild animal on the hunt. Alex had never been so frightened or so angry.

"David Hensley wasn't that old. He had the body of an athlete. He was the one touching her, and she was loving it. That's what you couldn't stand, wasn't it?" She had to goad him; it was her only chance.

"Shut up, bitch! I should have killed you a long time ago, after I saw you at the nurse's funeral." He lunged for her. She slid her right foot forward, pushing it between his legs and sweeping it to the side with all her might. He lost his momentum, stumbling backwards. He slipped in the pool of bloody water on the floor and struggled to stay on his feet. It gave her just enough time to slide out from the end of the table. He reached for her, but she was just a second faster. She turned and ran for the kitchen.

She needed a weapon. Her mind raced over the possibilities. He was right behind her. There was no time for hesitation.

She knew that the broom was just inside the doorway to the kitchen. She rounded the doorway and grabbed the handle. Still moving, she turned and swung the broom with all her might. He saw it coming and flung his left arm up to deflect the blow. The broom handle connected with his left forearm. The knife flew out of his hand and slid across the ceramic tile.

He bellowed in rage and disbelief, moving toward the knife. But Alex was closer. She dove for it, picking it up and rolling to her feet. "You love how it feels when you're slicing through someone's flesh, don't you? It gets you all hot, doesn't it? Well, let's see how excited you are when it's your flesh being carved," Alex said, gritting her teeth.

Death scenes flashed through her brain, the women he'd mutilated and killed, the euphoric expression she'd seen on his face. He lunged for her. She brought the knife down on his arm, felt the sickening slide of the blade as it cut through muscle and skin. Her stomach heaved, but she kept the pictures of the dead women firmly in her head. She could do this. He couldn't be allowed to walk out of there. She wouldn't let him do those things to anyone else ever again. Drake grabbed his arm, looking at her in amazement. "You cut me! With my own knife."

She heard banging on the front door, but she didn't look away from him. "That's right, I did. Did you like that? I hope so, because every time you come near me it's going to happen again." He advanced on her again. He tried to grab her wrist, but she swung it out and around him, this time cutting him on the upper arm. He cried out in pain, clasping a hand over the fresh cut.

She could hear someone battering against the front door. She prayed that they would get through soon. The adrenaline rush that had allowed her to continue the fight was fading fast. She was still bleeding, and she was beginning to weaken.

As he rushed toward her, she pulled a chair out from behind the kitchen table and pushed it between them. She heard the sound of the front door crashing open. Drake knocked the chair aside sending it clattering to the ground. He grabbed her wrist and twisted, shooting fire up her arm. She heard the snap a moment before she felt the new onslaught of pain. The knife fell from her injured hand. Drake bent and picked it up, raising it high in the air above her. She tried to back up, but only bumped up against the kitchen table.

So she was going to die after all.

She saw the knife descending as if in slow motion. Bringing her arms up, she made one last attempt to grab his arm, but her left hand was slippery with blood and the pain in her other wrist was too intense. She couldn't hold on.

This was it then. She was never going to be able to tell Jace that she'd fallen in love with him. The knife was descending. A shot rang out. Alex watched in fascinated horror as one side of Drake's forehead exploded. Blood, bone, and brain matter sprayed everywhere. The knife stopped inches from her chest. Though half his face was gone, Drake's body still stood, suspended there for a split second... and then he dropped to the floor.

Alex stood, watching the growing puddle of blood seep from what was left of his head onto the white ceramic tiles of the kitchen floor. He was dead! She was safe. The last of the adrenaline drained from her body. Her knees gave out. Someone caught her before she fell and then strong arms were around her, holding her close. She saw Detective Stone and Ray Jeffers barking orders at people she couldn't see.

"Lexi, thank God we got here in time. When I touched Drake's ski cap and I 'saw' him leaning over you with the knife, I thought I was too late," Jace said, kissing her forehead. His energy flowed through her, spilling warmth into the icy cold that had begun to pervade her body. He picked her up and raced outside to the waiting ambulance.

"Jace." Alex opened her eyes. Tears rolled from her eyes and disappeared into her hair. "I need to tell you something, just in case."

"Save it, Alex. You're going to be fine," Jace said fiercely.

"Sir," the EMT said, "she's lost a lot of blood. We need to get her to the hospital."

"Then let's get the hell out of here!" Jace said, closing the door and sitting down next to Alex.

Chapter 39

"I want to propose a toast," Eli announced, raising his bottle of beer. They all raised their drinks. Eli chuckled. "I can't get used to seeing both of you in casts."

"I must admit, as much as I wanted it, it's not my favorite fashion accessory," Olivia smiled ruefully.

"Okay, here goes." He raised his beer a little higher. "Here's to successful apprehension of one of the most heinous and elusive serial killers in all of New York, Ohio, and Pennsylvania. And we should mention, the capture of the slimy rapist/stalker as well. We rock."

"Cheers." They all clinked their bottles and glasses against each other's and took a drink.

"I talked to Jeffers this morning. He told me that by the time we made it to Drake's hideaway, Noah Hensley had already turned himself in to the police. He's told them everything he knows. Apparently the FBI is cutting him a deal. If he agrees to testify about what he knows about Paul Drake and the people he murdered, they'll drop all the charges pending against him for using forged instruments, false identity, and tax evasion."

"He also told me that thanks to Paul Drake's hideaway and his trophies, they've been able to get to the bottom of all of the murders that we already knew about and several that we weren't even aware of." Jace paused, taking a swallow of his beer. "Unfortunately quite a few of the bodies will never be recovered. We think that Drake used the same method of disposing of the bodies that he did with Ann. His lips tightened in disgust. "That guy was a genetic freak. He should never have been born."

"That's one bad boy who's never going to hurt anyone again," Eli said.

"Thank you, God!" Alex added.

Olivia drained the rest of her margarita, setting the empty glass on the table. "What I don't understand is how they even met Kevin Freeman and how he was involved in the whole mess?"

"Kevin Freeman was Paul Drake's roommate in college. Paul was taking business courses, but he had a double major, art being his other one. Kevin was an art major also. When he found that his talents lie in the media of ceramics, he realized that he needed a kiln. Paul had family money. He agreed to loan Kevin the money to build the kiln in the house that Kevin's parents had left him, if Freeman would agree to let Drake store some things there and come and go as he pleased."

The waitress came by to see if they needed anything else. Jace shook his head no and asked for the check. When she was gone he continued, "Where was I? Oh yeah, so then later Drake talked Freeman into teaching the twins how to handle clay and ceramics in exchange for the rest of the money Kevin owed Drake. By the time Kevin had cleared up his debt to Drake, he knew too much about Paul's dirty little secret. He was afraid he would become the next one. So he took Noah's advice, bought a new identity, and disappeared."

"Noah said he had turned in a tip about the murders of Ann and David Hensley right at the beginning of all this. If so, I wonder why nothing ever came of it?" Alex wondered.

"I talked to Tom Shaffer about that," Eli said. "He told me that they had checked out the tip, along with about a thousand other tips. The truth is, though, that there was absolutely no proof of anything. They had no bodies. Ann's boss had reported that she had sent him an email resigning her position, saying that she was leaving the state. Obviously, Drake must have sent that from Ann's laptop in order to cover his tracks. And then there was the fact that the housekeeper confirmed that Ann's purse, a suitcase and most of her clothes were gone. The kiln really did come in handy for Drake. So it appeared that the tip was just one of many false leads."

"Wow. So many lies and secrets kept for so many years. It seems so incredible to me," Olivia said. "I guess I shouldn't be surprised, with the people I meet in my profession."

Chapter 40

It was late and the only bit of light in the bedroom was a sliver of moonlight filtering through the partially closed curtains on a window across the room. Alex lay with her head against Jace's shoulder, his hand idly tracing the curve of her body under the blanket.

"You awake?" He asked.

"Yup."

"I think you should move in with me."

She raised her head to look at him. "You do?"

"You're here all the time anyway. And it would save us time going back and forth from your house."

She lay her head back down, sighing sadly. "I'll never feel quite right there again. I have to remember to block every time I even step into the kitchen." She was quiet for so long, he started to pull away.

She pressed him back down. "I'll think about it."

"You'll think about it?"

"Yes, I will, but I think we should give it a little more time."

"Why? I don't need more time."

"Jace, be reasonable. I'm more than tempted to take you up on your offer, but there's been so much going on lately that I can't even think straight right now. Let's see how this works out and if things go well, then we'll talk more about moving in together."

He was quiet for a minute. "Okay," he sighed, "but I as far as I'm concerned, things are working out just fine."

They were quiet again for a minute and then she said, "Do you ever wonder what John would think of this? Us, I mean? Do you ever feel guilty about it?"

This time he raised his head, looking down at her. "No, do you?"

"Sometimes," she whispered, "just a little."

Moving her aside, he got out of bed.

"Where are you going? Are you mad?"

"No, I'm going to get something. I'll be right back."

He left the room and she could hear him in his office shuffling through papers, obviously looking for something. Then she heard his bare feet padding back towards the bedroom.

He joined her in bed again, turning on the bedside lamp. She pushed up to sit with her back against the headboard. He handed her a piece of paper.

Looking down, she realized that it was the letter that John had written to Jace before he died, the one that she had delivered to Jace on the fateful day. She looked up at him.

"I want you to read it," he said.

"Are you sure?" she asked him.

"Very sure."

She just held it for a minute before she slid her fingers inside the envelope. She took the letter out and began to read.

Jace,

I know that you'll probably think it's strange that I'm writing you this letter when I see you all the time, but there are

271

things I can't bring myself to tell you to your face and I've always thought that you deserved to hear them.

Not to get all sappy and girly here, but first I wanted to say that you've been the best friend any guy could ever have. I've always valued your friendship above all else. That's why I'm writing this letter of apology to you now. God knows if I'll ever have the guts to actually send it to you.

From the very second that I met Alex, I knew that she was the woman I wanted. I needed her, had to have her. She always looked at me like I was the most intelligent, the biggest stud, the most put together man she'd ever met. The fact that I was none of those things when I met her was what made me strive with everything I had in me to be that man. She was just everything that a man could ever ask for and more. And that's why I couldn't stop myself from stealing her away from you.

I knew how you felt about her. I could always read you like a book. I saw the look in your eyes whenever she was around. I could even feel the electricity in the air whenever you two were within three feet of each other. But I closed my eyes to that and ruthlessly pursued her right in front of you. I even shoved it in your face every day, by forcing you two to do things together. For that, I am truly sorry. It kills me a little inside to know what I had to do to get what I needed.

Alex swiped at the tear running down her face, but one fell onto the page, causing the ink to run. Carefully, she blotted the page with the sheet and continued to read.

I'm sorry that I had to make a choice. More than that, I'm sorry that I couldn't choose you. I'm deeply humbled that you've stuck by me in spite of what I've done to you. I can't regret my life with Alex because I simply wasn't strong enough to let her go, as you were. I hope that after you read this you can be the bigger man, as you always have, and forgive me my sins.

Alexandra is and has always been the love of my life. If there's ever a time when I'm no longer around, I hope with all my selfish heart that you will be the one there to love and protect her as I would. You've always put my wishes first. I hope that you will be willing to do it again, if the need arises.

John

Alex set the letter down on the bed next to her. Raising her hands, she broke down and sobbed. Jace took her gently into his arms and she held on tight until the storm had passed. She leaned back, gazing up at him, moisture clinging to her dark eyelashes. "Is all of that true?"

"Of course it is. You know I could never keep any secrets from John. He knew me through and through, the same way I knew him."

"But you never showed it. You never said a word to me."

"John loved you, and you loved him."

"That's it? That's why you never said or did anything?"

"I loved you both. I couldn't have lived with myself if I had ruined my friendship with John and made you both unhappy."

"I can't believe that I was so blind all those years." She laid her palm against his cheek and kissed him tenderly. "I love you, Jace. Thank you for sharing John's letter with me."

"I love you too, Lex." He gathered up the letter, carefully sliding it back into the envelope. He laid it on the nightstand. And then he gathered her close and made slow, sweet love to her.